Books by Shirleen Davies
Historical Western Romance Series
MacLarens of Fire Mountain

Tougher than the Rest, Book One
Faster than the Rest, Book Two
Harder than the Rest, Book Three
Stronger than the Rest, Book Four
Deadlier than the Rest, Book Five
Wilder than the Rest, Book Six

Redemption Mountain

Redemption's Edge, Book One
Wildfire Creek, Book Two
Sunrise Ridge, Book Three
Dixie Moon, Book Four
Survivor Pass, Book Five
Promise Trail, Book Six

MacLarens of Boundary Mountain

Colin's Quest, Book One,
Brodie's Gamble, Book Two

Contemporary Romance Series

MacLarens of Fire Mountain

Second Summer, Book One
Hard Landing, Book Two
One More Day, Book Three
All Your Nights, Book Four
Always Love You, Book Five
Hearts Don't Lie, Book Six
No Getting Over You, Book Seven
'Til the Sun Comes Up, Book Eight, Releasing 2016

Peregrine Bay

Reclaiming Love, Book One
Our Kind of Love, Book Two

The best way to stay in touch is to subscribe to my newsletter. Go to *www.shirleendavies.com* and subscribe in the box at the top of the right column that asks for your email. You'll be notified of new books before they are released, have chances to win great prizes, and receive other subscriber-only specials.

Kindle Readers: Sign up to follow me on Amazon to be notified of new releases as they become available. It's the Follow button just under my photo on the left side.

Promise Trail

Redemption Mountain

Historical Western Romance Series

SHIRLEEN DAVIES

Book Six in the Redemption Mountain

Historical Western Romance Series

Avalanche Ranch Press, LLC
PO Box 12618
Prescott, AZ 86304

Book design and conversions by Joseph Murray at 3rdplanetpublishing.com

Cover design by Kim Killion, The Killion Group

ISBN: 978-1-941786-38-3

I care about quality, so if you find something in error, please contact me via email at
shirleen@shirleendavies.com

Description

Promise Trail, Book Six, Redemption Mountain Historical Western Romance Series

Bull Mason has built a life far away from his service in the Union Army and the ravages of the Civil War. He's achieved his dreams—loyal friends, work he enjoys, a home of his own, and a promise from the woman he loves to become his wife.

Lydia Rinehart can't believe how much her life has changed. Escaping captivity from a Crow village, she finds refuge and a home at the sprawling Redemption's Edge ranch...and love in the arms of Bull Mason, the ranch foreman. For the first time since her parents' death, she feels cherished and safe.

In an instant their dreams are crushed...

Bull is resolute in his determination to track down and rescue Lydia's brother, kidnapped during the celebration of their friend's wedding. He's made a promise—one he intends to keep. Picking the best men, they are ready to ride, until he's given an ultimatum.

Choices can seldom be undone...

As their journey continues, the trackers become the prey, finding their freedom and lives threatened.

And promises broken can rarely be reclaimed...

Can Bull and Lydia trust each other again and find their way to back to the dreams they once shared?

Promise Trail, book six in the Redemption Mountain historical western romance series, is a full-length novel with an HEA and no cliffhanger.

Visit my website for a list of characters for each series.
http://www.shirleendavies.com/character-list.html

Acknowledgements

Many thanks to my editor, Kim Young, proofreader, Alicia Carmical, and all of my beta readers. Your insights and suggestions are greatly appreciated.

As always, many thanks to my wonderful cover designer, Kim Killion, and Joseph Murray who is superb at formatting my books for print and electronic versions.

Promise Trail

Prologue

Montana Territory
1865

Billy grabbed Lydia's arm, propelling her forward. "We must keep moving."

"I'll kill myself before I go back." Lydia gasped for breath, digging her nails into his arm.

"Don't talk like that. Besides, who'd take care of your brother and sister if you weren't around?" Looking behind him, Billy nodded at Sam, Lydia's fourteen-year-old brother.

Holding Billy's seven-year-old sister, Margaret, in one arm, grasping nine-year-old Selina's hand with the other, Sam never complained, always watchful of the two young girls. From what Billy had seen, Sam and Lydia's younger sister, Selina, had more courage than many braves in the Crow village where they'd been held captive.

Having scant food and less water, the orphans had been running on fear for weeks. They'd been given food and then turned away by one white family after another for fear of what would happen if the Crow warriors tracking them discovered they'd helped the group of runaways.

To the settlers, the orphans were tainted, not worth the risk of helping. For Billy, the betrayal ran deep. Lydia felt different, taking the food and occasional blanket, understanding the fear behind the rejections.

As the oldest at eighteen, she should've been leading them. Instead, she'd slipped down a ravine the day before, spraining her ankle. The scratches didn't bother her. The excruciating pain when trying to run slowed them all down until Billy and Sam had taken turns carrying her. At fifteen and fourteen, neither had reached their full height or weight, yet both were bigger and stronger than Lydia. Neither allowed her to fall behind.

"Listen to me, Billy." Lydia yanked on his arm. "White Buffalo wants me. They'll turn back once he gets what he wants."

"No."

"Think of Margaret and Selina."

He slipped an arm around Lydia, helping her up a path of loose rock. "I *am* thinking of them." When they reached the top, he stopped and waited for Sam and the girls to catch up. "We haven't seen any sign of them for well over a week. Maybe they gave up."

She settled against a large rock, resting her arms across her knees and closing her eyes. Lydia had meant it when she said she'd kill herself before letting White Buffalo take her. Full of hate and cruel beyond reason, Red Tail had promised her to the Crow warrior. The ceremony had only been days away when she'd decided to escape with her brother and sister. Billy learned of it from Sam and refused to stay behind. He'd wrapped Margaret in a blanket, slung her over his shoulder, and left.

Sam set Margaret down, dropping to his knees beside Lydia. "Billy and I are going further up." He pointed to what appeared to be the crest of the hill. "We won't be gone long."

It didn't take the boys more than a few minutes to get their first view of what they'd later describe as the most beautiful sight they'd ever seen. Running back down the path, they collapsed next to the girls, smiles breaking across both faces.

"Let's go." Sam picked up Margaret and started back up the hill, Selina following close behind.

Billy reached out his hand to Lydia. "Come on."

Her eyes wide, she gripped his hand. "What did you find?"

He smiled. "I think it might be heaven."

Weeks later, suffering from lack of food and decent shelter, Billy's enthusiasm had vanished. Their trek toward the distant mountain range had taken them through the most beautiful valley any of them had ever seen. It had taken considerable effort to cross the vast acreage without being spotted by the ranch hands tending the massive herd.

They'd been beyond exhausted by the time they'd crossed a surging creek, finding a winding trail up the mountain. Discovering the cave had been easy. Finding food and keeping a supply of fresh water had been their biggest challenge.

Raiding nearby ranches had been easy...until a day before when Billy had gone alone and not returned.

"You'll be careful, right, Sam? I don't know what we'll do if something happens to *you*, too." Lydia covered her mouth, choking out the last words. She hadn't told anyone about her stomach cramps or tightness in her chest, although Sam's worried glances told her he knew.

He knelt next to his sister, drawing the blanket up over her. "I've no choice. We don't know what happened to Billy. He could be hurt and needing help."

"Or one of the ranchers may have caught him stealing their food."

"We must eat, and game is scarce this high up. Besides, it's not truly stealing." He stuffed an old, torn shirt into a tattered bag, then stood up.

"Taking food from people *is* stealing, Samuel. No amount of denying the fact will change it."

Sam cringed at his older sister's words. She'd been his and Selina's salvation after the Crow killed their parents and took them captive. Over time, the three had formed a strong bond with Billy and Margaret. He hated the disappointment on her face.

"Billy and I take what we need to survive. Nothing more." He let out a deep breath, dragging a hand through his long hair. "I'm wasting time. I need to find Billy and—" He stopped at the sound of someone entering the cave. "Billy..." His words trailed off when his friend bent over, gasping for breath.

He scanned the room, eyes wild as he focused on Lydia. "We have to leave."

"Billy, we were so worried about you." Margaret ran up and wrapped her arms around him. At seven, she was the youngest in the group, was devoted to him, and was the reason Billy had stayed in the Crow camp for three years. She'd just turned four when they were captured. Her age and small stature never would've allowed her to escape before.

"We can't leave now. Lydia is still sick, won't eat, and feels hot. I don't know what to do." Sam ran both hands through his long hair, clasping them behind his neck. "Where have you been?"

Billy swung his gaze to Lydia. Selina sat cross-legged on the hard ground, gripping her older sister's hand, eyes full of worry. He looked back at Sam.

"They caught me. I wasn't able to get away until this morning." Billy took a few steps toward Lydia, noticing her red-rimmed eyes. He felt his stomach clench as he turned back toward Sam. "We have to leave. I'm sure they've followed me."

"Who caught you?" Lydia asked, trying to sit up.

"Some ranchers. Pelletier is their name. I know they're close behind me. We have to go. Now."

"I already told you that Lydia can't move and won't eat. We can't take her out of here." Sam paced a few feet away, then swung back around. "What are we going to do?"

"You'll come with us. We'll help you."

The deep voice got everyone's attention as Dax Pelletier walked into the cave, followed by his brother, Luke, and the sheriff, Gabe Evans. He didn't stop until he stood over Lydia, looking down at her prone form. He dropped to his knees, causing Selina to scoot away, although she didn't drop Lydia's hand. Dax placed a hand on her forehead and shot a look at Luke.

"She has a high fever. We have to get her to Doc Worthington."

"You're not taking her anywhere." Billy stepped between Luke and Dax, daring them to interfere. "She's not leaving."

Gabe strode forward, fixing Billy with a hard look. "She's sick. Dax's wife is a nurse, and her uncle is the town doctor. They won't hurt her, but you will if you insist on keeping her in this damp cave without adequate food and medical supplies."

Sam stepped forward, grabbed Billy's arm, and spun him around. "Lydia needs help. They're offering and I think we should accept it."

Billy scrubbed a hand over his face, his stomach knotting as his eyes settled on Lydia. He didn't want to count on help from the type of white men they'd encountered over the last few months, yet these men hadn't turned them away. They'd taken him into their home, fed him, and gave him a place to sleep. Now they were offering their help again.

"You're right, Sam." Billy glared at Dax and took a step closer. "You'd better not hurt her."

"She'll be fine. You need to trust us." Dax wrapped the blanket edges around her, taking care to keep her feet and hands covered. "Does she have a bonnet?"

Selina jumped up and pulled an old, worn bonnet from a leather bag, handing it to Dax. He fitted it over her head and tied the strings, catching her watching him.

"Hello, Lydia. I'm Dax Pelletier. This is my brother, Luke, and our friend, Gabe Evans. We're going to take you to the doctor."

She closed her eyes and swallowed, not making any effort to answer.

Gabe looked at the others. "Gather your belongings."

Sam, Margaret, and Selina scrambled to do as Gabe ordered, grabbing their meager belongings and stuffing them into grimy sacks.

"You, too, Billy." Gabe eyed the boy, not at all sure what to expect. If he ran, they didn't have enough men to follow him. Their primary obligation was getting Lydia to the doctor.

Billy fought conflicting emotions, knowing he had just one choice. He'd never leave Margaret, and he'd formed a strong bond with Sam, Selina, and Lydia. He swung away from Gabe and began to gather what he owned—an old hat, an extra pair of moccasins, and a few other items still inside his worn, leather sack.

"We're ready." Dax lifted Lydia into his arms and caught Luke's attention. "You go through the opening first, then I'll hand her to you."

Gabe led the way through the tunnel toward the passage to the outside. He glanced over his shoulder to make sure no one had stayed behind, then slipped through the opening.

Sitting on his horse, holding the other horses' reins, Bull's gaze fixed on the woman in Luke's arms. His body stilled and his breath caught when she lifted her head from Luke's shoulder.

Her eyes widened at the sight of him. His gaze seemed to bore right through her, his soft brown eyes studying her as if she were the most fascinating woman he'd ever seen.

"She'll be riding with you, Bull." Luke held her toward him, chuckling softly when he saw the anxiety in his friend's eyes. "Lydia is your responsibility now. Take good care of her."

Chapter One

Splendor, Montana
1868

"Take my hand, Lydia. I won't let you fall." Bull stood on a large, flat rock on the opposite side of Wildfire Creek, adjusting the saddlebags on one shoulder before extending his hand, encouraging her to take the leap. "Come on, sweetheart. I'll catch you."

Biting her lower lip, she took a deep breath and leaned forward, her gaze focusing on Bull's eyes...the same soft brown eyes that had always given her strength and provided comfort. Reaching her hands toward him, she jumped. His strong arms wrapped around her waist, pulling her tight against him, a chuckle vibrating in his chest.

"I knew you could do it." Smiling, he placed a kiss on her forehead, then gripped her hand.

Leading him up the embankment, Lydia took a narrow deer trail, following the creek for a good distance before veering away into the dense forest.

"Are you sure you remember the spot?" Bull glanced around, committing their route to memory for the return trip.

"Yes. I've come up here many times since living at the ranch." She let out a yelp as Bull tugged her to a stop, pinning her with a hard stare.

"Tell me you haven't been coming here alone."

"Of course not. Selina and Margaret usually tag along." She tried to turn away, but his grip held firm.

An exasperated sigh escaped as he thought of the danger. "How come you've never mentioned it to me? I would've come with you, or sent one of the ranch hands along."

"And that's exactly why I never said a word to you, Bull. Sometimes I need to get away, clear my head. I can't do that if you're around."

"No?"

Pulling her hand free, she crossed her arms, tilting her chin up. "No. You can be a, well...a distraction when I'm trying to think."

Reaching out, he slipped his arm around her waist, drawing her close before lowering his lips to hers. After a moment, he lifted his head, smiling at the dazed look in her eyes. "And what kind of distraction am I?"

Placing her hands on his chest, she laughed as she lightly shoved him away, careful of his still healing injury. Weeks before, he and their friend,

Noah Brandt, had been ambushed, shot, and left for dead. The fact both had lived was a miracle.

"You know exactly the kind of distraction you are, Bull Mason. Now come on. It's not much farther."

Ten minutes later, she cut through a stand of pine trees, then stopped as the forest opened into a small clearing sprinkled with wildflowers in white, vibrant magenta, and pink.

"Isn't it beautiful? The perfect spot for a picnic."

He had to agree, although the idea of her coming up here with two young girls worried him. On his treks through Redemption Mountain, he'd spotted mountain lions, grizzlies, and wolves—all fierce and dangerous to humans.

Noticing his furrowed brow and dark expression, Lydia took a step toward him. "Bull, don't you like it?"

Ignoring her question, he settled his hands on her shoulders. "Don't ever come up here again without me or one of the ranch hands."

"But—"

"This isn't a discussion, Lydia. It's not safe for you and the girls up here alone. I won't have you putting yourself, and them, in danger. Do you understand me?"

She didn't like it, but the concern on his face and the way his fingers dug into her shoulders told her how important her safety was to him.

Reaching up, she kissed his cheek. "If it will ease your mind, then yes, I'll let you know if I want to come up here."

The relief she saw on his face felt good. From watching Rachel and Dax, and Luke and Ginny, she knew there'd be many disagreements after they married. Some would be worth fighting for. This wasn't one of them.

"Thank you." Bull adjusted the saddlebags she'd filled with food and a blanket, then looked around for a spot to lay everything out. "How about over there?" He nodded to a spot a few feet away.

"Perfect," she breathed out, taking his hand.

An hour later, Lydia sat on a corner of the blanket, Bull's head resting in her lap as he dozed. Brushing a strand of molasses-colored hair from his forehead, she leaned down. Brushing a kiss over his lips, she squealed when strong arms wrapped around her. Shifting, Bull tugged her down next to him, deepening the kiss. Gathering her close, he held her against him, her arms encircling his neck.

Burying her hands in his hair, she sighed, losing herself in the passion of the kiss. Heat ripped through her as she struggled to get closer. Pleasure took control as his kiss became more demanding, creating a need she couldn't define.

Loosening his grip, he let his hands roam up and down her back, one settling on her waist, his touch possessive. Blood pounded in his brain, fogging his senses.

"Bull, please..."

He knew what she wanted, what she needed. Breaking the kiss, he waited until she opened her eyes. The desire he saw stoked the fire roaring through him, yet he held back.

"We should wait. It's only a few weeks, sweetheart." They planned to marry soon, although today, lying next to her, it felt like forever.

Sure of what she wanted, Lydia pulled him closer. "Is that what you want?"

"No," he ground out. "It's what I think is best." His deep, ragged voice confirmed his desire ran as deep as hers.

"I don't want to wait any longer. I love you, Bull. Make love to me. Please."

"Ah, sweetheart. I don't want you to regret our first time."

Her soft smile felt like a kick to his stomach. "I'll never regret loving you. I can't think of a better place for our first time. I want you, Bull."

"I want you, too, Lydia." Leaning down, he claimed her lips, crushing her to him before raising his head once more. "You're mine. You've always been mine."

Redemption's Edge
Two weeks later...

"Come on, Bull. The women didn't work you *that* hard." Luke Pelletier slapped his foreman on the back. Less than three months before, Bull and Noah Brandt had been brutally attacked. Today, he'd hauled tables and benches from the barn, doing whatever else the women asked in preparation for Cash and Alison's wedding.

"*You* take a bullet in the chest, then we'll see how much you can do after a few weeks." Bull placed a hand over his chest, narrowing his eyes while chuckling. "It's good to be outside and doing something useful. If Dax would just let me saddle Abe and join the men..."

"It won't be long. I have strict orders from my boss to make you take it easy." Dax Pelletier walked up, stopping next to Bull. He and Luke owned Redemption's Edge, the largest ranch in western Montana. "You know how tough Rachel can be."

"Believe me, I know. You've got one of the toughest women in the territory."

"In the entire country, Bull." Dax turned at the sound of the fiddler starting a new tune, spotting Rachel, Ginny Pelletier, and Lydia Rinehart walking toward them.

Ginny unconsciously rested a hand on her expanding stomach. In a few months, she and Luke would be adding to the Pelletier family, giving Rachel and Dax's son, Patrick, a playmate.

"It's been such a lovely day. Cash and Allie look so happy." Lydia's eyes locked with Bull's. As always, her heart beat faster when he was near. Today, she couldn't help thinking how far she'd come since escaping the Crow camp. From a scared orphan, near death, lying in a damp cave in the mountains above the Pelletier ranch, to finding a home and falling in love with Bull Mason.

"Too bad you and Bull didn't want to join Cash and Alison, getting both weddings over with at once." Rachel laughed as she placed a hand on Lydia's shoulder. The Pelletiers had given the orphans a home and made them a part of their family, discovering them after they'd escaped the

Crow camp. It had been a miracle they all survived.

Lydia's eyes lit up when Bull slipped an arm around her waist. "It would've been easier, but we wanted our own special day. A day I know will always be Bull's and mine."

Lydia had lost so much after being taken captive when her parents were killed by the Crow. She'd become mother and father to Sam and Selina, kept them together, then found sanctuary with the Pelletiers.

Rachel put an arm around Lydia's shoulders. "You and Bull deserve such a day."

"If you all will excuse us, I believe I'll take my girl for a walk." Bull's gaze never left Lydia's as he turned her toward the dance platform he'd helped erect earlier.

He'd fallen in love with her the day they discovered the orphans in the cave, cradling her in his arms as they rode down the mountain. By the time they reached the ranch, he'd already made up his mind. Someday, the young woman would be his. She'd been sick, shivering the entire trip, and all he could think about was finding a way to make her life better.

In reality, Lydia had been the one who inspired him. He'd begun to see himself as more than an ex-Union soldier with memories he'd rather erase. Because of her, he'd accepted the ranch foreman position Luke and Dax offered, which included a small house. He saved the majority of his monthly wage, stashing it in an account at the bank. When he'd saved enough, Bull asked Lydia to marry him. The ceremony would take place in six weeks. It would be the longest six weeks of Bull's life.

"Everyone is having a wonderful time." Lydia leaned into him as they walked.

Bull leaned down, placing a kiss on her forehead. "Dance with me."

Clasping Lydia's hand, he led her into the middle of those dancing. Wrapping her in his arms, not caring what people thought, he pulled her tight. He'd hear about their closeness later, probably through Rachel or Ginny, after the church ladies made their comments. Right now, nothing else mattered except for the feel of her close to him. He had everything he ever wanted right here in his arms.

Movement next to them had Bull looking up, seeing Cash and Alison join them on the dance floor. Bull nodded, then turned his attention back to Lydia as the song changed to a lively jig. Cash and Allie continued to dance next to them, clapping along with the rest of the guests.

Cash pulled Allie to him as laughter filled the air. Ignoring anyone who might be watching, he brushed a kiss across her lips, then repeated it until she placed her palms flat on his chest to stop him.

"Mr. Coulter, I do believe you're trying to seduce me." She flashed him a brilliant smile.

"You would be right, Mrs. Coulter." Cash started to lower his head again when ear-piercing screams had him stepping away, pulling Allie behind him.

"Help! Someone help us!" The panicked cries came from behind the barn.

"My God, Cash. It's the children." Allie started to dash toward the barn when Cash pulled her back.

"You stay here, Allie. Let me see what's happening." Cash didn't wait for a response as he, Bull, and most of the men took off at a run.

Rounding the barn, they stopped at the sight before them. Billy lay on the ground, blood flowing from a gash on his head.

"Somebody get Doc Worthington," Dax shouted as he dropped to a knee next to Billy, checking his pulse, then tearing off his shirt, holding it to the wound. "He's alive."

Jackson, Lena and Gabe Evans' seven-year-old son, stood ramrod straight, his gaze focused on the horizon, pointing. Selina, Lydia's eleven-year-old sister, stood beside him, her face streaked with tears.

"Jack?" Gabe knelt beside him, drawing the boy to him. "What is it, son?"

Jack's vacant gaze moved to Gabe.

"They took him," Selena sobbed.

"Who, Selena?" Bull asked, kneeling down, turning her toward him.

Her panicked face, flushed and wet with tears, tore into Bull.

"Sweetheart, tell me what happened," Bull coaxed in a soft voice as Lydia ran up to them, then placed an arm across her sister's shoulders.

Glancing around, Lydia's heart began to race when she didn't spot her brother, fifteen-year-old Samuel. Her voice shook as she turned Selena to face her. "Where is Sam?"

A haunted look crossed Selena's face. "They took him, Lydia," she choked out. "The Indians took Sam."

Chapter Two

"I'm going with Bull."

"I figured you would, Luke." Dax thought of who else they could spare from the ranch. "Take Tat and Johnny with you. You'll need to leave Dirk at your place."

Luke nodded, glancing at a group of their ranch hands standing several yards away. The Pelletiers owned two large ranch houses. Dax and Rachel lived in one, while Luke and Ginny lived in another a few miles to the east. Bull was the foreman for Dax, and Dirk Masters handled the job for Luke.

"With Bull gone, we'll definitely need Dirk to stay here. I'd like to take Mal. He's a good tracker."

"Who else?" Dax asked.

"No matter his injury, Billy won't be left behind. He recognized White Buffalo, the brave Lydia had been promised to before the orphans ran away. Billy said White Buffalo made life hard on Sam, probably taking it real personal when they ran away." Luke drew in a deep breath. "There's no telling what the brave has planned for him as punishment, but it won't be good." He spotted Bull near the house, his hands resting on Lydia's shoulders, his features stern. "I'd like to take Travis, but I'm not sure we can spare him." Luke watched as the group of men moved his way. Judging by the look on each face, he knew they'd all volunteer to go.

"What can we do?" Travis stepped forward, hands resting loosely at his sides, his eyes signaling the anger he felt.

"Travis, I'd like you, Mal, Tat, and Johnny to ride with Bull, Luke, and Billy. This is a request, not an order. It will be dangerous. Some of you might not make it back." Dax looked at the men who circled Luke and him. "It's no problem if you choose not to go."

Travis crossed his arms and stepped forward, his face set. "I'm going."

Mal, Tat, and Johnny joined him.

"I'd like to ride along, too, boss." Dirk moved next to Luke.

"We can't spare both you and Bull. I'll be counting on you to help Dax and keep watch on Ginny while I'm gone."

"I'll do whatever you need, Luke."

"Then it's settled." Dax didn't like what lay ahead, but the thought of Sam being tortured, or worse, caused a hard knot of anger to build in his gut. "Get your gear, saddle your horses, and meet near the barn in fifteen minutes. The sooner you move out, the sooner Sam will be back home with us."

Luke, Billy, Travis, Mal, Tat, and Johnny milled about outside the barn, their horses restless as they waited for Bull. They knew the cause of the delay, although none ventured forth to give their opinion.

"What do you think, Luke?" Travis settled his hat low on his forehead, watching Bull and Lydia. From what he could tell, they weren't having a friendly conversation.

"She's determined to go, and Bull's equally determined she stay behind. As much as I don't like it, my money's on Lydia." Luke raised his eyebrows as Bull's voice carried toward the group of men.

"You aren't going. No argument, Lydia. I won't be able to put my full attention on finding Sam if I'm worried about you." Bull leaned toward her, his eyes pleading for understanding.

"I don't want to cause you more worry, but Sam is my brother. I won't be left behind." Lydia crossed her arms, chin tilted up in defiance.

"What about Selina and Margaret? Who'll watch after them with both you and Sam away? With so many men gone, Dax will need everyone who's left to keep the place going."

She shifted her gaze toward Dax, his arm around Rachel as they spoke to Luke and the others. Letting out a sigh, Lydia closed her eyes. As much as she hated leaving them with one less person to help, she needed to search for Sam.

"I won't be able to sleep while you're gone. Please understand, Bull. I *need* to go with you. Besides, I'll follow if you don't let me ride along. It's your choice."

Bull raked a hand through his hair, settled both hands on his hips, and looked up at the sky, trying to calm the fear he felt at the thought of her going along. She'd become a decent rider and could handle a gun with accuracy. Still...

"Listen to me, Lydia. We'll be riding hard and fast with few breaks and little sleep."

"I understand."

"You'll slow us down. Is that what you want?"

"I'll keep up. No matter what happens, I won't slow your pace."

Bull looked at her as if she were crazy, which she very well might be given the circumstances. Out of all of them, Lydia knew more about what could happen if White Buffalo got his hands on her. Bull's biggest fear centered on what he believed was the true reason the Crow raiding party took the risk of riding into a settlement of white men. White Buffalo wanted Lydia, and Sam could be his way of getting to her.

Taking a step forward, he wrapped his arms around her, resting his chin on top of her head. "He wants *you*, Lydia, not Sam."

Resting her cheek on his chest, she closed her eyes, tears threatening. "I know."

"He'll use Sam to get to you. Maybe offer a trade. If you aren't with us, his bargaining power is gone. We'll have nothing he wants."

Clutching his arms, she pulled away, looking up into stormy brown eyes, wishing they hadn't been put in this situation. Their life at Redemption's Edge had been good, much of the physical and emotional scars healed by the love and friendship of those at the ranch. White Buffalo had opened old wounds, forcing choices no one wanted to make.

"Please, Bull. Give me ten minutes." Turning, she ran up the steps and into the house.

Bull watched her leave, tempted to get on his horse and ride out with the others before she had a chance to return.

"What's going on?" Luke stepped beside him.

Bull sighed, dragging a hand down his face. "Lydia refuses to stay behind. Hell, she even threatened to follow us if I don't let her go."

"Where is she now?"

"I don't know what she's doing, but she asked me to wait. I've half a mind to..." His voice trailed off as Lydia emerged from the house. At least he thought it was Lydia. He'd never seen her in men's clothing. The image would've been funny if they didn't face such a dangerous journey.

"What do you think?" She stretched her arms out and turned around. "Do I look like a man?"

Luke's wide grin said it all. "Sorry, Lydia. But I think it's going to be real hard to hide your, uh...well, your..."

"That's enough, Luke." Bull's snarl stopped him from saying more. "Where did you get those clothes?"

"They're Sam's. It's the best I could do, but it should work to make White Buffalo believe I'm one of the ranch hands." The hope in her eyes squeezed Bull's heart. He didn't want to take Lydia with them, but he couldn't find it in him to leave her behind.

"If you're determined to go, then yes, you'll need to dress the part. *And* you'll need to do exactly what I say, when I say it. In fact, it won't matter if it's me, Luke, Travis, or any of the other men. You'll do what you're told. No arguing. Do you understand?"

"But I—"

"Those are the terms, Lydia. If you don't accept them, I'll tie you up, leave you in the storage shed, and post one of the men as guard. And trust me, you'll never find our tracks."

Crossing her arms, she glared up at Bull. "I accept your terms. Can we leave now?"

"We need to get a horse for you."

"Uh, Bull...it's already done. I asked Travis to get her horse ready." Luke didn't wait for a response as he turned, smirking, and strode toward the barn.

Cursing under his breath, Bull slapped his hat down on his head. "You stay with me. I don't want you more than two feet away."

"I understand." Stepping forward, Lydia wrapped her arms around his neck and placed a soft kiss on his lips. "Thank you, Bull."

"We'll see what you say a few days from now." He pulled her tight, then dropped his arms. Nodding toward Dax, Bull walked to the barn, taking the reins to Lydia's horse and helping her up. "All right. If we're all ready, let's go find the group of Crow who stole our boy."

Pulling his slicker tight, Bull cursed the sudden downpour for obscuring the tracks they'd been following for several hours. Glancing at Lydia, who rode between him and Luke, he felt a ripple of embarrassment at his outburst. In their two days on the trail, she'd been quiet, never voicing a complaint, keeping her focus on finding Sam.

"We need to get moving, Bull, before the rain destroys what little tracks I can find." Mal had been riding ahead, keeping them on the right path—at least until now.

"You ride ahead as far as you need to, Mal. The trail is already slick and getting worse. I don't know how much faster we can go." Turning in the saddle, Bull waved his arm, gesturing for everyone to pick up the pace.

"I'll ride back as soon as I can." Mal reined his horse around and disappeared in the fading light. The rain had started as a drizzle, increasing in force until Bull knew they'd have to find shelter if it didn't let up.

"I'll go with him. Try to stay as close as possible." Luke kicked his palomino stallion, Prince, guiding him up the trail until he, too, disappeared from view.

"Stay close, Lydia. No telling what will happen if—"

A flash of lightning crashed into the trees a hundred feet away. Lydia's horse reared back, its eyes wide with panic, dancing on its back hooves.

"Lydia, hold on!" Bull brought his older horse, Abe, under control with little effort, then slid to the ground. Tossing the reins over a nearby bush, Bull approached the startled animal, his hands raised. "It's all right, girl. Nothing will you hurt you, Angel." His relaxed voice did little to calm the horse as she reared again.

As soon as Angel's hooves landed on the ground, Bull grabbed hold of her mane and swung up behind Lydia, grabbing the reins from her. Pulling down, he again repeated his calm words, his weight adding an extra reason for the mare to settle.

"That's it, Angel. Nice and easy, girl." A few more seconds passed before Bull eased up on the reins, then slid to the ground, continuing to talk calmly, watching for any sign she might bolt. By then, Travis, Billy, Tat, and Johnny had joined him, circling the animal.

Stroking a hand down Angel's neck, Bull glanced at Lydia. Her hands were so tight on the saddle horn, her knuckles had turned white. Her eyes, wide with fear, found his and held.

"Lydia, sweetheart, you're all right." As Bull began to move toward her, Billy appeared. His hands settled on Lydia's waist, lifting her from the saddle, cradling her in his arms. Walking away, he placed her on the ground and looked into eyes that didn't seem to focus.

"Lydia, look at me." Billy waited a moment, then repeated his request. This time, her eyes met his.

"Billy…"

Wrapping his arms around her, he held her close. "You're fine now. Bull has Angel under control. It was just a little lightning, nothing more."

"I can take care of my own woman."

At the irritation in Bull's voice, Billy dropped his arms and stepped away. Bull knew Billy meant nothing by it, even though both understood if he were older, he'd go after Lydia himself. Although young, his feelings for her had been obvious from the time the men had discovered the orphans in the cave. Billy had grown older, become a strapping young man who turned the heads of girls in town—all except the one he wanted. She only had eyes for Bull.

"I'll, uh…" Billy didn't finish. Instead, he strode to his horse and grabbed the reins, swinging into the saddle to join the other men.

Bull encircled Lydia in his arms, watching the younger man stalk away.

"You did good, sweetheart."

Lydia wrapped her arms around Bull's neck, burying her face in his chest for a brief moment before pulling back.

"I couldn't get her under control."

"Angel's still young. I don't know that she's ever been under saddle during a lightning storm. Believe me, you did real good." Stroking her hair, he placed a kiss on her forehead, then looked up at the sky. The rain had stopped, the clouds moving away to reveal a star-filled sky. "Are you all right to ride?"

She blew out a shaky breath. "I guess it spooked me as much as Angel, but I'm fine now."

"Good girl. Let's get you back up on her and find the others."

Sam didn't know how much farther he could go without collapsing. They'd bound his wrists, the rain-soaked leather thongs tightening to a painful degree as they dried, cutting into the skin. He'd been made to run or, if he were lucky, walk since being taken from the ranch. Cursing his stupidity at being captured, he'd replayed the scene over and over.

They'd just started playing a game of hide-and-seek. His chores around the ranch gave him little time to play with Selina or Margaret. The wedding had brought several more children to the ranch, and he couldn't say no to their pleas to participate. Even Billy had agreed to play. Sam had been chosen to hide while the others counted to a hundred. Getting caught up in the fun, he'd ventured to the far end of the corral, ducked under the fence, and hid in a thick copse of brush and trees. Not once had he thought danger lurked just a few feet away.

Without warning, White Buffalo and two of his braves swooped down on him. Fear took over and he let out a blood-curdling cry. His shouts had been the only warning the others got about the party of Crow on Pelletier land. Before they'd ridden away, Sam had spotted Billy, running as fast as he could, trying to catch them. Sam blew out a sigh of relief his friend hadn't made it. Nothing good would've come from Billy being taken.

The first night, they'd whipped him with thin branches, shoving him around in the center of a small circle until he'd fallen to his knees, exhausted. The goal had been to frighten him into submission rather than cause injury. It hadn't worked. Knowing what to expect, he hardened his resolve, promising himself he wouldn't bend to fear.

A sudden shove from behind had him sprawling on the ground, his head missing a large rock by inches. Sam knew White Buffalo and his men spoke enough English to get by, but they preferred to use force to communicate.

The Crow people had resolved to work with the white man, deciding they'd never be able to stop the vast number of settlers from moving west. Many had learned English, become scouts for the army, and done their best to live alongside the settlers. The band led by White Buffalo's uncle, Red Tail, had disagreed with their chief, believing the white man couldn't be trusted. Their hatred resulted in a small number splintering off, living apart from their tribe, seeking revenge for perceived wrongs. They conducted their own isolated raids on farms and ranches, stealing horses and cattle, taking the occasional hostage.

When Red Tail's son had been killed by Sam's father during one such raid, he'd taken Lydia, Sam, and Selina captive, promising Lydia to White Buffalo.

They'd been naïve to think White Buffalo would give up trying to find Lydia. Sam's instincts told him Lydia had been the target. He was a weak substitute, but one White Buffalo could use to his advantage. Sam would not let that happen.

"Up."

Sam shielded his gaze to see White Buffalo standing over him, the familiar menacing scowl indicating his impatience.

Pushing himself up, Sam staggered forward, almost losing his balance a second time when White Buffalo shoved him, then laughed.

"Go." He shoved Sam once more, then leapt onto the back of his horse. Circling Sam twice, he spat on the ground, a clear indication of his irritation with their progress. Sam didn't care. The longer he could delay the journey, the better the chances he'd be found. He never doubted the Pelletiers would come for him.

When he, Lydia, and Selina had been taken hostage, White Buffalo insisted Sam stay with the women and children. Unlike Billy, who'd been captured a couple years before, Sam had been forbidden from learning the skills of a warrior.

Living with the Pelletiers not only provided him with a home, but training in handling a variety of weapons. Bull had made certain he could ride as well as any of the ranch hands, protect himself, and survive in the wilderness. When the time came, Sam planned to use those skills to get away—and make certain White Buffalo never came for them again.

Chapter Three

"What did you find, Mal?" Bull reined up beside him, leaving Lydia with Luke and the others. Of the group, Mal Jolly had the most experience tracking, volunteering to take on the role.

"I got lucky." Mal slid to the ground, then knelt, pointing to a spot before him. "Right here is where they changed directions. They've been heading north, following Wildfire Creek for much of the way, then veered west. This is where they cut east."

"To avoid Running Bear's village?"

"That'd be my guess." Mal stood up, his attention on the trail to the east.

As chief of the local Blackfoot tribe, Running Bear held no love for their enemies, the Crow. Unlike the Crow, most of the Blackfoot didn't trust white settlers. Running Bear's beliefs were different than the majority of his tribe, and certainly those who lived further north and east. He'd forged a peace with the surrounding ranchers. Most notably, the Pelletiers.

"How far ahead of us do you think they are?" Bull reined Abe around, pointing him toward the east.

"Half a day at most." Mal turned to look at Bull. "Sam is walking, which is why we've been able to get so close. And he's not doing well."

Bull's gaze narrowed on Mal. "What do you mean?"

"He's barefoot, limping, and if I'm not mistaken, they've beaten him. Look here." He walked over to a clearing on the other side of the trail. Bending down, he picked up three branches, each stripped of their leaves, all with dark brown stains near the tips. "I hope I'm wrong, but it looks like they whipped him with these."

Bull dismounted, grabbing the sticks from Mal. His stomach lurched. Cursing, he threw the branches aside.

"We have to find Sam and get him back before they do worse than whip him."

Mal nodded, then swung into his saddle. "What will you tell Lydia?"

"Nothing. And neither will you."

Bull leaned against the trunk of a large pine, watching Lydia sleep. He'd wanted to bed down with her, hold her in his arms, but even though they were to be married in a few weeks, propriety wouldn't allow it. Instead, he took the first watch, hoping he could get at least five hours of shuteye before the sun rose over the distant hills.

He hadn't been able to sleep more than a couple hours since they started the search, and neither had Lydia. Tonight, exhaustion finally claimed her. He glanced up as Luke came up next to him. Holding two cups of coffee, he lowered himself to the ground, offering one to Bull.

Luke kept his voice low as he leaned toward him. "Mal told me his suspicions of what White Buffalo is doing to Sam."

Bull took the cup, not meeting Luke's eyes. "Nothing I didn't expect. He'll rough him up, try to break him, but he isn't crazy enough to kill him." His voice hissed out, low and bleak. "Sam is the one chance White Buffalo has to get Lydia back."

"We won't let that happen. As long as she does what she's told, lets us protect her, she'll stay safe." Luke rested his arms on his bent knees, wondering how Ginny would react under the same circumstances.

He'd hated leaving her. She'd just reached six months in her pregnancy. Even though she'd never voiced it, he knew the thought of having the baby early, without him present, scared her. Their one consolation was Rachel. As part of her work at her uncle's clinic in Splendor, she helped deliver numerous babies. The death toll for infants was high in the frontier, yet she'd managed to do her work with little loss of life. As an ex-Union nurse, she had experience beyond the normal small town midwife.

"Lydia's sick with worry. She knows what White Buffalo is capable of and his blatant hatred of Sam. That's why I don't want her to know what Mal suspects. It would only confirm what she already fears." Bull rubbed his eyes with the palms of his hands.

"Then we keep it from her. When we find out Sam's location, we'll leave one of the men with Lydia to keep her as far away as possible. If White Buffalo suspects she's part of the search party, he'll bring the entire village down on us." Luke tossed out the last of his coffee and stood. "Guess I'd better get some sleep. Wake me in a couple hours."

Bull nodded, knowing he'd let Luke rest as long as possible. Leaning his head against the tree, he stared up at the sky, murmuring a prayer for Sam's safety and that of the people scattered around him. They'd been putting in long days, the urgency to find the boy weighing heavy on each of them. Timing was critical.

"Bull?"

Lydia's eyes focused on his as she sat up, drawing a blanket around her, studying the worry on his face. She made no move to look away when he stood and walked to her, kneeling, putting his arm around her shoulders.

"You should be resting." He kissed her forehead, stroking his hand up and down her arm.

"I heard you and Luke talking. Is everything all right?"

He didn't want to lie, but telling her what Mal found wasn't an option. "It will be once we find Sam."

"He must be terrified of what will happen to him. I don't know what I'll do if White Buffalo..." She leaned her head on Bull's shoulder, closing her eyes, working to stem the knot of fear in her stomach.

"Sam's grown into a young man since living at the ranch, Lydia. White Buffalo has no idea how capable he is or what he'll do to defend himself. You must have faith in him, and in us."

The sound of pounding hooves caught Bull's attention. Mal had refused to bed down with the others, deciding to ride ahead a few more miles. If the sky had been dark, he wouldn't have bothered, but the full moon illuminated the trail, providing the light needed.

Bull dropped his arm from around Lydia and walked over to where Mal had reined to a stop.

Noting Lydia several feet away, Mal leaned over in his saddle, keeping his voice low. "You need to come with me, Bull. There's something you need to see. You might want to bring Luke."

Bull glanced over his shoulder, seeing Lydia walk toward them, the blanket wrapped firmly around her.

"Let me get him."

"Did he find them?" The hope he heard in her voice squeezed his chest.

"Not yet. Mal found something he wants to show Luke and me. I'll ask Billy to keep watch on the camp while we're gone."

She grabbed his arm when he tried to move past her. "I'm coming."

"No. We won't be gone long, and I don't know what Mal wants to show us."

"But—"

"Lydia, please. Stay here with Billy and the others. We won't be gone long." He ran a hand over her hair, then kissed her cheek.

"You'll tell me what you find, right?"

He sucked in a breath, not wanting to promise what he might not be able to deliver.

"Bull, we need to hurry." The impatience in Mal's voice created an urgency to his request.

"What is it?" Luke walked up next to Bull.

"We need to ride out with Mal. Shouldn't take long. Ask Billy to keep watch on the camp." Bull grabbed his hat off the ground, then took

Lydia's elbow, guiding her back to her bedroll. "We'll be back as soon as we can."

"Down there." Mal stood next to Bull and Luke, pointing to a glow in the distance. "Could be anyone, but my instincts say it's White Buffalo's camp. He's just arrogant enough to keep a fire goin'. Probably figures we'll never catch him."

"Or he's setting a trap." Luke didn't like it. Only a fool, or someone with a plan, would keep a fire going knowing others were after them.

"Appears to be a couple miles." Bull looked through his field glasses, scanning the distance, then passed them to Mal.

"Two, maybe three. We're real close." Mal sighed, considering Luke's comment. "Luke may be right. White Buffalo's got to know we aren't far behind."

"There's one way to find out." Luke grabbed Prince's reins and swung into the saddle. "I'll meet you two back at camp."

"The hell you will." Bull's hard voice barely registered with Luke as he turned Prince toward the east.

Bull's chest hurt like the dickens from the months' old bullet wound as he mounted Abe and took off after him. There was no way he'd let Luke go alone. A moment later, he glanced over his shoulder, not surprised to see Mal a few yards behind.

They rode through thick trees and shrubs for close to an hour before coming to an open valley. Staying within the cover of the forest, they dismounted, walking to the edge of the prairie, spotting the fire a couple hundred yards away.

"Cocky bastard," Mal muttered, settling his hands on his hips. "His camp is surrounded by open grassland. They'll be able to spot anyone who gets within a hundred yards."

"Coming from the west." Bull stared at the glow of the fire, then turned his attention to the adjoining tree line. "What if we come in from the north?"

Luke studied the vista. "It'll take us at least three hours to move in a wide enough arc so we won't be spotted. He's baiting us, hoping we'll ride in and get caught in his trap. Three of us aren't enough to grab Sam and get away." Luke settled a hand on Bull's shoulder. "We know we're close. Let's get back to camp, get an early start, and catch them tomorrow."

"I'm staying here." Mal walked to his horse, untied the bedroll, then turned around. "I'll keep watch and wait for you. If I'm not here, it'll be because they packed up early."

"Don't do anything foolish, Mal. We need every man to go after Sam."

"Don't worry, Bull. I'm not crazy enough to take on a passel of braves alone. You get the others. I'll be waiting for you."

Lydia rubbed her hands up and down her arms as she paced around camp. It seemed like hours since Bull left, although Billy insisted the men hadn't been gone that long. He'd done his best to keep her mind occupied with talk of the ranch and the upcoming wedding, but he'd gotten little response.

"I've talked to Dax and Luke about moving back to Redemption's Edge." This got Lydia's attention.

"I thought you loved working for the Frey brothers."

"Frank and Hiram have been real fair with me and I've learned a lot, but they're not young anymore, Lydia. Fact is, they're ready to sell the ranch, move into town, and live out their old age in peace." Billy slid both hands into his pockets, kicking the dirt. "I'd buy it if I had the money."

"Maybe they can work something out with Horace Clausen." Lydia knew how much Billy wanted a piece of land of his own. The timing just didn't seem to work.

"I'm seventeen with a handful of money saved up. Even if I could work out a deal with the banker, I wouldn't have enough to pay the men and keep the place going. It's best if I move back."

Lydia crossed her arms, letting out a sigh. "Do they have a buyer?"

"Not yet. My guess is Dax is going to talk to them. He and Luke buy up whatever they can, paying a fair price."

Her eyes lit up at the thought of the Pelletiers buying the ranch. "Well, there you have it. They purchase the Frey ranch, and you stay on to run it."

"There are three others older than me with more experience. No way I'd work for any of them, except maybe Travis. If Dax and Luke take over, I'll come back to their ranch. Besides, it's time I was closer to Margaret. It won't be long before the boys come sniffing around. I want to be there to warn them off."

Lydia rolled her eyes. "She's *nine*, Billy. It will be years before the boys come around."

"Trust me. It's never too soon to start sending messages to all those randy boys in town."

"Billy!" Lydia choked out, her eyes wide.

He started to laugh. "I'm joking with you. Still, it's time I behaved as a big brother and not an almost stranger who shows up every few weeks for supper."

Shifting at the sound of approaching horses, Billy reached for his gun with one hand, pushing Lydia behind him with the other. "Get back in the bushes until we know who it is. Don't come out until I come for you."

She started to protest, then stopped at the concentration on Billy's face. Reminding herself she promised Bull to do as the men asked, she dashed behind the thick shrub, then pulled her gun from its holster.

Travis, Johnny, and Tat joined Billy as she disappeared. All focused their weapons on the approaching riders, then let out a collective breath when they recognized Bull and Luke.

"Where's Mal?" Travis asked as he slipped his gun back into its holster.

"Luke will explain. Where's Lydia?" Bull scanned the area.

"I told her to get back behind—" Billy stopped at Lydia's shout.

"I'm here, Bull." Rushing to him, she wrapped her arms around his waist. "What did you find?"

"Mal found their camp."

Dropping her arms, she jumped back, her eyes wide with excitement. "Then let's go."

"Hold up." Grabbing her arm, Bull pulled her back to him. "Listen to me, Lydia."

"But we have to leave."

He narrowed his gaze at her, waiting until he had her full attention. "We're close to finding Sam, which means the danger will increase. White Buffalo took Sam to get to you."

Lydia's patience diminished with each word. "I understand the danger, Bull. We already talked about it. Can't we just leave?"

"Not until I know you'll do what you're told when we find Sam. Do I have your word?"

Pulling out of his grip, she took a step back, crossing her arms. "I already gave you my word."

"But will you *keep* it once Sam is in sight?"

Lydia bit her lip, unable to meet his gaze. All she'd thought about since leaving the ranch was finding Sam, getting him back home. She hadn't meant to lie to Bull, but she didn't know what would happen once they found Sam.

"It's important White Buffalo not know you're with us."

Stepping away, she raised an eyebrow, gesturing to the clothing she wore. "Do you think he'd recognize me in this?"

Bull's face softened as he reached out, tucking a stray strand of hair under the well-worn hat Lydia wore. "I don't know what I'd do if anything happened to you."

"It's time we leave, Bull." Luke stood a few feet away, Prince's reins in his hands.

Bull nodded, looking down at Lydia. "Let's go find your brother."

The knot in Lydia's stomach tightened as they approached the spot where Bull and Luke had left Mal. The fact White Buffalo had allowed Mal to get so close nagged at her. He might be brutal with a nasty temper, but the Crow warrior was far from stupid. Lydia believed he knew the search party had gotten close, setting a trap to take another captive. She found herself praying she wasn't right and they hadn't found Mal.

"There's no sign of Mal or White Buffalo's camp." Luke pulled up close to Bull, signaling for Travis to join them as they continued on the trail. The sun touched the tops of the mountains to the east, its rays beginning to warm the chilly early morning air. "I figure they pulled out early and Mal followed. I want to ride ahead with Travis, see if we can catch up to him. I don't like the idea of him being out there alone."

"Go ahead. We won't be far behind." Bull glanced behind him, seeing Billy, Tat, and Johnny close behind.

Lydia watched Luke and Travis ride out, an uncomfortable dread settling over her. She shoved the hat further down on her head, making certain none of her strawberry blonde hair had fallen loose. She cringed, remembering the times White Buffalo had fingered her hair, staring at the locks as if they were a mystery. He'd called her Golden Bird, refusing to use her white name. Fear gripped her when she thought of what would happen if he ever got her back.

As much as she tried to fight the panic, her thoughts kept returning to Sam and what White Buffalo may have already done to him. She knew the kinds of punishment he exacted against those who challenged him. The humiliation of the orphans escaping and his inability to recapture them must have cut deep, costing him the respect of the tribe and his uncle, Red Tail.

Digging her heels into Angel, she moved forward, pulling alongside Bull. Lydia had to have faith the man she loved would do as he promised—find Sam and bring him home. She would not allow herself to focus on the danger awaiting them around the next bend.

Chapter Four

"It doesn't look good, Luke." Travis circled around the spot where he'd seen Mal's tracks. All horses on Redemption's Edge were shod with shoes made by Noah, stamped with the initials RE. The hoofprints of several other horses, all without shoes, caused a burning in his chest.

"They circled back and captured him." Luke didn't attempt to hide the anger in his voice.

"Let's hope that's all they did." Travis turned his horse off the trail, searching the bushes, looking for any sign of Mal.

"Over here!" Luke slid from his horse, spotting the familiar hat Mal always wore. Picking it up, he slapped it against his thigh, cursing at the discovery. "How could I have been so stupid as to leave him out here alone? This is my fault."

"The hell it is. Mal accepted the risk and volunteered. It does us no good for you to second-guess yourself."

Luke swallowed the bile in this throat. "We need to go after him."

"We do, but not by ourselves. That's what White Buffalo wants. To separate us, pick us off one at a time."

Luke knew Travis was right. They needed to wait for Bull and the others, be smart about how they continued.

"Do you know how many took him?" Luke tied the hat behind his saddle, his senses on alert.

"Best I can tell, three. Mal believes there are six or seven in the raiding party."

"We still have six. Good enough odds to get our boys back." At the sound of approaching horses, Luke pulled his shotgun out of its scabbard, pointing it down the trail.

"It's Bull." Travis holstered the gun he'd drawn, relieved he didn't have to use it.

"Where's Mal?" Bull dismounted, then helped Lydia from her saddle. His face drained of color at the sight of Mal's hat tied to Luke's saddle.

Luke waited to answer until Billy, Tat, and Johnny joined them.

"White Buffalo has him."

"How do you know?" Lydia stepped forward, grasping Bull's arm.

"Travis found the tracks, and this was lying a few feet off the trail." Luke nodded at Mal's hat.

Lydia gasped, a hand coming up to cover her mouth as her stomach churned.

"So he's alive?" Bull wrapped an arm around Lydia's shoulders and pulled her close.

Luke nodded, not wanting to speculate any further in front of Lydia. "Capturing Mal had to slow them down. I doubt they're more than a few hours ahead of us."

"But where?" Bull knew Mal was their best tracker. He thought of Cash's offer to ride along. His tracking skills were better than anyone else's. Alison would have understood, yet there was no way Bull would've asked that of the newlyweds. Travis had skills, but not nearly as good as Mal's or Cash's.

"Looks like they're heading northeast. I'm good with riding ahead."

"No, Travis," Luke answered. "We ride together from here on out."

"All this because he wants me," Lydia murmured, then turned away from the group, walking back to her horse.

Bull let her go. Nothing he could say would make her feel better. Rescuing Sam, and now Mal, was what it would take to put all this behind them.

"We need to move out. Every minute we wait allows them to get further away." Johnny had become close to Mal, his agitation evident by the tone of his voice and impatient stance.

"White Buffalo won't get too far ahead, Johnny. He *wants* us to find him." Bull glanced behind him, making certain Lydia couldn't hear them talking. "He wants Lydia. Sam and Mal are his way of getting to her."

"A trade?" Johnny asked. "I'd heard the story, but never thought he'd go this far to get her back."

"I don't know if it's as much wanting Lydia as restoring his pride. No one is more arrogant or vengeful than White Buffalo." Billy lowered his voice, turning his back to Lydia. "Red Tail promised her to him. The wedding ceremony was planned for a few days after we ran away." His jaw worked as he seemed to wrestle with some inner turmoil. When he spoke, his voice was hard and anxious. "I should've known he'd come for her. Why didn't I know?"

Luke settled a hand on the young man's shoulder. "It's not your fault, Billy. None of us believed he'd come for her after all this time."

"I don't understand how he found out she was at the ranch. We never saw him after we left the mountains." Billy let out a deep sigh, shrugging off Luke's hand.

"Right now, none of that matters. We need to get Sam and Mal back, making certain White Buffalo gets nowhere near Lydia."

"Bull's right." Luke pulled out his gun, checking his ammunition. "We find their camp, figure a way to get our boys, then get out. Billy, when we ride in, I want you to stay with Lydia.

Don't let her out of your sight and *don't* let her follow us. Understood?"

"But I—"

"I know you want to ride in with us, but White Buffalo can use you the same as Sam. Both you and Lydia need to be out of danger when we make our move."

Billy let out a breath, nodding. "Sure, Luke. I'll keep her safe."

Bull clasped Billy's shoulder. "She's not going to like it."

Billy's chuckle came out as more of a groan. "Neither do I, but it's the way it has to be."

"Travis, you take point. Stay close enough so we can see you. Let's move out." Luke swung up on Prince. "Billy, you ride with me. Johnny and Tat, you're at the back. I don't need to tell you how important it is for everyone to stay alert." Reining his horse around to follow Travis, he glanced at Bull. "You and Lydia need to stay in the middle. I don't have a good feeling about this."

Bull nodded, lines of worry creasing his face. "I don't either."

By late afternoon, they reached the top of a tree-covered hill, an open valley spreading out before them. A group of riders were visible a mile ahead. Even from this distance, Bull could make out Sam and Mal on foot, their hands bound, stumbling to keep up.

Lydia stopped alongside him, her heart racing when she spotted the band of braves. Pointing, she rose out of her saddle, letting her horse move out of the cover of the trees.

"I can see Sam...and Mal." Her voice rose with excitement as she glanced over her shoulder at Bull.

"Which means they can see us. Move back next to me, Lydia."

"We should keep going..." Her voice trailed off as Luke rode up next to Bull. She turned back to see the Indians move toward another set of low hills, Sam and Mal laboring to keep up.

"They're drawing us to them, leading us somewhere." Luke kept his gaze locked on the retreating riders.

"Directly to Red Tail's camp." Bull's eyes narrowed as the group began to disappear. "They're staying in the open and far enough ahead so they can be alerted to any attempt at rescue. White Buffalo is daring us to ride in after them."

"Once he reaches Red Tail, we'll be outnumbered." Luke grabbed his water flask, taking a swallow. "We either make our move before they reach the village or go back for more men. Everything changes once they reach Red Tail.”

“We can’t let them reach him. Please. We must rescue Sam and Mal before they get to the village.” Lydia’s plea felt like a knife in Bull’s chest.

Riding directly at them would be suicide. White Buffalo had planned his route well, not giving the search party a chance to attack. Taking Mal had been brilliant. Two hostages made the rescue more difficult and more dangerous. Bull took off his hat, raking a hand through his hair, blowing out a deep breath. They needed more men.

As if reading Bull’s mind, Luke spoke first. “We’re being drawn into a trap, Lydia. There’s only one reason they camp in the open and never ride fast enough to lose us. White Buffalo *wants* us to follow him. There are six of us, and I counted eight Crow. Plus, they’re holding two of ours. White Buffalo needs Sam, but Mal? He’d be killed the minute we rode in.”

“He’s doing all this to get to you. That’s why it’s so important he not learn you’re with us.”

“But he doesn’t know I’m with you, Bull. How could he?” She indicated her clothing.

“Somehow, he knows. He may have had a scout watching us the entire trip, reporting back to him. All it would've taken was for you to remove your hat one time. Plus, you're not exactly built like a man, sweetheart."

Her gaze shot to Bull, seeing concern mixed with warmth. She felt her face flush. They planned to marry in a few weeks, build a life together on Redemption's Edge, and start a family. Her life was perfect, certain of a future with a man she could depend on and love until they grew old. She turned her head, focusing on the spot where Sam had disappeared a few minutes before. Her future now seemed anything but certain.

"It will be dark soon. We'll camp here tonight." Luke slid from his horse, motioning for the others to do the same.

"But, Bull—"

"Luke's right, Lydia. We've been riding since sunrise. The horses and the men need rest. Trust me...White Buffalo will not get too far ahead. He wants us to know where he is."

Bull slid to the ground, then helped Lydia down. Grabbing both bedrolls, he walked into the woods, placing them next to each other under a tall pine, a good distance away from where the rest of the men had set down their gear. It was private, quiet. He hoped the location would give Lydia a chance to finally get some rest.

She glanced around, noticing the distance he'd put between them and the rest of the men. Until now, Bull had been careful to place her bedroll several feet away from his, doing his best to keep up a certain amount of propriety. A slow smile spread across her face when she realized he'd decided to push all manner of decorum aside. Tonight, she hoped to feel his strong arms around her, pulling her close, making her feel safe.

"It'll be dark in an hour. Walk with me." Bull tugged at her hand, drawing her into the woods, careful to keep the others in sight.

They'd spoken little since beginning the journey days before, and what was said focused on Sam. Although always just a few feet away, she felt the loss of Bull's closeness. She missed what they'd had—their quiet conversations, his laughter. Neither of them had laughed since White Buffalo rode into the ranch and took Sam. The joy had disappeared from their lives, replaced by dread and determination.

Lydia knew what the men whispered about when they gathered together. She knew they spoke of White Buffalo and the reason he'd taken Sam, then Mal. He wanted her. The warrior had made his desire known from the moment he'd lifted her onto his horse after Red Tail killed her parents.

In his own way, he'd courted her, earning Lydia the wrath and disdain of the Crow women. More than once, she'd been spit on, pelted with rocks, and pushed aside when tending her chores. She suspected White Buffalo knew, but chose to ignore the actions against her. He'd been brutal to Sam, humiliating him, making him do women's work instead of learning the skills of a brave. With each shameful taunt, she'd grown to hate him more, until the sight of him made her recoil in disgust.

The time at Redemption's Edge and her love for Bull had lulled her into believing she'd found safety, a haven from a loathsome future. She'd been blind to believe White Buffalo wouldn't come for her. As they walked, she gripped Bull's hand tighter, the beginnings of a plan formulating in her mind. The idea of going through with it sickened her, yet she knew of no other solution.

"We'll bring Sam and Mal home, Lydia. I promise you."

She glanced over at him, her eyes showing fear and something else Bull couldn't define.

"Don't make promises you can't keep."

"Have I ever made you a promise and broken it?" Bull turned her to him, his hands resting on her shoulders. "I'll do whatever it takes to bring Sam home to you."

She looked away, unable to hold his gaze, her voice barely above a whisper. "White Buffalo wants me."

"Look at me, Lydia." He waited until she lifted her face. "He isn't going to get near you. We'll do whatever is needed to get Sam and Mal back, keeping you safe. Do you understand?"

She nodded, already feeling an intense sense of dread tightening her chest. Bull was a good, honorable man who worked hard, taking care of those he loved. He'd jump in front of a bullet if it meant protecting her or any of those he considered family. She glanced behind him to the other men huddled together, talking in low voices. At that moment, she realized each one of them risked his life to bring her brother home and protect her. And they could all die for their efforts. She knew of only one solution. Swallowing the fear at what needed to be done, she nodded.

"Yes, I understand."

He pulled her to him, wrapping strong arms around her, holding her close. Circling her arms around his waist, she rested her head against his chest, taking comfort from his warmth and strength. He'd honored her with his love, asking her to be his wife. Sucking in a ragged breath, she closed her eyes, knowing there would never be another man for her. Bull was her life, the only man she ever wanted and would ever love. In that instant, it became important he understood how she felt. Tonight might be her last chance to show him.

Bull rested his chin on her head, stroking a hand down her hair. "Let's get something to eat, then sleep. Tomorrow will be a long day."

Stepping away, Lydia grabbed his hand, forcing a smile as she looked up at him. An odd sense of peace consumed her as she accepted her decision. Tonight would be about her and Bull. By the time the sun rose over the eastern mountains, their lives would change...and neither of them would ever be able to go back.

The camp had quieted, the fire reduced to a few burning embers as everyone slept. Well, everyone except her and Travis, who rested his back against a tree trunk several yards away, his rifle in his lap, his gaze fixed on the distant horizon.

Lydia propped herself up on her elbows, looking around, relieved to see the others sleeping with their backs to her. Scooting closer to Bull, she reached a hand out to touch his chest, letting her fingers slip between the buttons. He jerked an instant before his eyes popped open.

Clear hazel eyes gazed into his, a timid smile tilting up the corners of her mouth. His breath caught as she played with the soft hairs on his chest.

"Lydia..." he whispered, his hand coming up to grasp her wrist. "This isn't a good idea."

Her smile broadened. "It's the best idea I've had in days." She rested her other hand on his arm, pulling herself toward him, placing a kiss on his lips. When he didn't respond, she brushed her mouth across his until he moved closer, placing a hand behind her head and deepening the kiss.

A soft moan escaped her lips as heat rushed through her. Raising her arms to circle around his neck, she drew him in so their bodies aligned, creating an exquisite friction.

His hands splayed across her back, he groaned into her mouth when her body writhed against his. Pulling back, he rested his forehead against hers, sucking in an unsteady breath.

"Lydia...we have to stop."

Her answer was to grip his head with both hands, searching his eyes.

"No." Drawing him back down, she brought her lips up to his, unwilling to stop.

"They'll hear us. Do you want that?" he murmured against her mouth.

"I don't care. I need you, Bull. Please, make love to me."

A whispered curse preceded his arms tightening around her as his lips traced a path from the corner of her mouth, along the curve of her jaw, and down the ivory column of her neck.

Kissing the pulsing hollow at the base of her throat, he felt himself surrender. He didn't know what tomorrow would bring—if luck would be with them, or if they'd face a cruel fate. Bull's only thought was the overwhelming desire for the woman in his arms, the unrepentant drive to love her, without regard to those sleeping so close.

Shifting her to her back, he hovered over her, searching her face one more time.

"Are you sure this is what you want tonight?"

Smiling up at him, she cupped his face in her hands. "It's what I want every night."

Chapter Five

Rolling over, Bull reached out, surprised when he didn't feel Lydia next to him. Sitting up, he scanned the camp, still seeing no sign of her.

The sun hadn't come up. Everyone except Travis, Luke, and Billy were still asleep. Tossing off the blanket, Bull stood, hands on hips as he made a slow circle, then walked toward the three men hovering over a small fire.

"Where's Lydia?"

Three sets of eyes shot up to meet his. Billy jumped up, his eyes wide. "I haven't seen her since last night."

"We thought she bunked down with you." Luke stood, walking toward the horses, turning abruptly to stare at Bull. "Her horse is gone."

"What?" Bull ran toward the horses, a string of curses spewing from his lips when he saw Angel missing. "Where the hell is she?" he roared, storming back to gather their bedrolls. "We've got to find her."

"Travis, see if you can find her tracks. Everyone else, get ready to ride." Luke walked up to Bull as he tied the bedding to the back of Abe's saddle. "We'll find her, Bull."

"Luke?" Travis came toward them, shaking his head. "One set of prints riding out." He looked over at Bull. "She's headed in the direction of White Buffalo's camp."

"But...why?" Bull scrubbed a hand down his face. "What is she thinking?"

"She's going to offer a trade." Billy moved next to Bull, his voice strained.

Grabbing Billy by his shoulders, Bull glared at him. "How do you know that?"

Billy's face reddened, both anger and fear evident in his voice as he pushed Bull away. "I don't—not for sure. But I know Lydia, and she'd do anything for family. Even giving herself to that miserable savage to free Sam and Mal."

Bull's chest tightened, his heart pounding as he bent forward, placing his hands on his knees, sucking in a deep breath. He couldn't think, could barely breathe. The thought of Lydia leaving him, riding out without a word to hand herself over to their enemy, couldn't find a place in his brain. Without saying the vows, he'd made her his in every way a man could. Now she was willing to share herself with another man. *In order to save her brother*, he reminded himself. The thought gave him no comfort.

"We'll get her back."

Bull heard Luke's words and slowly rose, his gaze locked on the mountains to the east. Straightening, he glanced at the men who waited for him to give an indication of his intentions. As much as he wanted to race after her, he couldn't put them in more danger. Even her leaving didn't change what had to be done—locate the Crow camp and determine their next move.

"Lydia leaving changes everything." Bull cleared his throat, shoving aside the hard ball of fear in his gut. "Assuming Billy is right, we need to ride hard, catch her before she reaches White Buffalo."

"I'm on point." Travis swung into his saddle, not waiting for Bull or Luke to respond.

Luke nodded at the others. Nothing else needed to be said. They'd ride flat out, doing their best to catch her before she made the greatest mistake of her life.

Lydia slowed Angel to a walk, glancing behind her, letting out a ragged breath. Her body shook with the knowledge she wasn't alone. She'd sensed a presence for the last hour, believing at least one of White Buffalo's braves was following her. Shifting in the saddle, a shudder rippled through her as she accepted how alone she felt and what she'd left behind.

Her thoughts locked on Bull. Lying next to him last night, wrapped in his strong arms, her resolve had almost faltered in the hours before dawn. Staring at the stars, she thought of every possible option, knowing the fate of Sam and Mal, perhaps the entire search party, rested with her and no one else. Her heart broke knowing the man she loved more than her own life would never understand her actions. She couldn't bear to think of Bull's pain when he found her gone.

Sneaking out of camp had been easier than anticipated. Travis had taken a position far enough away to not notice her tiptoeing around the sleeping men. Angel made no sound as Lydia climbed onto her back, guiding the horse in a wide circle around Travis, following the tree line until she found a trail east.

Riding alone had given her ample time to consider what she'd done, what she'd thrown away. Standing on the crest of the hill, looking down on the valley below, knowing it wouldn't be long before she traded her freedom for the release of Sam and Mal, she wondered if she'd made the right decision. Bull had promised he'd bring Sam home. He'd asked her to trust him.

It felt as if they'd started their journey ages ago. In reality, they'd only been on the trail a week—a week where they'd had the Crow camp in sight each night, and a good man had been captured. She wanted it to end. She wanted to find Sam and Mal, rain havoc on White Buffalo, and escape to the shelter of Redemption's Edge.

But the men were cautious, serious in their quest, and not prone to act without thinking. They planned to take Sam and Mal back, no matter the time it took or if they had to follow the Crow to Canada. To a man, they were patient, unwavering, and loyal.

She placed a hand on her chest, trying to calm her erratic breathing as she allowed herself to consider everything that had happened. Had she given the search party enough time? Had her decision to leave been reckless and selfish? They were good men, putting their lives in jeopardy to rescue others. Glancing over her shoulder, her heart raced at the thought she'd made a mistake by giving up too soon.

Any doubts she had about continuing disappeared the instant two braves emerged from the brush, rushing toward her, pulling to an abrupt stop. She recognized both as close friends of White Buffalo. Neither spoke as their gazes wandered over her body. One grabbed Angel's reins as the other rifled through the saddlebags.

Satisfied she carried nothing to harm them, her wrists were tied together with a leather thong. The one she knew to be Strong Eagle moved close, nudging his horse against Angel's side, causing the mare to dance away.

Tall with strong arms and muscled thighs, he'd made no secret of his desire to have her, despite her being promised to his friend. Lydia knew if White Buffalo didn't claim her, Strong Eagle would. Either way, she now faced a life she'd run from, hoping to never return.

Letting out a deep laugh, Strong Eagle stared at her, his voice strong, intimidating.

"Golden Bird, you made a good decision to ride from the white men. White Buffalo will be pleased." Without giving her a chance to speak, he nodded to the other brave.

An instant later, they were riding fast and hard away from the spot she'd left Bull only hours before. Gripping the saddle horn with her bound hands, she held on tight, unable to swipe at the tears of fear, regret, and hopelessness streaming down her face.

As the wind whipped over her, drying the moisture on her cheeks, she pushed aside her doubts, making the hard decision to focus on the reasons she rode away from her life with Bull.

Giving herself to White Buffalo would be a small price to pay for Sam's and Mal's freedom. It would guarantee they, and the search party, would have safe passage back to Redemption's Edge. No matter how much Bull might hate her, be repulsed by the turn of events, Lydia knew, deep in her heart, her actions were justified.

"Right here." Travis pointed to the spot where one horse approached the top of the hill, but three rode away. "This is where they found her." He rode several yards ahead. "And this is the direction they took."

"Straight to White Buffalo's camp." Bull sucked in a harsh breath, then let it out, his hands clenching on the saddle horn.

"All we have to do is follow and we'll find her." Luke had pulled his horse alongside Bull's, seeing the unshod tracks of Crow horses. "Can't say how we'll get all three back, but we will."

"You know as well as I do her intention is to trade herself for Sam and Mal. By the time we reach them, the boys will be on foot, heading to the ranch, and Lydia..." Bull couldn't say the words. He knew exactly what would happen to Lydia the moment Sam and Mal were released...if they were released. "White Buffalo may keep Lydia, as well as Sam and Mal. There's no real reason to let them go."

"Except knowing we'd continue to chase them. He might believe we'll give up if he has already taken Lydia as his wife." Luke saw the pain cross Bull's face and wished he could pull the words back. "I'm sorry, but that's what I believe. We can't do what's needed if we don't accept what we might be facing. I've got to believe he'll let the boys go. Once we have them, we can make our plans for getting Lydia back." A play of emotions washed across Bull's face. "You *would* want her back, right?"

"Damn right I want her back. I don't care what happens or what White Buffalo does. Lydia is mine, Luke. She'll always be mine."

Luke clasped a hand on his friend's shoulder. "Lydia loves you, Bull. She's doing this to save Sam and Mal. That's all."

Bull nodded. Hearing the words was easy. Accepting them in his heart posed a bigger challenge.

Strong Eagle let out an ear-piercing cry as the three rode into the Crow village. Lydia's spine stiffened, her body shaking as she lifted her gaze to see women and a few children rushing toward them. Gathered together outside one tipi, older men stood and made their way over. She recognized most, seeing a few more children than when she and the others had run away.

She continued to search faces, her gaze darting around the encampment, not seeing Sam or Mal. A scuffle on the right drew her attention. Turning in the saddle, her breath seized at the sight of White Buffalo striding toward her.

Behind him stumbled Sam and Mal, both being shoved harshly by four braves walking behind them.

Sliding from his horse, Strong Eagle spoke to White Buffalo, whose gaze never left Lydia's. After a moment, White Buffalo nodded before walking to her, roughly pulling her off Angel's back. He didn't try to help her when she lost her footing and fell to the ground.

"You bastard!" Sam's curse rang through the village, yet White Buffalo only laughed, saying something to Strong Eagle before Sam was shoved to the ground, a foot in the middle of his back holding him down.

"His mouth has grown loud since you left. Scared Boy is no longer one who works with women." White Buffalo used Sam's Crow name as he threw out the warning. Some would take it as a compliment. Not Lydia. She understood his intent was to humble Sam, break his spirit, and force him to cower as he did when he'd been held captive. Smirking, she lifted her chin, not giving him the satisfaction of a reply.

White Buffalo grimaced as he walked around her, his gaze drifting up and down her body as if assessing a horse, determining if it were suitable to ride. Coming to a halt, he fisted her hair in his hand, forcing her to within inches of his face.

"Golden Bird should not have run. Now you must learn your place."

She didn't give him the satisfaction of grimacing or showing fear. Instead, Lydia hardened her gaze and stared into his eyes.

"I came here to ask a trade."

Roaring with laughter, White Buffalo released her. Strong Eagle stepped forward, then backed away at his friend's gesture. As quickly as the humor filled his face, it disappeared, replaced by an arrogant smile. "You have no power to trade."

"Then I will run."

This time, he didn't laugh. Wrapping a strong hand around her arm, his fingers dug into her skin as he tugged her close. "You *will* do as I say, Golden Bird."

She grimaced in pain, even as her resolute gaze never left his. "Then I will appeal to Red Tail. He is a wise man. He will listen to me."

White Buffalo's brows rose slightly before he steeled his features. Shoving her away, watching in dispassionate silence as she landed hard, he nodded to Strong Eagle.

"Bind her. Take her to my—"

"She will be brought to me."

Lydia's gaze shot to the familiar voice of the band's chief, Red Tail. Shuddering at the unyielding look he sent White Buffalo, her unease grew as the older man's attention moved to her. His features didn't soften as he studied her, as if she were a new and unfamiliar creature.

A hard man who'd experienced much suffering, she knew he could show a great deal of compassion or kill without remorse. Working alongside the other women during her previous captivity, she'd understood enough Crow to know he'd anguished over the decision to break from the Crow tribe and forge a separate life with over a dozen braves and a few women. A few years later, their village still survived by raiding white settlements, stealing from the nearby Blackfoot, and moving frequently. He held no love for the white man, yet had never lifted a hand to any of the white captives living in his camp.

"Strong Eagle, you will bring Golden Bird to my tipi. I will hear what this woman has to say."

Letting out a breath, she shrieked in pain when Strong Eagle yanked her up, pushing her toward Red Tail's tipi. A few minutes later, she sat on her heels before the chief. An elder she recognized sat to his right, another she didn't to his left. White Buffalo walked in behind her, said something to Red Tail, then took a seat when he nodded.

Red Tail looked at Strong Eagle, who stood inside the tipi's entrance. "Cut the ties."

Strong Eagle didn't make the mistake of glancing at White Buffalo before doing what the chief ordered. Rubbing her raw skin, Lydia winced at the redness and bruising before letting her gaze wander over the three elders before her—the men who would decide her fate, as well as Sam's and Mal's.

The silence grew as the men stared back at her, their faces a collective mask. Lydia dropped her gaze to the ground, feeling the growing dampness on her forehead. She refused to show any weakness by wiping it away. Instead, she closed her eyes, focusing on what needed to be said—the request for a trade, and her promise not to run again.

Red Tail lit a pipe, passing it to the other two elders. Each took it and inhaled, then passed it back, never uttering a sound. Minutes ticked by before Red Tail set the pipe aside.

"You will speak, Golden Bird."

Licking parched lips, Lydia cleared her throat, forcing an unwavering gaze at Red Tail as she tried to ignore her fear. Opening her mouth, she clamped it shut as an unbidden image of Bull flashed through her mind. Lingering on it for a brief instant, she shoved the pain aside, clearing her throat a second time.

"Running from the people was a mistake. I have returned freely and will accept whatever punishment you feel is just." Her gaze sharpened as she continued. "However, I ask a trade. I will stay, promise not to leave, but I ask that you release my brother and his friend. They have not harmed the people. They are innocent." She felt her body shudder as Red Tail and the other two elders continued to watch her, saying nothing. "I—"

She stopped when Red Tail held up his hand. The three men spoke in whispers, nodding, shaking their heads, then appearing to agree. Red Tail shot a look at White Buffalo before speaking.

"It will be as you ask."

She let out a breath, her shoulders relaxing before jerking to attention when Red Tail continued.

"You will be bound to White Buffalo. That is our decision." Reaching for his pipe, Red Tail began the process of cleaning it, a sure signal the meeting was over.

She nodded, knowing he'd say nothing more. A brief moment of elation washed over her, knowing Sam and Mal would soon be free. The joy disappeared when a strong hand gripped her arm, forcing her to her feet and out of the tipi.

"Wait." She tried to wrench free. "I want to see Sam and Mal. You have to let me see them."

Ignoring her, White Buffalo roughly pulled Lydia next to him, then opened the flaps to another tipi, tossing her inside as if she weighed no more than a feather.

"You will not leave." His menacing glare told her what would happen if she tried.

Lydia paced in a circle in the small space, her heart pounding. She needed to see Sam and Mal, explain to them what happened, ask them to give Bull a message. Knowing she had little time, Lydia started for the entry flaps, stopping when an older woman appeared, a buckskin dress draped over her arm. Lydia recognized her as White Buffalo's mother. Without a word, the woman set the dress aside, stepped in front of her, and delivered a painful slap to Lydia's cheek.

Her face stinging, eyes watering, Lydia stumbled away from the woman. As her mind cleared, she straightened, planning to shove past the older woman to find Sam and Mal before it was too late. Taking a tentative step toward the opening, she froze when two more women she recognized entered the tipi. Neither moved from the entry, blocking her path—and her last chance to see Sam one more time.

Chapter Six

Time passed in a blur as the three women worked to prepare Lydia for the ceremony binding her to White Buffalo. Washing her body, cutting her hair short in the Crow tradition, then dressing her in the elk tooth buckskin dress seemed to take hours. When a respectful voice preceded a young woman stepping inside the tipi, Lydia realized the sun still shown outside.

"White Buffalo says it is time." She spoke to the older women, then glanced at Lydia. The unmistakable look of disdain clear in her features, her eyes sparking with hatred. It was at that moment Lydia recognized the woman. She'd grown up with White Buffalo, been promised to him as a girl, only to be pushed aside by the warrior when Lydia had been taken captive.

"Tell my son this woman is ready." White Buffalo's mother stepped next to the younger woman, whispered in her ear, then nodded at the flap. She sent Lydia one more hateful look before disappearing outside, leaving the flap open.

Lydia heard singing, drums beating, and children's laughter, feeling the breeze begin to cool the heated air. It all seemed so normal, when everything about her life was about to change. Her mind wrapped around one thought—never seeing those she loved again. Sam would be fine. He'd grow into a strong man who'd take care of Selina. He'd work the ranch, fall in love, marry, and raise a family. Selina, already a proficient rider and budding cook, would also fall in love and marry. And Bull...her heart twisted painfully at what she knew would be his future.

The man she loved would recover from her betrayal, meet another woman, and transfer the love they shared to someone else. She sucked in an unsteady breath, gripping her chest. Even as she told herself the sacrifice was worth it, Lydia knew she would never recover from losing Bull.

"Down there." Luke handed Bull the field glasses, pointing to the Crow camp nestled among the trees in the valley below. Billy and Travis lay on their stomachs next to them, while Johnny and Tat watched the horses.

Bull trained the glasses on the village, scanning each tipi and all movement, looking for any sign of Lydia, Sam, or Mal. Movement out of the corner of his eye had him swinging the glasses in that direction. Two riders on a single horse raced from the camp. Sharpening his gaze, he sucked in a breath and looked at Luke.

"It's Sam and Mal. They're riding right toward us."

"Are they being followed?"

Bull raised the glasses, focusing on the Crow camp. "No." The air left his lungs.

No explanation was needed. They all knew what it meant for Sam and Mal to be riding away. Lydia's plan had worked.

"I'll have Johnny and Tat meet them. The rest of you stay here." Luke pushed back from the ledge, then stood, retracing his steps to the horses.

"Can you see Lydia?" Billy asked, his voice anxious.

Bull saw children running around, groups of men talking, women finishing chores outside their tipis, but no sign of Lydia. Then his gaze lit on a lone figure standing with his arms crossed and feet apart. His face was painted, his clothing appearing to be more ceremonial than that of a brave.

"Billy, take a look at the warrior in the center of the camp." Handing the glasses over, Bull continued to stare, even though he couldn't make out anything at this distance.

Billy adjusted the glasses a couple times, moving them across the camp until they focused on the figure Bull described. "White Buffalo." He lowered the glasses, casting a somber look at Bull. "He's wearing ceremonial clothing."

Bull swallowed the bile in his throat. "What ceremony?"

"Marriage."

As if in a trance, Lydia let the women guide her to a place several feet away from White Buffalo. As a captive, she'd seen the brief marriage ceremony several times, vowing to herself she'd never participate and certainly never be the bride. Yet here she was, bound to the one man she never wanted to see again.

She knew it would be short. Their traditions were nothing like the white man's. White Buffalo would offer her a horse, Red Tail would take their hands and fold them together, then the medicine man would announce Lydia and White Buffalo were now bound together. They were then free to stay and celebrate or disappear—whichever White Buffalo decided.

The sounds of the drums and singing pounded in her head. Her stomach roiled at the chatter of those surrounding them. Then silence. She glanced up to see Red Tail, along with the medicine man, emerge from his tipi. To her right, Strong Eagle appeared, leading a horse toward

White Buffalo. It was an offering she cared nothing about.

Lydia understood their tradition of the husband returning to the bride's mother's tipi to live, wondering what it meant for her. She had no mother, no tipi...no home.

"White Buffalo, you agree to be bound to this woman, Golden Bird?" Red Tail stared at the warrior, his features stern, unmoving.

"Yes."

Red Tail then turned to Lydia. "Golden Bird, you agree to be bound to this man, White Buffalo?"

She hesitated, knowing there was but one answer. Offering herself in exchange for Sam's and Mal's freedom hadn't taken hold until this moment—a moment when a promise became real.

Glancing at White Buffalo, she saw the anger begin to burn in his eyes. Incurring his wrath would be a monumental mistake.

Clearing her throat, she nodded. "Yes."

Red Tail took her right hand, then White Buffalo's, holding them together as he looked at the people of his village.

"This man and this woman are now bound." The chief stepped back, turning, walking back to his tipi.

White Buffalo did not release her hand. Tugging her to him, he leaned in close, warning her with his eyes. "You will come with me." Not waiting for a response, he pulled her to a tipi near the far side of the village. Opening the flap, he didn't turn to her as he stepped inside.

Lydia came to an abrupt halt, her body rigid. "No. Wait." She knew this moment would come, had told herself over and over not to resist, knowing the consequences could be severe.

Faced with the reality of what would happen inside the tipi, she found her legs wouldn't move. Her breathing stalled, her gaze darting around as she searched for an escape. White Buffalo's mother told her Sam and Mal had been released. By now, they would be safely back with Bull and the others. Red Tail had honored her request.

By her words, she'd fulfilled her promise to be bound to White Buffalo. Could she go through with being bound to him physically? Her life would cease to exist once she crossed into the tipi. The only alternative was to run, which she felt certain would result in death.

One hard tug caused Lydia to stumble across the threshold. Brutal hands grasped her arms, shaking her until she felt her teeth rattle. He glared at her as if he'd been able to read her thoughts.

"It is too late for escape, Golden Bird." With those words, he tossed her to the ground and closed the flap.

Bull wanted to rage at the world, shout that Lydia was his and no other man had the right to her. Watching her disappear into the tent with White Buffalo was too much to bear.

When he started to push from the ground, a hand clamped across his mouth before strong hands pulled him away from the ledge, wrestling him back to the ground. Luke and Travis worked to control what could be a deadly situation if Bull acted on his emotions.

As he struggled to gain freedom from their hold on his arms, Tat and Johnny dropped to their knees, each grabbing one of his legs, holding him still.

"We *will* get her back." Luke stared at his close friend, his gaze unwavering as hate poured from Bull's face. "Going in there now will only get us all killed, and Lydia will still be with White Buffalo."

Bull shook his head, his body convulsing as he tried to wrench away from their grasp.

"Dammit, Bull. You have to get control. Besides, we have something White Buffalo doesn't." A small grin pulled up the corners of Luke's mouth when Bull's eyes went wide. "Now, if you're ready to listen, we'll let go."

Bull cursed, stopping his attempts to break free. The others backed away when he stood, not knowing what to expect from a man who'd always been slow to anger and reticent to use his fists. He turned to Luke, a look on his face none of them had ever seen before.

"You tell me what we have that will change any of this." The look in his eyes was hostile, yet pleading. He needed to hear a solution, something that would take away the pain seizing his heart.

"There's nothing that will change what we just saw, but we do have a way to get her back." Luke watched Bull's eyes narrow. "Unless you won't take her back after what you saw."

"Hell yes, I want her back. I don't care what he does to her. She'll always be mine."

Luke studied Bull's face, seeing bleak despair and unfathomable loss. "Who hates Red Tail and White Buffalo even more than we do?"

Bull shook his head, a humorless laugh escaping his lips. "No one hates them more than me."

"You're wrong. There's one man who's never made a secret of his disgust of the renegade Crow band. Hell, he has no love for any of the Crow people, but especially not Red Tail.”

Bull's gaze left Luke's as he thought about those he knew with a grudge against the Crow. A slow surge of understanding had him straightening, his eyes widening.

“Running Bear...” Bull breathed out the name as if it were a small slice of salvation.

“That's right. The Crow band has been raiding his village for years, stealing horses, food, and...” Luke paused, letting Bull recall why else they might garner the support of the Blackfoot chief.

“They tried to take Running Bear's granddaughter when she'd been alone at the river.” Bull remembered the incident of a few months ago. “If we hadn't come along, scattering White Buffalo and his braves, they would have succeeded.”

“Running Bear promised whatever we need, all we had to do was ask.”

Bull thought about the consequences of asking the Blackfoot for help. The tribe aligned themselves with the Sioux and Cheyenne, traditional enemies of the Crow. Asking Running Bear for help would trigger a conflict beyond anything imaginable. Many would be killed to reclaim one woman. His woman.

"I won't ask Running Bear to put his people in danger. I can't accept the responsibility of the lives that will be lost." Bull closed his eyes, then shook his head, turning his back to Luke. "Taking Lydia back is up to me and no one else."

Luke crossed his arms, bracing himself for Bull's reaction. "Can't let you go in alone."

Bull spun around, taking a threatening step toward Luke. "You don't have a choice. I'm going after her—*alone.*"

"The hell you are." Billy moved to one side of Luke.

Travis flanked Luke's other side. "Sorry, Bull. You can't make the decision for us."

"For any of us."

Bull turned at the sound of Sam's voice. He and Mal staggered toward him, their clothes torn and filthy, their bodies riddled with cuts and bruises. Walking to him, Bull wrapped his arms around Sam, emotion overwhelming them both.

Sam dropped his arms and stepped away. "I'm going after my sister, Bull. You might as well accept it."

"We're all going." Mal dropped to the ground. "Just give me a few minutes to rest up."

Bull stared at Mal. He'd been captured, brutalized, then released. He shouldn't want to return, putting himself in more danger.

"Did they beat all common sense out of both of you?" Bull asked.

Sam scrubbed a hand down his face. "Might be, but it doesn't matter. I'm getting my sister away from that sorry sonofabitch."

"If it were Ginny or Rachel, what would you do?" Luke's gaze met Bull's, challenging him.

Accepting a hard line had been drawn by the men around him, Bull let out a slow breath. "I'd go after her."

Luke clamped a hand on Bull's shoulder. "Then it's settled. First light, we ride west to find Running Bear."

Chapter Seven

"It's been almost two weeks, Rachel. I thought they would've been back by now." Ginny rested a hand on her protruding stomach as she lowered herself onto a kitchen chair. "Do you think they're all right?"

Rachel glanced over her shoulder, noting the deep lines at the corners of Ginny's eyes and the signs of worry on her face. She'd stayed with Rachel and Dax since Luke left with the search party. Each day added more stress to her already drawn features.

"I wish I knew, Ginny. I'm as worried as you, but Dax says it could take weeks for them to find Sam and return."

"He's not anxious about them being gone so long?" Ginny had watched Dax as he left each morning, then returned for supper. On the outside, he seemed calm, unconcerned about his brother and the others. As an ex-Confederate general, she knew he'd school himself to show no signs of weakness or doubt. She wondered if he felt the same inside.

Rachel dried her hands on her apron, turning to face Ginny. "If he is, he's doing a good job of hiding it." Taking a seat, she grasped Ginny's hand and squeezed. "Luke would've sent someone back for help if they were in trouble. None of them are the type to make rash decisions or put themselves in more danger than necessary. They'll do what's needed, then come home."

If she were being truthful with herself, Rachel had slept little the last few nights for worry over the men. Like Ginny, she'd thought they'd find Sam, take him back, and return within a few days. According to Dax, her expectations were idealistic at best, naïve at worst. At this point in Ginny's pregnancy, she needed as much encouragement as possible, not an increase in her worry.

"Let's walk out to the barn. Dax is with the men on the north pasture and asked me to check on the new colt. I'm not sure why. I don't think I could tell if he had a problem." Rachel laughed, taking Ginny's arm and helping her stand, leading her out of the house.

With so many gone, few men worked close to the house during the day. Most were needed to ride fences or keep check on the herd. Dax had asked Dirk to move the cattle from the eastern section of the ranch to the west and north. It meant the cattle had to be rotated more frequently, but it made it easier to keep track of the large herd.

"You haven't been out to see the colt, have you?" Rachel stopped when Ginny's face contorted in pain. "Are you all right?"

Clutching her stomach with both hands, Ginny bent over, crying out.

Wrapping an arm around her waist, Rachel helped her to the side of the barn where Luke and Dax had built a small bench. "Sit down and tell me what you're feeling."

Ginny sucked in a breath as another sharp pain gripped her stomach. She looked up at Rachel, her eyes wide with panic. "Something's wrong. This shouldn't be happening...should it?"

Rachel bit her lip, not wanting to say anything until she knew more. "Let's get you inside. I need to do a quick check before we jump to any conclusions."

"Now, lay back and take deep breaths. This won't take long." Lifting Ginny's skirt, it only took one glance for Rachel's heart to sink. The telltale spotting indicated a real problem—one needing more expertise than as a nurse. "I'll be right back." Returning a few minutes later with warm water and a rag, she cleaned Ginny as best she could, then helped her sit up. "We need to see my uncle. I'll get the wagon ready."

Harnessing her horse to the wagon, Rachel pulled it to the front porch, secured the lines, then dashed inside to grab blankets from a chest. After spreading them out into a makeshift bed in the back of the wagon, she returned to help Ginny.

"I feel warm, Rachel."

"What's going on?" The women had been so focused on getting Ginny into the wagon, they'd failed to see Dax and Dirk ride up.

"She has a fever." Rachel glanced at Ginny, then ran into the house, Dax following close behind while Dirk stayed by the wagon. "I need to wake Patrick and get water." She turned to Dax. "She's spotting. I'm afraid she's losing the baby."

Dax nodded, cursing under his breath. "I'll get Patrick. You pack whatever else she'll need before we head to town." Dax took the stairs two at a time to get their son ready for the trip.

Within minutes, Dax sat on the wagon bench, the lines in his hands. He glanced over his shoulder at Rachel, holding Patrick, sitting next to Ginny in the back.

"Are you ready?"

"We're good, Dax."

He shifted his gaze to Dirk. "You're in charge while I'm gone. We'll be at the clinic. Don't know when we'll be back."

"I'll take care of everything, boss. Do what you need to." Dirk leaned over the saddle horn, suspecting their reason for the trip to town. His thoughts went immediately to Luke, knowing he'd blame himself if anything happened to Ginny or their baby while he wasn't around. *What a damn mess*, he thought before turning his horse around and heading back to work.

Ginny moaned, gripping Rachel's hand so hard her knuckles turned white. Pulling her knees up to lessen the pain, her panicked gaze locked on Rachel.

"I'm losing the baby."

"We don't know what's happening, Ginny. I know you're in pain, but try to relax as much as you can. It won't take long to get to town." She continued to hold Ginny's hand as Patrick squirmed on her lap. "Patrick, sweetheart, please settle down. How would you like to visit Miss Suzanne when we get to town?"

Old enough to walk, he still didn't talk much, but nodded his head vigorously. Suzanne Briar, the owner of the local boardinghouse, had a way with children, even young ones like Patrick. Rachel prayed Suzanne would be able to watch him while she and Dax were at the clinic with Ginny.

"What will I do if I lose the baby? Luke will...he'll..." She sobbed, unable to continue.

Rachel didn't reply, knowing Luke would understand and be supportive, as Dax would. The worst would be the guilt she knew Luke would feel for not being here. *At least she has us*, Rachel thought as she turned to look over Dax's shoulder, seeing Splendor come into view.

"Two more minutes. How's she doing?" Dax asked, glancing behind him. Rachel shook her head.

Sucking in a breath, Dax thought of his brother. Luke hadn't been off his mind for more than a few minutes since the search party left. He thought he'd done a good job of hiding his concern from Rachel and Ginny, letting them believe he wasn't worried. After two weeks, worry over Luke and the others all but consumed him. And now Ginny might lose the baby. Even if Luke were here, there wasn't anything he could do to change the outcome.

"We're here. I'll help with Ginny." Dax secured the lines, then climbed over the seat into the back as Rachel dashed into the clinic with Patrick. "Come on, Ginny. Let's get you inside."

"Uncle Charles, are you here?" Rachel pushed through into the back room. Seeing no sign of him, she went out the back door, taking the short walk to his house behind the clinic. She could smell something cooking the moment she stepped inside. "Uncle Charles?"

"In the kitchen, Rachel." He set down the spoon he'd been using to stir the stew, then turned, his smile fading when he saw her face. "What is it?"

"Ginny may be losing the baby." Her voice broke.

Charles wasted no time scooping Patrick out of Rachel's arms. "Come with me, lad. Let's go check on your Aunt Ginny." Walking into the clinic, he found Dax bending over Ginny, holding a cool rag to her forehead. "Here you go, Patrick." He handed him to Dax, then went right to work.

"Why don't you take him to Suzanne, Dax? I'm sure she'll be glad to watch him." Rachel stroked a hand down Patrick's thick, dark hair.

"I won't be gone long."

As Dax disappeared through the front door, Rachel rolled up her sleeves and washed her hands. Swallowing her concerns, she steeled herself for the news she feared.

"Who do we have here?" Nick Barnett walked into the boardinghouse, his heart almost coming to a stop when he saw Suzanne bouncing a boy on her lap. He'd lived in a room at Suzanne's since coming to Splendor to run the Dixie Saloon. Since then, he'd become a well-respected businessman with a significant investment in the town. He'd long since outgrown his need to live upstairs, purchasing land near the Pelletier place in the hopes of someday talking the beautiful woman before him into becoming his bride.

"You recognize Patrick Pelletier, don't you?" She smiled up at him, the brilliance sucking the air from his lungs. "Nick, are you all right?"

Shaking his head, he knelt before her, taking a good look at the laughing little boy. "I'm fine, Suzanne, just surprised at how much he's grown since I last saw him." He looked around, expecting to see Rachel or Dax. "What's he doing here?"

Suzanne's face fell. "Ginny's at the doc's."

"Isn't it too soon for the baby?" Nick stood, removing his hat, unconsciously adjusting the patch over his left eye.

"Yes, it is."

Her flat voice and change in mood had him studying her. He rested a gentle hand on her shoulder. "Are you going to tell me what's going on?"

Blowing out a breath, she stood, setting Patrick on his feet and taking his hand, lowering her voice. "She may be losing the baby."

Nick didn't respond as he thought of how much Ginny and Luke wanted this baby. He'd liked Ginny from the first time he'd met her when she lived in a tiny room at the boardinghouse with her younger sister, Mary. Suzanne had provided it in exchange for Ginny's help cleaning rooms. Then she'd met Luke and her life changed, although Nick and Luke had almost come to blows over an unfortunate misunderstanding. Since then, Nick had become good friends with both of them.

"And Luke hasn't returned?" Nick walked alongside her as she guided Patrick into the kitchen. She pulled a cookie out of a canister, handing it to the boy.

"No, he hasn't. The Pelletiers seem to be getting hit hard from every direction right now."

"You know Luke will blame himself if anything happens to Ginny or the baby while he's gone. That man's got more pride than any five men." Nick had learned that first-hand. His jaw hardened at the injustice that might befall the young couple.

"I just pray Luke, Bull, and the others get back with Sam soon. If she loses the baby, Ginny's going to need Luke by her side." She thought about all that had happened over the last few weeks. Cash and Allie's wedding, Sam being kidnapped, the search party leaving at a time when Dax needed all the help he could get, and now Ginny. "Lydia's another one I'm worried about, Nick. Who knows what she'll do if those Indians hurt her brother." She glanced at him, her eyes showing a spark. "You know she'd die before letting any harm come to him or Selina."

Pouring a cup of coffee, Nick took a seat at the small table against one wall, thinking of all the people he now considered friends. Everyone in Splendor came west for a different reason. Each story distinct, the reasons for staying diverse. Suzanne had come with her husband. When she lost him and their daughter in a freak blizzard, she'd buried her heart, putting all her energy into the boardinghouse and helping as many people as she could. Nick had always been drawn to her big heart and giving nature. The fact her beauty took his breath away didn't hurt.

"Bull isn't going to let Lydia do anything foolish. They took a good number of men, all experienced. I'm sure it will turn out all right." At least Nick hoped it would. There was no telling what would happen if the search party returned without Sam or lost anyone else. Setting down the empty cup, Nick stood. "I'm going to head to the clinic."

"You'll let me know how she's doing?" Her worried expression caused his chest to constrict.

Taking a step closer, Nick bent down, brushing his lips across hers, then drawing back, hearing her gasp. "You'll be the first person I talk to." Touching a finger to the tip of her nose, he turned, strolling out, leaving Suzanne with her jaw hanging open.

Nick hadn't made it twenty feet down the boardwalk when Dax came through the clinic door. He watched as his friend scrubbed a hand down his face, then let out a feral oath. Continuing until he stood a couple feet away, Nick waited for Dax to speak.

"She lost the baby, Nick. Dear God. What am I going to tell Luke?" Rubbing his eyes, Dax leaned against the outside of the clinic, his eyes haunted.

Cursing under his breath, Nick debated responding before deciding Dax needed a dose of encouragement. "The truth. Luke's a good man, married to a wonderful woman. It won't be easy and they'll have rough times, but they're both strong. Real strong, Dax. Now, what can I do to help?"

"Ginny doesn't want to go back to the ranch. She needs a little time to herself, but Doc says she can't be left alone. Does Suzanne have a room until she's ready to come back?"

"Ginny's room is vacant."

Dax's eyes narrowed. "Ginny's room?"

"The room Ginny and Mary lived in when they first came to town. It's how Suzanne refers to it. I'm sure she'd be welcome to it or another empty room upstairs." With the expansion he, Gabe Evans, and Gabe's wife, Lena, had helped fund, Suzanne had added several more rooms and expanded the restaurant. He liked being one of Suzanne's partners, maybe more than he should. "I'll let Suzanne know. Bring Ginny over whenever she's ready. When she's well enough to head home, Suzanne and I will bring her back."

"Don't know if that will be necessary, but thanks. I believe Rachel will be coming to town each day Ginny's here." He blew out a breath. "Well, guess I'd better head back inside." Dax started to turn, then stopped. "You know, I'd like one month...just one month when life seems easy, Nick. No hard choices, no illness, no death, and none of this bull going on with Sam. Is a month too much to ask?"

Nick let his gaze move up the street, then back down, drifting over the many businesses, thinking of the people and the lives they lived.

Danger, tragedy, and difficult choices were all part of their daily life.

"Never thought I'd hear an ex-Confederate general gripe about the facts of life. Especially not an arrogant, hard-headed man like you."

Dax straightened, his mouth tilting up slightly at the corners, although there was no joy in his eyes. "You know, Nick, you are one brutal man. But...well said." With that, Dax walked back into the clinic, closing the door quietly behind him.

Chapter Eight

"Running Bear's village is over the next hill." Mal reined to a stop next to Luke and Bull. For two days, he and Travis had scouted the trail to the Blackfoot village. "We're being watched. Two small groups."

"Ignore them. They won't stop us when Running Bear realizes who we are."

"Are you certain about that, Luke?" Sam joined them, his gaze darting about, looking for any type of danger. Since his release, he'd been tense, unable to sleep or eat more than a few bites.

"Running Bear isn't a threat to us, Sam. His enemy is the Crow."

"If you say so." Sam shifted in his saddle, unable to control his unease. The Blackfoot distrust of white settlers was well-known, although he hadn't heard of any raids in a long time.

"Luke's right, Sam." Bull's voice held an edge, as it had from the moment he'd realized Lydia had ridden away. His total focus was on getting her back by any means available. "Besides, we have little choice but to ask for his help. We don't have enough men to go against Red Tail and White Buffalo, and I'll not rest until Lydia is back with us. We're wasting time. Let's get going." He didn't wait as he reined Abe back onto the trail, heading toward Running Bear's village.

Luke hurried to ride alongside him. "You calm enough to talk?"

Bull sent him a scathing look, then nodded.

"We should all ride in, but only you, Sam, and I should approach Running Bear." Luke guided Prince toward the camp a few hundred yards ahead, seeing people emerging from tipis, young children running to be with adults.

"As long as he agrees to help, I'll do whatever seems right."

Stopping a hundred yards away, Luke turned to the others, explaining the plan. The expression on Sam's face wasn't what he expected. His fifteen-year-old frame straightened in the saddle, but the fear in his eyes gave him away. Bull noticed it, too.

"Would you rather stay here with the other men, Sam?" Bull moved toward him, getting close and lowering his voice. "You don't need to go in with us." The young man had been through a lot. Bull knew he felt a great deal of guilt about Lydia's decision, although no one else blamed him.

Sam's eyes locked on Bull's, his face hardening. "I'm going with you."

Luke looked at the others, each of them eyeing the village with a mixture of curiosity and unease. "Stay here. Don't come closer unless Bull or I signal you. Leave your hands where the braves can see them, away from your weapons."

"Whatever you say, boss." Travis glanced at the rest of the men, who nodded in agreement.

The three continued to the edge of the village before several Blackfoot warriors charged forward on horses, circling them. Raising lances and yelping, they did their best to intimidate them. Luke and Bull stayed calm, not letting the antics bother them, but Sam began to panic, pulling back hard on the reins, causing his horse to dance around.

"Easy, Sam. This is the way they always act when we ride into their village." Bull's deep, soothing voice had the desired effect. Sam sucked in a slow breath, relaxing in the saddle.

A few moments later, Running Bear emerged from one of the tipis. Walking toward them, he spoke to the warriors, who immediately stopped their yelling and backed away.

"Running Bear, it is good to see you again." Luke slid to the ground, followed by Bull and Sam.

"It is good to see you, Luke Pelletier." His gaze shifted to Bull, a slight smile curling his lips.

"And you, Bull Mason." Then his eyes caught Sam's. "Is this boy of your family?"

"Yes. Samuel is one of us and a friend to the Blackfoot."

Running Bear knew there was more, but the introduction satisfied him...for now. "Come. We will talk."

As was his custom, Running Bear didn't return to his tipi. Instead, he took the path toward the river, knowing the three would follow. Sam let Bull and Luke go first. Looking behind him, he was surprised to see no one trailing them.

The chief stopped at the water's edge, watching for several minutes, not speaking. Turning slowly, he waved his hand in the direction of the river.

"This is a good home to my people. We have food, shelter. We have made friends." Running Bear let his gaze linger on each man, letting them know he referred to them. "We have found many moons of peace. I think this will change. You have come here to ask for my help."

Bull's eyes widened. "How did you know?"

"We do not sit silent in our tipis. To keep our enemies away, we watch. We know of your woman, Bull Mason."

"You know of Lydia and White Buffalo?" Bull asked, still not quite believing the chief knew of his anguish.

"We know he took this one." He nodded at Sam, then looked back at Bull. "We know your woman rode into the Crow camp. This one rode out with another. Now you are here."

The air around them stilled as each absorbed Running Bear's words. Bull's throat worked, trying to dislodge the ball of hatred choking him. Whatever he'd done in the past to calm his anger vanished, replaced with a desire for revenge so strong, it frightened him. Choking on pride as thick as his fear, Bull stepped forward.

"I would ask for your help rescuing my woman."

Running Bear studied his face for long moments, his own face a mask. "Perhaps this woman does not want to return."

Bull's eyes widened an instant before his gaze narrowed at the chief. "She gave up her freedom for her brother. She does not want to stay with White Buffalo."

"She is now his woman." Running Bear's face remained impassive, as if what he said didn't cut Bull like a sword piercing his heart.

Planting his feet shoulder width apart, he glared at the chief. "She will *never* be his woman.

Lydia is mine. She'll always be mine." He spat the words out, then turned to pace several feet away.

"Then you are willing to die for this woman?"

Whipping around, Bull took a few steps forward, then stopped. "Yes."

Running Bear stared into Bull's eyes, studying his resolve, then nodded. "Then it will be so." Without another word, he took the path back to the camp, nodded to a group of older men, and entered his tipi. In seconds, several of his people followed, closing the flaps behind them.

Bull stood frozen in place. He had no idea what had been decided, if anything. Cursing, he ran a shaky hand through his hair, then slammed his hat down on his head.

"What now?" His gaze sought Luke's, but he saw no answers in his friend's face.

"We wait."

"Will he help us, Luke?" Sam straightened his shoulders as his voice shook.

"I don't know."

"He's had braves following us most of the time. They were there the morning Lydia left. They saw everything." Bull couldn't believe no one in the search party heard or saw them. They knew someone followed, always assuming it had been White Buffalo's men. Letting out a stream of vile curses, which seldom crossed his lips, he turned to Luke. "I can't wait any longer. I'm riding back to the Crow camp."

Luke walked up, gripping Bull's shoulder. "The hell you are. We're all in this together—with or without Running Bear's help. For now, we wait for his decision."

Bull rounded on his friend, his words dying on his lips when Running Bear emerged from the tipi. His expression didn't change as his gaze moved from Sam, to Luke, then to Bull.

"Tomorrow, we go after your woman."

Bull's jaw dropped open, his voice catching when he tried to speak.

"We will be ready," Luke answered as Running Bear turned to return to his tipi. "Come on, Bull. It's time to tell the others."

Lydia huddled in White Buffalo's tipi, fighting tears. He'd stormed out minutes before after another morning of brutal treatment. Her arms and upper body showed the results of what he expected. Each time he took her, she forced all images of the vicious warrior from her mind, instead focusing on Bull. She wrapped herself around memories of him, as if his presence in her heart could make him real.

Over a week had gone by since White Buffalo had taken her as his wife. The torturous nights and agonizing days felt like years. Every muscle ached, she couldn't sleep, and hadn't been able to keep down more than a few bites of food since before she left Bull. Her weight had dropped, as it had when she'd been held captive. Choking down her regret, she accepted death as preferable to staying alive in what would be her future. Even if she ran, she had no place to go. Bull would never take her back, not after what White Buffalo had made her do. No matter the love, she could never look Bull in the face, seeing his trusting eyes, knowing what she'd done.

Even if he took her back out of pity, it would never be the same. She wouldn't be able to face her friends or handle the scorn directed at her. If he took her back, Bull would also endure the disdain of those he'd always called friends. The people of Splendor would turn against her, as she'd heard other towns doing when white women had been captured and taken as Indian wives. As supportive as they'd been when Bull and the Pelletiers found the orphans hiding in the cave, she doubted Reverend and Mrs. Paige would allow her to return to church.

Her decision freed Sam and Mal, but abolished all chance for a normal life in the white man's world. Killing herself would be a mercy.

Lydia's stomach growled, threatening to rebel at the lack of food. She could try to eat, but the result would be the same—throbbing pain ending in her bending over, losing all she'd taken in. Instead, she focused on getting away. Dying in the wilderness would be preferable to a slow death inside the Crow camp.

Running fingers through her short, tangled hair, she grabbed what needed to be washed and walked to the river. She already knew what to expect.

The women would shun her, some even throwing rocks. The children would run around in circles, taunting her, calling her names for which there was no white man's meaning. Sometimes White Buffalo would lean against a tree and watch. Other times, he'd walk past, not acknowledging her. He never intervened. His lack of action revealed his disrespect for her, as well as his approval of what the women and children were doing.

Today, though, they'd see a different Lydia. She'd made up her mind. She'd stand tall, ignore all their insults, knowing it would be her last day in camp. Tomorrow, after White Buffalo left, she'd go for berries, take the path along the other side of the river, and disappear.

Bull tossed and turned, unable to get comfortable on the hard ground. It was well past midnight. In a few hours, the raid on the Crow village would commence. Running Bear had selected to camp a couple miles away, confident Red Tail's guards wouldn't spot them. Before sunrise, they'd ride into the village, kill as few as possible, leaving with the prize they sought. If all went well, Lydia would be back in his arms by nightfall.

Turning onto his back, Bull folded his arms behind his head and stared up at the star-filled sky. Nothing had changed from one night to the next. The stars still twinkled, the moon still moved, yet his world had been changed forever. He thought of those back home, knowing the worry this trip caused them. Luke hadn't complained, but Bull knew his friend missed Ginny terribly and wanted nothing more than to return to her and the baby who'd arrive in a few months.

Sucking in a shaky breath, Bull remembered how he and Lydia talked of having children. He wanted four or five. She'd been thrilled with the idea of a large family, their children running around, causing havoc. Now, all he wanted was to have her back in his arms.

His thoughts were so wrapped around Lydia, he didn't realize he'd finally drifted to sleep until Luke shook him awake.

"It's time, Bull."

The Blackfoot made no sound as they mounted their horses. Luke turned to Sam, Billy, Travis, Mal, Johnny, and Tat. "Last chance to wait here. None of you need to ride after Lydia."

Travis glanced at the others before stepping forward. "No offense, boss, but we're wasting time. Running Bear's men are ready, and so are we."

"He's right, Luke. It's time to bring Lydia home." Sam mounted his horse, riding toward the group of braves, ready to go after the warrior who'd caused him and his family so much pain.

"It's settled." Luke swung up on Prince, nodded at Bull once, then rode to join Running Bear. "We are ready."

Lydia rubbed her eyes, stretching to loosen her sore muscles. Peeking outside, she guessed it would be at least an hour before the sun rose. White Buffalo and several braves had ridden to the east late the night before to raid a farm a day's ride from camp. She wouldn't have even known that much except his mother took great joy in talking about his plans, knowing he told Lydia nothing.

Once White Buffalo left camp, she gathered her meager belongings, deciding it was better to rest and make sure her husband didn't return. The little food and small flask of water she'd been able to hide wouldn't last long, perhaps two days, maybe three. It would have to be enough.

Reaching into a basket concealed along one section of the tipi, she withdrew a knife, smiling at the one piece of good luck she had. As careful as White Buffalo was around her, he'd left it behind in his haste to ride out with the others. It wouldn't protect her from large animals, but it was all she had. Tucking it into her buckskin clothing, she glanced around one more time, seeing nothing else worth taking. She'd travel light and run fast, taking only what she needed to get away from the Crow camp and the prison she'd willingly walked into.

Pulling open the flaps of the tipi, she jumped at the sound of horses. Stumbling backward, her heart pounded, fearing White Buffalo had returned. Turning, she hid the food and water, leaving the knife secure in the folds of her clothes, then huddled down, drawing the blanket around her.

Holding his gun steady, Bull rode through the village, searching for White Buffalo. He'd dispatch the warrior first, then find Lydia. While the Blackfoot, Luke, and the others surrounded the confused people, keeping them occupied, he'd grab Lydia and ride out.

Reining to a stop in front of White Buffalo's tipi, he fought off two Crow men who came after him with knives. Older, neither showed much fight when Bull relieved them of their weapons, leveling his gun at them.

"Don't move." His deep growl and unwavering hand had the desired effect. Neither budged, even as their gazes darted around, watching as Running Bear's braves gathered the people into a circle in the center of the village. "I've come for the white woman. Where is she?"

Although their eyes shifted to the tent behind him, neither spoke.

"I've got them, Bull. You find Lydia." Luke rode up next to him, Sam and Billy on either side.

Still holding his gun, Bull turned back to the tipi, ready for his encounter with White Buffalo. Not waiting, he opened the flap and peered inside. At first, he saw nothing, then his gaze landed on a small form wrapped in a blanket, making no move to attack. Bull took a cautious step forward.

Lydia's heart squeezed when she heard the familiar voice outside the tipi. *Bull.* He'd come for her. In her excitement, she'd almost tossed the blanket aside, then reality gripped her. She couldn't let him see her like this...wouldn't leave with him. Fear ripped through her, knowing the disgust he'd feel at the sight of her. He'd say nothing, but Lydia knew what Bull would think. She'd betrayed him, given herself to the enemy to free her brother. Nothing could change what she'd done, how she'd suffered, but she refused to drag Bull into it.

The sound of Luke's voice had her scooting further back into the tipi, holding the blanket up so Bull couldn't see her face. Hearing someone draw aside the flap, she drew her knees tight to her chest, praying he wouldn't find her.

"Lydia?"

She jerked when he called her name. White Buffalo and those in the village called her Golden Bird. The sound of her name on Bull's lips had her trembling.

"Lydia, is that you?"

She could hear him move farther inside, knowing he stood just feet away. Clutching the blanket, her mind screamed for him to turn around, leave, even as her heart beat wildly, reaching out to him.

Feeling the blanket begin to lift, she jerked away, a futile attempt to avoid him discovering her.

"Lydia, it's Bull. I've come to take you home."

In one quick motion, the blanket was ripped away and tossed aside. Unable to bear his scrutiny, she lowered her forehead onto her knees, shaking her head. Tears spilled down her cheeks. Lydia knew she couldn't endure what she'd see when his eyes met hers. Sensing him crouch before her, she continued to shake her head, letting out a low keening sound when his hand rested on top of her head.

Chapter Nine

The first thing Bull noticed was her hair. The glorious, long strawberry blonde locks had been cut away, but he had no time to comment before his head exploded at her ear-piercing scream.

"Lydia, stop. It's Bull. I'm taking you home."

Holding both arms above her head to fend him off, she didn't look up, panic taking control. "I won't go back. I'll never go back."

Ignoring her words, he slipped an arm around her back, attempting to pick her up. Instead, her body jerked, arms flailing as she tried to push him away.

"No, no, no. I don't want to leave." Her words cut through him, but didn't deter Bull's response.

Capturing her wrists in one hand, he drew them above her head, searching her eyes. The pain, fear, and panic he saw might have deterred a weaker man. That man wasn't Bull Mason. Behind the anguish and terror, he could still see the love, the Lydia he'd want until the day he died.

Tightening his grip, he leaned closer. "I'm not leaving you here. You can walk or I'll toss you over my shoulder, but you are coming with me."

Fear turned to resolve as she glared back at him, her voice rising. "I won't go back to the ranch or Splendor or anywhere with you."

"Of course you're going back." His grip loosened a little. Big mistake.

Hardening her heart, she said the only thing she hoped would stop him. "I don't love you anymore."

She saw pain flicker across his face, her chest constricting at his agonized expression. An instant later, to her dismay, it was replaced by a look of pure determination.

"To hell with this." His muttered words were followed by him picking her up, flinging her over his shoulder. Exiting the tipi, he felt her hands beat on his back, her feet connecting with his legs. "Stop it, Lydia. We're going home. You can tell me how much you hate me later."

Shocked at what he saw, Luke rushed toward him. "What's going on?"

"She says she doesn't want to go."

"I *don't* want to leave. Put me down."

Bull raised a brow at Luke.

"We can't have Running Bear thinking she wants to stay." Luke reached into a pocket, pulled out a handkerchief, and grasped the back of Lydia's hair. "Sorry, darlin." When she opened her mouth to speak, he stuffed the cloth inside, silencing her. Luke glanced around, seeing

Running Bear's attention focused on the Crow they'd surrounded. "Hand her to me while you get on Abe. You need to ride out fast. Don't stop to talk to anyone."

Bull grabbed Abe's reins, hoisting himself into the saddle, then took Lydia from Luke. Placing her face down across his lap, he leaned forward.

"Don't fight me, Lydia. I'm taking you back to the ranch, and that's the end of it."

Kicking Abe, he sped past everyone, out of the village, and into the open.

Riding fast and hard, Bull put as much distance as possible between them and the Crow camp before stopping to rest and wait for Luke. He'd removed the handkerchief from Lydia's mouth a mile from the village, expecting her to yell and scream. To his surprise, she had stayed silent. Instead, she reached behind her in an attempt to hit him. Putting a large palm on her back, he'd pressed down until she stopped. When she continued, he swatted her on the rump, stilling her motions.

Dismounting, he lifted her from the saddle, then placed her on the ground, holding her arms tight to her sides. He wanted to wrap his arms around her, hold her to him, and never let go. Instead, he found himself in the role of her captor. Watching closely, he noted her gaze not meeting his as she searched their surroundings. On a deep sigh, he pulled her wrists together, holding them with one hand, gripping her chin with the other.

"Look at me, Lydia."

When she didn't oblige, he tightened his hold on her chin, lifting it so her eyes met his. "Do I need to tie you up?"

She shook her head until he loosened his hold, although he refused to release her wrists. Her lower lip trembled, her gaze falling to the ground.

"You should have left me." Her strained whisper was almost lost in the breeze.

"I would never have left you. Not ever."

"It would have been better if you had." Her shoulders slumped when he let go of her wrists. Taking a few unsteady steps backward, she turned away. "I can't go back. Please don't force me."

Walking up behind her, he placed his hand on her hips, but she jerked away. "I don't understand. Why would it be better?"

A spasm of emotion rolled through her. She wanted to scream, hammer his chest with her fists, rage at the injustice. The man she loved stood before her, had risked his life to rescue her. But Lydia knew it wasn't enough to heal the hurt. Nothing would ever erase what had happened in the course of a few days. She could never forget, and neither would he once he heard the truth. Bull needed to understand how she felt, what the future would be like if he kept her with him. Taking a deep breath, she turned to face him.

Before she could start, he moved forward, cupping her face in his palms. "I love you, Lydia. No matter what happened with White Buffalo, it won't change how I feel." Bending, he brushed a kiss across her lips. When she didn't try to stop him or pull away, he settled his mouth over hers, letting out a sigh at the familiar taste and feel.

He felt satisfaction when her hands reached up to clench his shirt. A moment later, she pushed away, stepping out of his reach. Her eyes filled with tears as she shook her head.

"I'm so sorry, Bull. So very sorry."

He choked down his reply at the sound of riders. Her despair and guilt at what happened tore through him, causing an ache too deep to define. Taking a quick glance over his shoulder to see Luke and the others ride up, he shifted back to Lydia.

"There's no time now, but know this. I will *never* walk away from you. It won't matter what you tell me. I'll always be here for you."

After a brief rest, the group continued on in silence. Running Bear had taken two horses from the Crow, giving them to Luke for Lydia and Sam. Having learned to ride bareback while with the Crow, Billy offered her his saddle, switching the familiar Indian rope bridle with his leather one. Sam took the second horse, easily handling the animal without a saddle.

Both Sam and Billy tried to approach her as the journey progressed. Lydia shook her head each time, turning away. She did ride between them, spurning Bull's request she ride up front with Luke and him.

"What did you tell Running Bear?"

"We spoke little." Luke reached behind him, grabbing a flask and taking a long drink of water. "I asked what he thought would happen when White Buffalo and Red Tail returned. He shrugged it off and smiled, saying how easy it had been with both the warrior and the chief out on a raiding party. I did get his promise he'd send for help if the Crow retaliated."

"Will he?"

"Doubtful. Red Tail's village is a splinter band of the Crow tribe. They are capable of sneak raids, but taking on Running Bear's village isn't the same. The Blackfoot have them outnumbered and the advantage of location. It would be hard for anyone to approach without them knowing."

Bull nodded. "As we already found out." Glancing over his shoulder, he saw Lydia riding between Billy and Sam, her head down.

"How is she doing?"

Turning back around, he shot a quick look at Luke. "Not good. She told me she's sorry and I should have left her there. Can you believe it?" His voice began to rise as anger clawed at him. "She said it would have been better if I hadn't come after her." He scrubbed a hand down his face, then rubbed his chin. "I know she was there too long, but I got there as soon as I could."

"Bull, don't punish yourself. You did all you could. She needs time to heal, understand we all still love her. I'm sure she's afraid. You've heard the stories of how some white hostages are shunned after they're rescued."

"You know that won't happen in Splendor, Luke."

"I'm not so sure, Bull. If you're honest with yourself, you know most will welcome her home, but some won't. It's the way people are."

Bull's blood boiled at the thought of anyone treating Lydia with anything other than respect. Still, he knew Luke spoke the truth. There would be people, God-fearing people who attended church and called themselves friends, who might look the other way when she walked toward them, maybe even cross the street to avoid her.

"I don't know what to do...how to help her."

"Give her time. She'll come around."

"And if she doesn't?" Bull knew there'd never be another woman for him. Lydia was it. If she shut him out of her life, he'd go on living, continue his life as he had before he met her. But he'd never be the same.

"You have to believe she will. If you love her, you won't give up."

The journey home took little time with everyone ready to return to the ranch, especially Luke. Almost a month had passed since they'd left. Bull knew he had never stopped worrying about Ginny, the same as Bull couldn't stop worrying about Lydia.

Nothing had changed between them. She stayed close to Sam and Billy, ignoring Bull and everyone else, as if they were the enemy. They'd rescued her, yet she acted as if she were still in prison, her tortured expression never changing.

Reining Abe around, he rode to the rear. He didn't say a word as he nudged his horse next to

Lydia's, sending a meaningful look to each of the boys.

"We're heading up front, Lydia." Sam shot a last glance at Bull, a subtle warning to tread carefully.

"Sam, wait..." Her voice trailed off when he didn't turn around.

They rode in silence for several minutes, Lydia never acknowledging him.

"We'll be home soon. I want you to stay with me."

Her gaze shot to his. "I can't do that. We aren't married. What will people think?"

"Everyone knows we plan to marry. There are two bedrooms. You can have one and I'll take the other."

"No. I'll stay in my old room at Dax and Rachel's." She looked away, her face clouding. "If they'll let me."

He sighed. At least they were speaking. "Of course they'll let you. Why wouldn't they?"

Pain flashed in her eyes. When she spoke, her voice was strained. "I'm married to a Crow."

"The hell you are." The words were out before he could stop them.

"It happened, Bull. You need to accept it."

"I do accept it, Lydia. I also know the Crow custom of ending a marriage with a simple declaration. You moving out of his tipi, leaving with me, is the same as a divorce. You're free."

"You don't understand. I'll never be free. Never." She spat the words out as if they were garbage in her mouth. Kicking her horse, she rode forward, leaving Bull behind. When she reached the front, she didn't slow down, riding past Luke, Sam, and Billy.

"Lydia, wait!" Sam called after her an instant before Bull dashed past him on Abe. When Sam started to follow, Luke held up a hand.

"Let Bull get her. They have a lot to work out."

They all knew Lydia had pushed Bull away each day. Even when she'd fought nightmares and Bull had been the first by her side, she closed up, refusing to talk.

"I just want her back the way she was."

"I know, Sam. We all do. Especially Bull."

Bull didn't slow down as he came up next to Lydia, grabbing the reins away from her, bringing them both to a stop. "What do you think you're doing?"

"I don't know," she shot back, tugging hard to pull the reins from him. "Getting away."

"Away? To where?"

"Anywhere but the ranch. I can't face them. I just can't face any of them." All the fear, pain, and anger she'd kept inside tore loose on a sob. Wrapping her arms around her waist, she bent over the saddle, allowing her agony to release through wracking cries.

Sliding off Abe, Bull pulled her off the horse and into his arms, carrying her to the shade of a large pine. Lowering them both to the ground, he cradled her in his lap, stroking her back, whispering how much he loved her. He didn't even notice the others ride by several minutes later, taking a path around them, allowing Bull and Lydia the privacy they needed.

He could feel her fingers dig into his chest when she gripped his shirt. If he could absorb her pain, take it from her, he would. Instead, Bull settled for doing the best he could to provide comfort, praying Luke was right and Lydia would someday return to the person she was before White Buffalo swooped down on the ranch, changing all their lives.

After long minutes, Lydia's body began to relax, her grip on his tear-soaked shirt easing. Looking up at him, her red-rimmed eyes spoke of the anguish she still suffered.

"You must let it go. Try to forget." He placed a soft kiss on her temple.

"I don't think I ever can. It was...he was..." The words caught in her throat, her body shaking at the memory.

"If you want to talk, I'm here, but you don't have to tell me any of it."

"I don't think I will ever be strong enough to tell you what he did to me. Even the thought of him touching me..." She buried her face in his chest, her stomach roiling, remembering White Buffalo's brutal treatment and what he'd forced her to do.

"Shhh, sweetheart. We'll get through this...you and me together, Lydia. You'll see. Someday, as we watch our children running around, this will be a distant memory." He swallowed the ball of fury he'd tried to choke down, hoping the future still included Lydia by his side, living in his house, and building a life together.

"Dax, look." Rachel held Patrick on her lap as they returned home from church. A group of riders approached from the opposite direction. "Oh my! It's Luke and Bull. And they have Sam!" As they got closer, she could see the weariness on each face as they spotted the wagon and waved. Then her gaze landed on Lydia. She didn't look toward her and Dax, her eyes fixed firmly on the ground as they approached the barn.

Pulling the wagon to a stop, Dax jumped down, enveloping Luke in an embrace the instant his brother hit the ground. Slapping him once on the back, Dax stepped away, relief clear on his face.

"I was about to send out a search party for you boys." Dax shook each hand, then turned to Sam, pulling him into a hug. "It's good to have you home."

Sam didn't break into a smile. Instead, his gaze shot to Lydia and Bull. "Thanks, Dax. I'm glad to be back."

Dax's gaze followed Sam's, settling on Lydia. Her short hair and buckskin clothing got his attention, as did the look of total desolation on her face. He watched as Bull helped her from the saddle, gently setting her next to him, his body shielding her from the others. She even turned away when Rachel approached with Patrick. Walking over to Luke, Dax motioned toward her.

"Is Lydia all right?"

Luke shook his head. "No, she's not. I want to get inside to see Ginny, then I'll explain it all. It's not a good story." He tossed Prince's reins over a post, then started toward the house.

"Hold up, Luke. I need to speak with you."

"Can't it wait until I've seen Ginny? After all, it's been..." He stopped at the anguished look on Dax's face. "What is it? Is it Ginny?" He stepped up to his brother, grabbing his shoulders. "Tell me."

"I'm sorry, Luke." He sucked in a breath, continuing in a strained voice. "Ginny lost the baby."

Chapter Ten

Dax, Luke, and Bull sat in the study long after dark, downing one glass of whiskey after another. Ginny and Lydia slept upstairs—at least the men assumed they were sleeping. Rachel kept watch on both women until exhaustion took over and she, too, went to bed.

Luke poured another glass with a shaky hand, brought it to his lips, then lowered it. "She won't talk to me. Barely looks at me. It's as if I'm a stranger." He rolled the glass between his hands, watching the amber liquid coat the sides before tossing it back, letting the warmth slide down his throat. "She kept telling me she's sorry."

Bull's head still spun from the news about Ginny. He never dreamed another tragedy could hit the people of Redemption's Edge so soon. His already shredded heart ached for his friend. They'd wanted a family, tried for a baby since the day they married. The impromptu party the men had thrown for Luke when he announced Ginny's pregnancy was still fresh in Bull's mind. The huge smile and joy on his friend's face. Bull glanced up, seeing a man as broken as him.

Dax looked between them. The news about Lydia had shocked them all. She'd given up a great deal to rescue her brother and Mal, sparing the others a confrontation with the Crow warriors. Although he didn't agree with what she did, he admired her courage. Sipping on his whiskey, Dax sighed at the way life had changed for everyone in the matter of a few weeks.

"Ginny's strong, Luke. Given enough time, she'll learn to live with what happened and continue on, the same as Lydia will. Doc said he sees no reason you can't still have children." Dax sounded more confident than he felt.

"Rachel said she was with Ginny when the pains began."

"It happened fast. I rode in, took one look at Ginny, and started for town. We had her at Doc's within an hour of the first pains. I thought the baby had a chance, but..." His voice faltered. He'd do anything to change the outcome.

"It's nobody's fault, Dax. Don't go blaming yourself. I don't." Luke tapped his fingers on the arm of the chair over and over until the tips felt raw. The peace he expected upon returning to the ranch eluded him, replaced by unimaginable loss and sorrow. Letting out a pained growl, he stood, pacing to the window. Staring out at the starry sky, Luke remembered the night Ginny had told him she was with child. He'd picked her up, twirling her around, her laughter filling the air.

They'd been so thrilled, so confident all would go well.

"Doc said depression is normal after a miscarriage. It could take weeks or months for Ginny to get over the loss." Dax leaned back in his chair, his intent look focused on Luke. "He said for you to talk to him when you returned. I think it's a good idea."

Luke spun around, his eyes flashing. "You don't think I can handle what happened?"

"I think you can use all the information available to help Ginny." Dax stood, walking to him and placing a hand on his shoulder. "Doc's willing to help. Accept his offer, Luke."

Bull tried to relax against the back of the large leather chair as he listened. Luke and his situation were similar, yet so different. Both women were smart and strong, willing to put up with the hard life on the frontier. He knew Ginny loved Luke with all she had, and Bull believed Lydia still loved him in the same way. The two separate events had brought all four to their knees, forcing them to face tough realities.

"Bull, you know Rachel and I will do all we can to help you and Lydia. Whatever you need—anything—just let us know."

Nodding, Bull stood. "I appreciate it, Dax. The best I can do right now is allow her time to rest, and be there for her." Shrugging, he inhaled a deep breath. "Maybe Rachel will be able to get her to talk. I haven't been able to."

"You're who she needs, Bull. Someday she'll realize it and you'll be waiting."

One day led into the next, little changing as both Ginny and Lydia fought their own internal demons. Luke spoke to Doc Worthington, reaffirming his understanding about how often miscarriages occurred. It didn't matter if you lived in a city or on the frontier, problems during pregnancy were common.

"I saw nothing that had me concerned or told me she couldn't have a child, Luke. For whatever reason, this pregnancy wasn't meant to be. There's no reason you can't have the family you want." Doc Worthington sipped his coffee, cradling the cup in both hands. He wouldn't tell Luke what Ginny had said right after learning she'd lost the baby. Her heart-wrenching sobs, her fear Luke would think she'd failed him. "That doesn't mean it will be easy for her to get over the emotional effects of losing a child. The instant a couple learns they're having a baby, it's normal for them to visualize the child, begin to see the boy or girl in their life. I know Rachel had been helping her prepare a room and sew clothes. A pregnancy of a few months can create the same sense of loss as one lasting much longer."

"How long, Doc?" Luke sat forward in his chair, ignoring his cooling coffee.

Worthington cocked his head. "Until she is herself again?"

Luke nodded.

"Some women recover more quickly than others. It can span from days to weeks or months. In a very few cases, the woman never recovers and gives up. I don't see that happening with Ginny." Setting his cup on a nearby table, Doc rested his arms on his knees, leaning forward. "It's been less than two weeks. Rachel says Ginny's eating better and resting. Both are good signs. Has she talked to you at all?"

"Only to say she's sorry. She won't look at me, as if seeing my face is too painful."

"Her response isn't unusual, Luke. She will get over the pain as long as you're there for her. Ginny needs to know she can count on you, and your feelings haven't changed."

"Nothing will change my love for her. Even if we're never able to have children, I'll still love her just as much."

The doctor rested his hands on his knees and pushed up. "You're a good man, Luke. Ginny knows this. Time and love can heal many things."

"I hope this is one of them."

Luke rode home, considering Doc's words, thankful he'd taken his brother's advice and spoken to him. Each night, he'd slept alongside Ginny, offering whatever comfort she'd accept. He'd woken more than once to the sound of her quiet weeping, his heart breaking with each sob. She never spoke, other than to repeat how sorry she was about losing the baby. His response was always the same—he loved her and would never leave. In time, he hoped she'd be able to talk about trying again.

"Dax asked me to ride with him to the Frey ranch. Hiram and Frank seem to be serious about selling, but Dax wanted to wait to talk with them until I got back." Luke spoke to Bull as they saddled their horses. "Are you fine doing the branding without me?"

Bull snorted. "I believe me and the boys *might* be able to handle it without you."

"Yeah, I guess you can." Luke shook his head at the ridiculous question. "Dirk's going to work with some of the men on the eastern border. Apparently, we've been missing some cattle since he separated the herd after we returned. He's trying to determine if they're straying or if they're being stolen."

"I spoke to Gabe and Cash yesterday when I went for supplies. They didn't mention anything about rustlers. It's probably strays," Bull guessed. The sheriff, Gabe Evans, or his deputies, Cash Coulter and Beau Davis, were the first people notified when rustling occurred anywhere near Splendor.

"I'm thinking the same." Luke swung into the saddle, almost ready to ride out. "They say anything about how Beau's doing since Caroline left for San Francisco?"

"As you'd expect. He's taking it pretty hard, spending his nights at either the Dixie or the Wild Rose. He received a telegram from her after she found a place to stay. Cash said that's when her leaving became real to Beau." Swinging up on Abe, Bull rode with Luke to the house, where Dax waited. "Guess the next time we speak, you'll be the owners of the Frey ranch."

"Could be." Dax reined his horse toward Bull, his mouth twisting into a smile, a brow arching. "Could very well be."

Rachel worked alongside Tat, mucking out stalls and spreading clean straw while Johnny stayed in the house, keeping watch on Lydia and Ginny. On a normal day, the two would've ridden off with Bull or Dirk to help with the herd. These days, nothing was normal. Since Lydia returned, the entire ranch had been on alert, anticipating White Buffalo attempting to reclaim her. Dax and Luke had gone as far as to hire three extra men, stationing them as lookouts on the north and east borders of the ranch.

"You don't need to be out here with me, Mrs. Pelletier. I can take care of this." Tat leaned on the handle of the shovel, swiping a shirtsleeve across his brow.

The weather had turned from a comfortable warmth to unseasonably hot, turning the barn into an oven. The faster the work got done, the faster the two of them could return to the comfort of the tree-shaded house.

Spreading another handful of straw on the floor of one stall, she wiped her hands and crossed her arms. "Tat, I've asked you several times to call me Rachel. As far as leaving you to finish alone, two of us will finish more quickly than one."

Picking up another handful of straw, she debated whether or not to ask Tat what had been on her mind for days. She couldn't ask Luke, Bull, Sam, or Billy. All four were too close to Lydia to separate their own feelings from what happened.

"What do the men say about what Lydia did? Does anyone seem to have an issue with it?"

Tat's motions stilled. Straightening, he set the shovel aside, taking the ladle from a nearby bucket to scoop out some water. Taking a sip, pouring the rest over his neck, he looked at Rachel.

"No one has a bad word to say about Miss Lydia. Fact is, the men think she's about the bravest person they know, what with trading herself for Sam and Mal." Grabbing the shovel, he continued his work, his mind back on the task.

Rachel had suspected as much. "Thanks, Tat. I appreciate you being honest."

He let out a breath, not glancing up. "Bull almost went crazy when he found her gone. I've never seen him as angry as when she fought him, trying to convince him to leave her at the Crow camp. He looked at her as if she'd gone mad, tossed her across his lap, and took off out of the village as if the devil were after him. No way was he going to leave her behind. In a way, I'm sorry White Buffalo wasn't there so we could've finished him off once and for all."

Rachel knew what he meant. She suspected part of Lydia's distress came from the fear the Crow warrior would return, wreaking havoc on the ranch, killing innocent men in an attempt to get her back. Rachel hoped Lydia wasn't considering sneaking away, returning to White Buffalo in an attempt to eliminate retaliation.

"You got her back for us, which is what's important, Tat. The rest will work itself out." Rachel thought a trip into town might be a good way of dispelling Lydia's fear of people rejecting her. Perhaps a visit with Suzanne and a stop at Alison Coulter's shop for a new dress might help. Staying cooped up in the house, hiding from everyone, wasn't helping. Rachel believed most everyone in Splendor would welcome her, marvel at her courage. Getting Lydia to believe it would be a slow process. A ride into Splendor might be a good start.

Lydia stared at Rachel, her eyes wide. "No. I can't possibly go to town. Not now. Maybe never."

"Of course you can go to town. There are many people who've sent messages, asking when they could come visit. You have a lot of friends, Lydia, and it's time you stopped ignoring them."

"Friends? Or people who are curious about the girl who gave herself to a savage?"

The misery on her face almost stopped Rachel from pushing. If she gave up now, Lydia would convince herself the fears she felt were justified.

"Do you truly believe Suzanne, Abby, Alison, or Lena think of you that way? They're all your friends. If nothing else, you should at least give them the benefit of letting them express their thoughts in person rather than pushing them away."

"I'm just not ready. It's too soon."

"There is no better time than now, Lydia. You've holed up in this house for days, convincing yourself you're unworthy. It has to stop." Rachel crossed her arms, not letting Lydia's beaten expression dissuade her. "Of course, if you'd be more comfortable, I can invite the ladies here."

"What about Ginny?"

"I'm talking with her next." The gleam in Rachel's eyes brought a softening to Lydia's face.

Wringing her hands, Lydia paced to the window. "Bull should have left me. It would have been better if he had." She touched her short hair, fingering the jagged ends.

Rachel walked up next to her, careful not to get too close and spook her. "Your hair will grow out, Lydia."

"I know."

"And Bull will always love you."

Lydia turned to look at Rachel, a pleading look in her eyes. "He may love me now, but he won't when he learns everything."

"Listen to me. You've got a good man who loves you, who put his life and that of others at risk to get you back. There is nothing you can tell him that will change his mind."

"Do you truly believe that, Rachel?"

"Yes, I do."

Lydia wrestled with Rachel's words well into the night, rolling them over in her mind as she struggled to find peace. Rachel might be right about Bull, but what if she wasn't? Perhaps he'd accept all that had happened at first, then change his mind as time went on, wishing he'd left her behind.

Rubbing her hands down her arms, Lydia had the strongest urge to take a bath, scrub her body until all feeling left. She'd felt this way since the first time White Buffalo grabbed her, dragged her into the tipi, and threw her to the ground. The constant feeling of being dirty and defiled never went away. If anything, the compulsion to constantly bathe, erase every memory of his touch, grew to the point she wanted to scream in frustration.

Tossing off the covers, she walked to the window, feeling the cool evening breeze pass through her thin gown. Rubbing her arms, more from unease than the chill, she wondered if Bull slept. If so, did he dream of her?

He'd come by for supper, encouraging her to join the others at the table. When she declined, he brought a tray with their meals into her room, staying later than usual. He told her of the missing cattle, of the Pelletiers meeting with the Frey brothers, and the pending purchase of their ranch. She listened quietly, hands folded in her lap, nodding her head on occasion. He didn't push her to respond or try to touch her, which Lydia told herself was for the best.

When she couldn't stifle a yawn any longer, he'd left, telling her he'd return for breakfast. For the first time since her rescue, she'd almost reached out to grab him, ask him to stay. Instead, she'd let the feeling pass.

At least she'd agreed to have her friends visit the ranch. Rachel planned to ride into town the following day to personally deliver the invitations. They'd set the date for the following Wednesday, Rachel feeling certain Alison and Suzanne could work something out with their businesses for a few hours.

Turning from the window, Lydia sat on the edge of her bed. She never saw herself as a coward, a woman who needed coddling. If only she could get the old Lydia back, she might be able to face the challenges ahead, even accept Bull back into her life and her arms.

Lying down, she pulled the covers up to her chin and shut her eyes, determined to find a way to get past the doubt. For the first time since her return, she felt a slight bit of hope that everything would turn out all right.

Chapter Eleven

Lydia woke to the aroma of bacon and eggs. She'd been eating better, a few more bites each day. This morning, her stomach rumbled. Tossing off the covers, she made short work of her ablutions. All the while she thought about Bull and their time together the night before.

She'd agreed to sit with him on the front porch, sharing a meal until he and Luke left to meet Beau in town. They'd spoken of his day, his plans to enlarge the house when they started having children, and how he might be traveling between the Frey place and Redemption's Edge until Dax and Luke decided if they needed another foreman to handle the additional land and cattle.

For the first time since leaving the Crow village, she didn't flinch at his continued desire to marry her and have children. The looks he sent her told Lydia how much he struggled at not being able to touch her—how much the enormous toll of fighting her demons had impacted him. There'd never been any doubt in her mind she loved him, only fearing her return would cause Bull tremendous suffering. She now realized pushing him away had done much worse.

A knock on her door had Lydia hurrying to button her dress. Running fingers through her short locks, she stepped to the door and took a deep breath before pulling it open.

"Bull..." Her voice trailed off as she let her gaze wander over him. He wore his shiny black boots, Sunday pants and jacket, and a starched white shirt finished with a thin black tie. Incredible didn't begin to describe the sight of him standing with his shoulders erect, an air of self-confidence she hadn't seen in weeks. When her gaze moved back to his face, she blushed at his knowing smile.

"Did you sleep well?"

"Um, yes...quite well. Are you going to church?" She felt a stab of disappointment at the possibility he'd be going without her.

"Not today, Lydia. I came to take my girl to breakfast and for a walk. If she'll let me."

"A walk?"

"I thought we'd take the wagon to the river and stroll the path by Luke's old house. I know how much you like it there." Bull held his breath, sending up a prayer she wouldn't refuse him.

Clutching her arms around her waist, she took a step back. "Bull...I don't know."

"Just you and me, Lydia. We'll return whenever you're ready."

Sucking in an unsteady breath, Lydia told herself she could do this. She could spend a morning alone with Bull. She loved the path by the river. At this time of year, there'd still be an abundance of flowers and berries.

"Can we pick berries for pie?"

Bull let out a relieved chuckle. "We can pick whatever you want, sweetheart."

"And breakfast?"

"Everyone has left for church. It's just you and me." Bull watched her eyes go wide as she figured it all out.

"You cooked the bacon I've been smelling?"

"I've been alone a long time. If I wanted to eat, I had to learn to cook. I promise it won't poison you." He held out his hand, willing her to take it.

For the first time since he'd taken her from White Buffalo's tipi, she allowed herself a small smile, the gesture racing straight to his heart. Then she reached out her hand, threading her fingers through his, and let him escort her to breakfast.

Lydia hadn't eaten so much in weeks. By most standards, it wasn't a lot, but it was almost three times what she'd been able to keep down.

Sitting on the wagon seat next to Bull, she held his hand, enjoying the ride to Wildfire Creek. His grip wasn't tight, more reassuring, and it occurred to her she never wanted to let go.

Rounding the last turn, her heart began to race at the sight of the house Luke had lived in before meeting Ginny.

"We'll leave the wagon here." Bull pulled back on the lines and secured the brake. Jumping down, he reached in the back and grabbed a bucket, then rounded the wagon. Setting it down, he reached up to settle his hands on Lydia's waist. As much as he wanted to, he didn't let his hands linger. Scaring her after this much progress wasn't going to happen. He did hold out his hand, which she willingly accepted. "Ready?" He reached down and grabbed the bucket.

Squeezing his hand, Lydia tugged enough for him to know the answer.

"You haven't told me what you thought of breakfast."

"How much did I eat?"

He laughed. "Much more than I expected. I suppose that's my answer."

She bit her lower lip and nodded.

He kept stealing glances at her as they took the narrow path to the river. She didn't talk much, yet he was thankful for each word. As more time passed and she felt more secure around him, he believed she'd let herself open up.

Bull didn't care if she told him what happened with White Buffalo. For many reasons, he didn't want to know. The past was behind them and couldn't be changed. He wanted her future. He just needed to keep his own desires under control and allow Lydia to heal at her own pace.

"Do you hear it?" He looked over at her, his soft brown eyes gleaming.

A careful smile curved the corners of her mouth as she nodded.

"There, through the trees." Bull inclined his head in the direction of the river, spotting the running water several yards ahead. "Shall we walk upriver or down?"

Lydia opened her mouth to respond, then clamped it shut, a hand going to her stomach. Bending at the waist, she dropped Bull's hand and turned away.

"Lydia, what is it?"

She sucked in a deep breath as nausea knotted her stomach. Shaking her head, she held up a hand to warn him away, taking a few steps off the trail.

"What can I do?" Bull's voice held a worried edge as he came up behind her.

Taking a few more deep breaths, she stood and turned toward him. It seemed the worst had passed.

"I hope it wasn't breakfast."

She blinked a few times and shook her head. "Maybe it's the change from being in the house for so long. I'm fine now." She did feel better. To her relief, the cramping in her stomach had been brief, leaving her a little shaken, nothing more.

"Do you want to go back?"

"No. Please. I'd like to stay a while longer."

Reaching out, he took Lydia's hand again, drawing her as close as she'd let him. "We'll stay as long as you like."

They'd stayed much longer than Bull anticipated. Lydia picked berries, filling the bucket to overflowing, then gathered flowers until her arms could hold no more. Setting it all in the back of the wagon, he helped her onto the seat.

"You certain there's nothing else you'd like to take back?" His eyes twinkled, letting her know he was joking.

Shaking her head, Lydia watched as he checked the harness, then climbed up beside her. "Thank you, Bull. I had a wonderful time."

"So did I, sweetheart." Turning the wagon around, he reached out, taking her hand, seeing her other resting on her stomach. "Are you still feeling all right?"

"Yes. I don't know what happened. I'm sure it wasn't your breakfast, though." She glanced up at him, doing her best to hide the tremors still rippling through her.

"You'll let me know if it happens again. Right, Lydia?" His eyes narrowed, his concern obvious.

"I just ate too much. Please, don't worry." Lydia truly believed it was nothing. Too much food, apprehension at being alone with Bull, maybe fear of someone seeing her.

Squeezing her hand, he decided to let it go...for now. Tonight, he'd ask Rachel to watch her for any signs of pain. As they took the trail toward the barn, Bull saw the other wagon, people milling around outside, and felt Lydia stiffen beside him.

"Remember, everyone here cares about you. There's no need to worry about what they're thinking because each one wants the best for you." He wanted to brush a kiss across her cheek. Instead, he settled for squeezing her hand before letting it go and bringing the wagon to a halt.

Lydia kept her head lowered, not meeting anyone's gaze until Rachel walked up with

Patrick in her arms. When Bull helped her down, the toddler didn't hesitate, reaching out his arms toward her.

"Guess he knows who he wants." Rachel laughed, transferring Patrick to Lydia. "It's so good to see you outside. Did you go to the river?"

Lydia nodded, shifting Patrick to her other side, balancing him on her hip.

"I think we may have created more work for you." Bull reached into the back of the wagon, taking out the bucket full of berries. "I'll take these into the kitchen, then come back for the flowers."

"Nonsense. I'll bring the flowers since Lydia has her hands full." Rachel lifted the flowers from the wagon, waiting until Bull was far enough away not to hear them. "Tell me how it went."

Lydia lowered her head enough to let Patrick play with her short hair, smiling as he giggled.

"You were right. Bull was wonderful, and walking near the river felt so good."

"It's been a while since you've spent any time outside. And it's a glorious day." Rachel glanced up at the blue sky sprinkled with a few white clouds.

"Bull fixed me breakfast."

"I know. He asked me yesterday if it would be all right." Rachel started toward the house, Lydia and Patrick keeping pace. "Is he a good cook?" She lifted her brows.

"Yes. Very good." Lydia didn't plan to say anything to Rachel about her stomach cramps, firm in her belief the pain resulted from overeating.

"There you are. I thought you two had decided to stay outside." Bull walked toward them, taking Patrick from Lydia's outstretched arms. "Hey, little man." Patrick giggled when Bull held him up in the air, then spun around. "This boy gets heavier each time I hold him."

"Ha! How well I know." Rachel continued to the kitchen, leaving Lydia with Bull in the living room.

"I should help with the berries."

"Lydia, wait." Bull held Patrick on his left side, reaching out his right hand, grinning when she linked her fingers with his. "Please come out for supper. Sit with me at the table."

Swallowing her remaining apprehension, Lydia nodded. "All right."

Bull watched her retreat into the kitchen, feeling better than he had in a long time.

"They're here." Rachel wiped damp hands on her apron, untying the strings as she dashed toward the kitchen where Ginny and Lydia finished dinner preparations. "Suzanna, Lena, Abby, and Alison are here."

"We're ready." Ginny finished cutting pieces of cornbread from the skillet, placing them on a platter alongside a tureen filled with soup. "Rachel, can you help me carry these to the table?"

Picking up the soup, Rachel followed Ginny to the table while Lydia arranged the chicken, carrying it into the dining room, setting it next to a bowl of vegetables. Untying her apron, she touched her hair, a habit she couldn't seem to break.

"You look wonderful, Lydia. Please, don't fret." Ginny touched Lydia's shoulder, noting her friend didn't flinch away as she would've a few weeks earlier. "Personally, I like your short hair."

Lydia started to reply when Rachel opened the front door. "It's so good to see you."

"We're so glad you invited us." Abby hugged Rachel, then walked into the living room. Without a word, she walked up to Lydia, wrapping her arms around the young woman. "You don't know how hard it has been to stay away, Lydia. Noah and I have been so concerned about you." Dropping her arms, Abby stepped back, a broad smile flashing across her face. "Oh my. I *love* your hair."

Lydia lifted a hesitant hand to touch the ends of her hair, tilting her head. "I'm getting used to it." She glanced over Abby's shoulder to see Lena, Alison, and Suzanne standing quietly next to Rachel and Ginny. They'd all come by to offer their encouragement to Ginny after she'd lost the baby, but had been asked to give Lydia more time to recover before paying a visit.

Stepping forward, Lena Evans, Gabe's wife, took hold of her hands. "We're so relieved you're home. If there is anything Gabe or I can do for you, all you need to do is ask."

Alison and Suzanne expressed the same before Rachel invited them to take their seats for dinner.

"Everything looks wonderful. You three must have worked all morning." Abby made it a point to sit next to Lydia. When she and Noah had their son, Gabriel, Lydia lived with them, becoming a true part of their family. It had taken every bit of self-control Abby possessed to keep away this long.

"We split the work. I think Lydia may have had the toughest job—preparing custard and stewed fruit for dessert. Suzanne, why don't you start?" Rachel placed a napkin on her lap, glancing around the table at the strongest women she knew. She considered each a close friend, a confidante, and trusted them completely. If anything could help Lydia return to the life she had before Sam's kidnapping, it was the support of these women.

"All right, Suzanne. I've been waiting days to find out what happened with you and Nick." Lena placed a forkful of chicken into her mouth, chewing slowly.

Suzanne's hand stilled in midair. "He's your business partner. I thought you would've heard something."

"What do you mean?" Lena's eyes widened, as did those of the other women. Nick Barnett had been smitten with Suzanne from almost the first instant he met her, and most believed she felt the same.

Suzanne set down her fork, inhaling a ragged breath. "He asked me to supper at the restaurant in your new hotel. I declined at first, knowing how hard it would be to get someone to take my place for the night. He wouldn't take no for an answer, figuring a way to have one of the morning servers work in the evening."

"It helps that he's part owner of the boardinghouse."

"It does, Alison. Anyway, I worried about it for days, then took hours to get my hair ready and select the perfect dress." Suzanne glanced at Alison, who'd altered one of the dresses in her shop to fit Suzanne's lithe form.

"What happened?" Lena had stopped eating. She'd known Nick since they were children trapped into living in a brothel with mothers who could barely provide food and clothing. If he'd done anything to hurt Suzanne, he'd be in a world of trouble.

"I waited until it became apparent he wasn't going to come for me. When I went downstairs to make certain the restaurant had been closed and the kitchen cleaned, I found him sitting at a table with a woman I'd never seen, sharing a bottle of whiskey. The look on his face made it clear he'd completely forgotten me...forgotten he'd invited me to supper." Her shoulders slumped. "Since then, Nick hasn't spent more than a minute around me, and hasn't offered an explanation or apology."

"That was Saturday night?" Ginny asked.

Suzanne nodded. She hadn't planned on discussing the disastrous event with her friends.

"Goodness, Suzanne. That doesn't sound at all like the Nick we know. Does it, Lena?" Abby couldn't miss the disappointment on Suzanne's face. Abby had known her for years, knew about the death of her husband and daughter in an unexpected winter storm, and watched her struggle to make a living. Not once had Suzanne shown any interest in a man—until Nick Barnett arrived in Splendor.

Lena cleared her throat, anger welling inside. "No. It doesn't sound at all like him. I wonder who the woman was. Did he introduce you?"

"He barely acknowledged me, Lena. Of course, I left the moment he noticed my presence."

"Can you describe her?" Lena pushed aside the unease she felt. She couldn't recall a time he'd ever treated a woman as he had Suzanne. Although she'd never betray Nick's confidence, she knew his love for her ran deep.

Suzanne closed her eyes, remembering the woman who'd captured Nick's attention. "Beautiful dark hair, almost as black as Nick's. I wasn't close enough to be sure, but I think her eyes were a shade of green. I didn't get a good look at her, but she seemed young, perhaps eighteen."

"Hmmm." Lena scowled. "Nick has never shown an interest in younger women."

"What do you mean?" Rachel sat forward in her chair, as mesmerized by the discussion as the other women.

Lena's face softened. "Nick has always come across as older than his years. He took on a lot of responsibility as a boy, including acting as my protector. He always seemed attracted to women close to his age or a little older. Younger women never appealed to him."

Suzanne felt a blush creep up her face. She'd intentionally pushed him away more than once, knowing he was younger, although she never knew by how many years. It had now become important to her. "Lena, how old is Nick?"

She tapped a finger on her chin. "Let me think. Thirty-seven or thirty-eight."

"Why, you're only a few years old than he is, Suzanne." Abby slapped a hand over her mouth and shook her head when everyone's gaze turned to her. "I'm so sorry. I didn't mean to blurt that out."

Suzanne's soft laugh cut the tension. "It's fine, Abby. The women here know I'm older than Nick. Regardless, it's been four days and he hasn't tried to speak with me or explain what happened. I honestly believe he forgot his supper invitation." Picking up her fork, she scooped up a hefty portion of vegetables. "Let's talk about something else, shall we?"

The room fell silent for a moment before Ginny spoke, her voice a whisper. "Luke wants to try for more children."

Rachel leaned over, placing a hand on Ginny's arm. "Of course he does, honey. Luke loves you. Do you think you're ready?"

A slow smile spread across her face. "Yes, I believe I am. I'm tired of feeling down over the loss, and I can't stand to see Luke so miserable.

I'm going to ask him if we can return to our house tonight—if you and Dax don't mind, Rachel."

"Why would we mind? I'm so glad you're ready to try again. Luke is going to be ecstatic."

"I think so, too. Even though it's been wonderful being here, he's ready to move back to our place and have some privacy."

Rachel glanced around the table at the empty plates. "I think it may be time for dessert. Lydia would you..." She didn't finish, seeing Lydia's face turn an odd shade of green, one hand on her mouth and the other on her stomach. Standing, she rushed over to her. "Are you ill?"

At first she shook her head, not wanting to ruin the day. When another wave of nausea hit, she nodded.

"Come on. Let's get you to the bedroom. Ginny, would you mind serving the dessert? I'll help Lydia, then come back out." Rachel wrapped an arm around her, helping her down the hall and into her room. Lowering her to the bed, she grabbed a bowl from a nearby table. "Here. Use this."

Lydia removed her hand from her mouth, shaking her head. "I'm already feeling better." She glanced up at Rachel, her red face signaling her embarrassment. "I'm so sorry. I don't know what came over me."

Rachel folded her arms, not budging. "How long, Lydia?"

"How long what?"

Pulling up a chair, Rachel sat down. "I'm not leaving until you tell me what's going on."

Chapter Twelve

Lydia's chest tightened, fear racing through her. Every day, she prayed the stomach pains would stop and her normal monthly would start. Neither happened. She didn't need a doctor, or Rachel, to tell her she was with child. Raising a shaky hand, she stroked her short hair, not wanting to face the possibility she could be carrying White Buffalo's child.

"Lydia, sweetheart. Let me help you."

Tears filled her eyes. "My God, Rachel. What am I going to do?"

Reaching out, Rachel took Lydia's hands in hers. "Is there a chance the baby could be Bull's?"

Lydia thought back to their last night together in camp. The night before she left him behind, riding to the Crow camp to make the trade she knew would spare Sam and Mal.

"Yes."

A rush of air escaped Rachel's lips as she thought through the implications. "So the baby could be Bull's."

Nodding, Lydia sucked in a deep breath. "Or White Buffalo's." Covering her face, she did her best to hold back the tears. Instead, heart-wrenching sobs shook her body.

Rachel moved next to Lydia, taking her in her arms. "It will be all right." She continued her soft, encouraging whispers, her own heart breaking at the injustice of what Lydia would be facing. Rachel couldn't imagine the challenges her friend would have to deal with, the hard decisions she'd have to make.

"Oh, Rachel...what am I going to do?"

Rachel found herself fighting her own tears. "I don't know, honey, but you need to talk to Bull. You can't keep this from him."

Lydia pulled away, swiping away the dampness on her face. "I can't believe this is happening. Not after the last few days with Bull. He doesn't deserve this. He..." Her shoulders began to shake. Slapping a hand over her mouth to stifle another sob, she closed her eyes, feeling the urge to retreat back into the shell she'd created weeks before.

"Bull will stand by whatever you decide, Lydia. Let him be strong for both of you."

"No, Rachel. I can't tell him. I just can't."

"Don't forget how much he loves you. I know he won't turn away."

"You don't understand. He hates White Buffalo. Bull will hate me if the baby isn't his." Her voice rose, agitation increasing with each sentence. "What kind of life will a Crow child have in Splendor? A child whose father has murdered whites and wishes nothing more than to force settlers to leave."

"He took you as his wife. White Buffalo must not hate *all* whites."

A bitter laugh escaped Lydia's lips. "His pride allowed him no other decision. White Buffalo has no feelings for me, and I have no desire to ever see him again. He's cruel and vile. If this is his child, White Buffalo must *never* know. I'll make sure of it."

Rachel's brows drew together as she thought of what Lydia's words meant. "What are you thinking?"

Standing, Lydia walked to the window, looking out at the beautiful vista, her gaze moving to Bull's home not far away. If all had gone as planned, it was to become her home where they'd raise a family, be happy, and never leave Splendor. It had all changed when White Buffalo rode onto the ranch, stealing Sam away.

Placing a hand on her stomach, she thought of the life growing within her. Some women might try to find a way to end it, seeing it as a mistake. Not Lydia. And she knew she'd never be able to force White Buffalo's child on Bull. It wasn't fair to him. He deserved so much more, such as a wife who wasn't tainted. She couldn't take a chance of ruining his life any more than she already had.

She couldn't tell Bull about the baby or her decision. Her only choice was to leave, and she knew the exact person who could help her.

"Rachel and Lydia went into town, Bull. I saw them leave not long after you took off with the men this morning." Johnny cast a worried gaze at the foreman, not liking the anger he saw building on the other man's face. "Should I have tried to stop them?"

"They've been gone all day?" Bull had left right after breakfast, returning in the late afternoon.

"Who's been gone all day?" Dax walked up, followed by Luke.

"Rachel and Lydia. They went into town this morning."

"What about Ginny?" Luke asked, turning to look at the house, smiling when he saw her walk out to greet him. They planned to move back to their own place after he and Dax finalized the purchase of the Frey ranch tomorrow. The sale had gone off without a hitch. Now they had to figure out the best way to work a ranch several miles from their own.

Shielding her eyes from the late afternoon sun, Ginny came toward them and walked into Luke's arms. "I'm glad you're back."

Luke kissed the top of her head, giving thanks for the way she'd turned some imaginary corner to get back to the woman he remembered. "Is everything all right, Ginny?"

"I'm a little worried. Rachel and Lydia should have been back hours ago."

"Maybe I should ride into town and find them." Bull put his foot in the stirrup and swung into the saddle.

"Let me water Hannibal, then I'll go with you." Dax walked his horse to the trough, letting him drink, then tugged on the reins. "Let's go."

Watching them leave, Luke turned to Ginny, slipping an arm around her shoulders. "The trip to town came up pretty sudden, didn't it?"

"I was helping Rachel with the breakfast dishes when she said Lydia needed to do something in town. She thought they'd only be gone a few hours." She leaned her head on his shoulder as they took the steps up to the porch.

"Did Lydia seem all right? Bull said she's been doing much better."

"Up until a couple days ago, I would've agreed with him. She's been so much better since they took their trip to the river. On Wednesday, when the women came to visit, it all changed."

Ginny looked up into Luke's face, her eyes showing her worry. "I don't know what happened, but whatever it was, I think it's the reason she wanted to go into town."

"I joined Lydia and Rachel for dinner. Rachel said something about waiting for a response to a telegram. She said they planned to visit Alison and Abby before going back to the ranch." Suzanne glanced between Bull and Dax. "Why? Is something wrong?"

"They've been gone longer than we expected. Bull and I wanted to make sure they were all right." Dax fingered the edges of his hat as his worry began to fade.

"It's understandable given all you've been through the last couple months." Suzanne glanced over their shoulders to a table in the corner where Nick sat alone, sipping his coffee. Her chest constricted at how he still hadn't mentioned a word about forgetting their supper almost a week before. Shaking off the disappointment, she focused back on the men in front of her. "They're probably up at Abby's now. It's been ages since Lydia has seen baby Gabriel."

"We'll head that way now. Thanks, Suzanne." Dax settled his hat back on his head as he and Bull walked outside. "Something's not right."

"My feelings exactly."

Bull had believed he and Lydia were over the worst until he'd stopped by the house for supper on Wednesday, finding her still in the bedroom, refusing to come out. She'd done the same Thursday, talking to him through the closed door, telling him she was ill. This morning, he'd left right after breakfast, not talking to her at all. When he'd asked Rachel about it, she'd deflected his concerns, telling him Lydia would be better in a few days and to give her time. The response hadn't been what he wanted to hear.

They took the trail up to Noah and Abby's house, Bull's heart pounding when they reached the spot where he and Noah had been gunned down a few months earlier. He'd recovered in a much shorter time than his good friend. Noah still faced months of healing to recover the use of his right hand and arm.

"What do you think is going on?"

"I don't know, Bull. Maybe nothing more than the two ladies getting away, visiting friends."

"Why would either need to send a telegram?"

"Rachel sends a message to her parents once a month, sometimes more often. They're getting older and she worries about them."

Bull knew Dax was probably right. He didn't need to pile more worry onto what he already felt for Lydia. Yesterday, she felt too ill to see him. Today, she felt good enough to ride a wagon into town and visit for the entire day. And she chose not to share her plans with him.

They spotted the Pelletier wagon the moment they emerged from the trail and into the open expanse of land around Noah and Abby's house. They also saw Noah's horse, Tempest, grazing outside the barn.

"Noah must be home." Bull reined to a halt next to the front steps, anxious to get inside and speak with Lydia.

"While you were gone, he hired someone to work the livery for him. His recovery is going much slower than he hoped." Dax joined Bull as they walked to the front door and knocked. "He's spending more time around here, doing as much as he can."

The door swung open, Abby's face freezing in place when she saw Dax and Bull. "Well...um...what a nice surprise. Please, come inside." She stepped aside, glancing behind her. "Lydia and Rachel are inside with Gabriel."

Bull followed Dax into the living room, coming to a stop when he saw Lydia bouncing Gabriel on her lap. The smile she had for the boy disappeared when she spotted him, causing Bull's stomach to plummet.

"We were wondering where you two had gone." Dax walked up to Rachel, bending down to kiss her cheek. "It'll be dark soon."

Rachel sent a quick look at Lydia before standing to put her arm through Dax's. "The day must have gotten away from us. It appears I should be leaving."

"With Lydia." Bull didn't take his gaze off hers. The hairs on the back of his neck prickled when she looked away, but not in time for him to miss the sadness on her face.

"Lydia will be staying with Noah and me for a few days." Abby sat next to Lydia, clasping her hands in her lap. "It's been too long since she's had a chance to visit with Gabriel."

Noah walked in through the back. He started to greet them until he saw the way everyone stared at Bull and the confused look on his face.

Bull took a few hesitant steps toward Lydia. "Is that true? You want to stay here?"

Nodding, she handed Gabriel to Abby and stood. Her heart broke at the apprehension in Bull's eyes. She loved him so much, knowing he felt the same. No matter how she tried to come up with a better solution to what fate had handed her, she couldn't. And until she knew the father of her child, she'd keep her pregnancy from Bull.

"Abby's right. I've been away a long time and Gabriel has grown so much. I'd like to stay a few days, maybe a week." She walked up to him, placing her hands against his chest. "You don't mind, do you?"

Clasping her hands, he shook his head. "Not if it's what you want, although I'd rather have you at the ranch with me."

"I know, Bull. And I'd rather be with you, too." She glanced at Rachel, knowing she understood Lydia's dire situation, even if Abby didn't. "It's just a short time. I'll be back before you know it."

A hard knocking on the front door stopped Bull's response.

"Let me see who it is." Abby opened the door to find Bernie Griggs, who operated the local Western Union office, standing outside.

"Pardon the interruption, Miss Abby. A telegram came for Miss Lydia. I thought it best to deliver it right away."

"Thank you, Mr. Griggs. You may give it to me. Lydia's inside." Taking it from his hand, she closed the door, looking down at the unopened message. Her brows knit together, wondering what was inside. Lydia had no family or friends outside Splendor, except perhaps one person. Returning to the others, she held the telegram toward Lydia. "It's for you."

Reaching out, Lydia's hand shook as she took the telegram and opened it. Reading the message quickly, a slight smile curved the corners of her mouth. "It's from Caroline."

"Caro?" Bull asked, bewildered as to why she'd be sending a message to Lydia.

"Yes. She heard we'd returned with Sam." Lydia bit her lip before raising her gaze to Bull's. "She's invited me to visit her in San Francisco."

"What?" Bull roared, unable to hide the shock and anger in his voice. "Doesn't she remember we're getting married?"

Swallowing her doubt, Lydia licked her lips, her voice shaky as she closed the distance between them. "She says it's lovely in San Francisco this time of year. I've never seen the Pacific Ocean. Maybe it would be good for me to get away for a little while."

"No. Absolutely not. We're getting married. If you want to see San Francisco, I'll take you as soon as I can get away."

"But, Bull—"

"No, and that's final. You can stay here a few days to visit with Gabriel, then you're coming back to the ranch and we're getting married." He ran a hand through his hair.

"Um...perhaps it would be best if the rest of us went into the kitchen and let you two discuss this." Rachel took Dax's hand, turning to leave.

"There's no need. The decision's already been made. Lydia is staying here, then I'll come get her in a week." Bull turned to Lydia. "Will that give you enough time?"

Clearing her throat, Lydia nodded. "Yes."

"I'll stop at the telegraph office on my way back to the ranch and send Caro a reply you aren't going to be able to come out right now."

"No. I mean, I'm sure Abby could take me to town so I can send it myself. It would be better coming from me."

"Of course I can take you to town, Lydia. Whenever you want." Abby's gaze shot between the two of them. She had to admit it sounded odd to have Caro invite her to California when she knew Lydia and Bull had plans to marry.

"See. It's all settled. Now, why don't you, Dax, and Rachel start back to the ranch while you have a little bit of sunlight left?" Lydia's heart thudded at the realization this might be the last time she ever saw Bull.

For an instant, her heart tried to take control. She began to doubt her decision, wanting desperately to stay and marry the man she'd been in love with for so long. Then her head took over, convincing her the right choice was to leave. After the child was born and she knew it was Bull's, she'd return, praying he'd understand and take her back. Until then, she had to spare him the agony and humiliation of watching her give birth to a child who might belong to another man.

"You're certain?" Bull asked, reaching out to take her hand.

"Yes, I am. Now, go ahead."

Cupping her face in his hands, he leaned down to kiss her, ignoring the others in the room.

"I'll miss you." His whispered words sent a tremor through her body.

How she wished it could be different. She loved Bull too much to force him into a life he might later regret.

"I'll miss you, too. More than you'll ever know."

Chapter Thirteen

"How many more are missing?" Bull, Travis, and Dirk had left early to do another count. They'd been losing a few head of cattle each week. Not enough at one time to cause great concern, but when added together, the number amounted to a sizable loss for Dax and Luke.

"Three in this herd. I don't know how much in the other two." Dirk rested his arms on the saddle horn, trying to figure out what had been happening. "I'd expect twenty or thirty to be missing at a time if it's rustlers, not three or four. Except we aren't locating the missing head or finding carcasses."

"Makes no sense." Travis whipped off his hat, dragging his arm across his brow.

"It's time for me to have another talk with Gabe. Maybe some of the other ranchers are experiencing the same." Bull reined Abe around. "I'm heading into town when we get back to the ranch. Lydia's waiting for me to bring her home. How's Isabella doing?" Bull knew Travis and Lena's good friend, Isabella Boucher, had been seeing each other for several months, although they tried to keep it quiet.

"I guess you didn't hear. She left a few days ago to visit Caroline in San Francisco."

Bull's gaze whipped to Travis. An unfamiliar dread began to work its way through Bull's body. "No, I didn't hear. Did she go alone?"

"Nope. Another lady went with her. Don't know who."

Before either Travis or Dirk could say another word, Bull kicked Abe into a run, heading straight for the ranch. Jumping to the ground before his horse stopped, Bull rushed up the steps to the front door, pushing it open without knocking.

"Rachel, are you in here?" He didn't stop until he stepped into the kitchen.

Turning from where she stood at the sink, Rachel's smile faded when she saw the stormy look on Bull's face.

"Bull, what is it?"

"Is it Lydia?"

She shook her head, not understanding. "I don't know what you mean."

He couldn't control his angst or the strength of his voice. "Is Lydia the woman who left with Isabella for San Francisco?"

"What's going on in here?" Dax stepped around Bull. "Are you *yelling* at my wife?"

Bull ignored him, taking a step forward. "Tell me, Rachel. Is it Lydia?"

Her shoulders slumped, giving him the answer without words. Clasping her hands in front of her, she nodded.

"You knew? You knew all this time and didn't say a word to me?"

Her voice shook as she reached out to him. "Bull...I—"

He held up his hands, barely able to control his rage. "I don't want to hear anything you have to say." Turning to leave, he stopped when Dax spoke.

"That's enough, Bull."

"No, it's not enough. She knew, Dax. Rachel knew Lydia planned to leave me and she didn't say a word." He glared at her, unable to comprehend how someone he considered a friend could betray him so easily.

Dax turned to Rachel, disbelief clear in his eyes. "Is it true? Did you know Lydia left?"

Tears began to pool in her eyes. Nodding, she took another step forward. "I hoped she'd change her mind. I thought, given a few days with Abby and the baby, Lydia would see how foolish it was to leave."

"So you chose to say nothing, *hoping* she'd change her mind to leave me? Did you know she left a few days ago with Isabella?"

She stared at him, tears running down her face. The misery Bull saw almost changed his mind, but he couldn't get around the fact she'd kept something so important from him. "Yes."

Mumbling a curse, Dax crossed his arms, sucking in a deep breath.

Bull's jaw worked, but he couldn't manage another sentence. He'd stayed away from town, given her time with friends, done all he could to make her happy, but she'd left him. "I'm sorry, Dax, but I can't stay around here right now." He pushed through the kitchen door into the dining room, then stormed toward the front door.

"Bull, wait." Dax followed, grabbing him by the shoulder to stop him. "Where are you going?"

He shook his head. "I don't know, but I can't stay here." Stepping out the front door, he turned. "Give my job to Travis. He's a good man."

"Dammit, Bull. Wait. I'm not giving your job to anyone. You're my foreman. Look, I'm not happy with what Rachel did either. I'm sure she has an explanation, but I know that's not going to solve what's already happened. Let me help you figure this out."

Bull swallowed hard. He needed space, distance from Rachel. He couldn't even look at her right now. "Lydia's gone, Dax. After all that's happened, she left anyway." Pinching the bridge of his nose, he closed his eyes, fighting for control. "I did everything I promised, but it wasn't enough for her." He sucked in an unsteady breath. "It just wasn't enough."

Taking Abe's reins, he walked to his house and disappeared inside. A few minutes later, he emerged, bulging saddlebags in his hands, a jacket slung over his arm, carrying his rifle. Dax watched as he placed it all on Abe, then mounted, riding toward him.

"I don't know where I'm going or when I'll be back. All I know is I have to get out of here."

Glancing at the front porch, he saw Rachel clinging to the porch rail, misery clear on her face as she swiped at her tears. He didn't care. In his mind, friendship meant nothing if there wasn't any trust. Trust and loyalty were everything to him. Apparently, he'd asked too much. He didn't look back as he took the road to town.

Dax watched him ride out, having no idea what else he could do or say. Resting fisted hands on his hips, he glanced at the ground, shaking his head before turning around to look at Rachel. Taking slow steps, giving himself time to calm down, he walked up the steps, stopping next to her.

"Do you want to tell me why you let this happen? We've lost a good man, a friend, and I don't know how to make it right."

Rachel saw the disappointment on his face and heard it in his voice. All week, she'd told herself she had to keep Lydia's secret, had to protect her request to stay silent. Now, she wasn't so sure. Lydia was young, ruled by her emotions, making decisions that should have been discussed with the man she so obviously loved and who felt the same. The reasons sounded solid when Lydia explained them. Right now, experiencing the loss of someone she cared about deeply, someone she admired and respected, Rachel realized how misplaced her silence had been. She should have fought harder for Lydia to do right by Bull and trust how he'd react.

Rachel's eyes were now open. Lydia hadn't given Bull the respect he deserved when she decided not to confide in him. She'd focused on her own fear instead of on the man she'd come to love. Rachel now knew how wrong that was. Bull would have never abandoned her, never disavowed a child, even if it weren't his. It wasn't in him to do either.

"I'm so sorry, Dax. So terribly sorry." Lowering herself onto the porch swing, she buried her face in her hands, trying to think. Dax didn't say a word as he sat beside her, resting an arm across the back of the swing, careful not to touch her as he normally would. She knew it wasn't accidental. He was still mad and frustrated, disappointed in the decision she'd made.

"Why, Rachel? She'd made so much progress. Why would she turn her back on Bull and leave now?"

Sitting up, she drew in a breath, then let it out slowly. The time had come to be honest. "She's going to have a baby."

Dax sat up, resting his arms on his knees. "All right. So they decided to be with each other before marriage. We did the same."

Rachel blushed, remembering the night in her uncle's house when they'd admitted their feelings for each other. Not long afterward, Doc Worthington had come home and confronted Dax.

"What I don't understand is why she felt the need to leave? She could've told Bull. He would've had her in front of Reverend Paige before she had time to—"

"She doesn't know if the child is Bull's or White Buffalo's."

The air left Dax's lungs. The thought the baby wasn't Bull's never entered his mind. *Will this nightmare never end*? he asked himself, feeling another wave of pain for his friend.

"Either way, Bull would have stood by her."

"I told her the same...more than once. By then, fear had taken over. She couldn't face Bull knowing she might be carrying another man's child."

"For God's sake, Rachel. He saw the ceremony with his own eyes. Don't you think he knew what could happen by the time he was able to get her out of there? He risked his life and those of many others to rescue her after more than a week of her being bound to White Buffalo. Knowing Bull, he thought all of this through and made his decision long ago."

"You're right. I wish I would've confided in you, forced Lydia to listen to what you just told me." She glanced at him. "You should have seen her face the instant she accepted the fact she was with child. It broke my heart."

"Because she couldn't be certain if Bull was the father?"

Rachel nodded. "Still, what she did to Bull by leaving will always haunt me."

"It won't if we get her back."

Her eyes widened. "Or send Bull to San Francisco. I know where Caro lives. Lydia and Isabella will be staying with her. Caro offered whatever Lydia needed, planning to sponsor her if she decides to make her home in California."

"Caro won't need to sponsor Lydia if we get Bull out there. He'll set her straight and bring her home."

Standing, Rachel looked down at Dax, a determined set to her face. "All right. What do we do next?"

"Probably one night, maybe two, Suzanne. I appreciate you making room for me." Bull reached into his pocket to pull out some money.

Suzanne held up a hand. "You can pay once we know how long you're staying." She pushed a journal toward him. "Sign here, then I'll show you to your room."

Shouldering his saddlebags, Bull signed, then followed her upstairs. The room she selected looked onto the street still filled with wagons, horses, and pedestrians finishing their day. For the first time since he could remember, Bull felt lost, unsure of what to do next. The woman he loved, would've given his life for, turned from him, leaving without a word of explanation. Worse, he'd severed ties with a family he considered his own, and he hadn't said a word to Luke, his closest friend, a man he saw as a brother.

Tossing his belongings onto the bed, he removed his hat, then poured water into the basin on the counter, splashing the cool liquid on his face. He wasn't hungry, but he did need a drink, maybe two or three. Drying his face, his brows rose at the loud pounding on the door.

"Open the door, Bull. We need to talk."

"Luke?"

"Yes, it's Luke...and Dax. Now, open up."

Pacing to the door, he turned the handle. "Is everything all right at the ranch?"

Both Luke and Dax ignored his question as they pushed past him, stopping in the center of the small room.

"What's this about you quitting your job?" Luke crossed his arms, glaring at him.

Bull glanced at Dax before returning his gaze to his closest friend. "I can't stay. Not with what I've learned. Travis is ready to take my place. He's good with the men and..." His voice trailed off when Luke held his hand up.

"We aren't hiring Travis as the foreman because we aren't letting you leave."

"Look, Luke. You and I may be close, but you still can't decide something like this for me. It's my decision, not yours."

Luke blew out a breath. "You didn't let me finish. We're sending you to San Francisco to get Lydia and bring her home. When you return, there'll be a wedding, then you're going to take over the Frey spread for us, live in that big house they built, and raise however many children you want."

Bull shook his head. "Lydia left me, Luke. She didn't just leave to move into town. She's traveling to California to start over. I'm not going after her."

Dax tossed his hat on the bed. "*Yes*, you are. She needs you now more than ever, even if she doesn't understand it."

Bull's bitter laugh didn't surprise either man. "She doesn't love me. It's why she left. I've got no intention of trying to change her mind. It's over and I'm moving on."

"Here you are." Suzanne appeared in the open doorway, a tray with a bottle of whiskey and three glasses in her hands.

"They aren't staying." Bull picked up his hat. "I'm heading over to the Dixie—*alone*."

"Hand the tray to me, Suzanne. Thanks for bringing it up." Dax took it from her, setting it on a nearby table.

Bull let out a groan of frustration when Suzanne closed the door as she left. He knew Luke and Dax were trying to help, being friends when he needed them most, but they didn't understand. Watching Dax open the bottle and fill three glasses, he sighed.

"One drink, then you two are leaving and I'm going to the Dixie." Taking the glass Dax held out to him, he held it, wanting nothing more than to toss it down his throat, then do the same with the rest of the bottle.

"You need to sit down for what I have to say next." Dax motioned to the bed. "Go ahead. Swallow it. Then I'll fill your glass again."

Bull's brows furrowed, his gaze narrowing on Dax as he sat, tipping back the glass, pouring it down his throat. "All right. What is it you have to say?"

Dax shot a quick look at Luke, who nodded.

"She didn't leave because she doesn't love you. Lydia left because she's with child."

Bull's jaw went slack, the glass slipping from his hands to bounce on the wood floor. "She's pregnant?"

"Doc Worthington's already seen her. He confirmed it." Dax grabbed the bottle, then picked up Bull's glass, filling it again. "Here. You're going to need this."

"But...why? Why didn't she tell me?"

"Because she doesn't know if the baby is yours or..."

Bull closed his eyes, a curse escaping his lips. Tossing back the whiskey, he cursed again, loud enough to be heard outside. "She believes the baby is White Buffalo's."

"She doesn't know and didn't want to burden you with a child if it isn't yours." Luke stood, pacing to the window, looking out at the crowded street. "What would you have said if she had told you?"

Bull buried his face in his hands, shaking his head before looking up, his eyes signaling his grief. "God forgive me, but I don't know. I just don't know." He stood, grabbing the bottle of whiskey, taking a long swallow. "I know it's not what you expected me to say, but right now, it's the best answer I can give."

Luke nodded, feeling a wave of compassion for his friend. He'd just been given news no man should hear. "Do you still love her?"

"Hell yes. I'll always love Lydia."

"Then you'll figure this out and do what you believe is best. That's all any man can do." Luke tossed Dax his hat. "Come on. You need food to go with the whiskey, and so do we. I'll even buy you another bottle if you need it."

"I'm not up for going downstairs."

"Suzanne's sending our meals to the Dixie. Any more excuses?" Luke clasped Bull's shoulder. "Let's go. You need to get out of here. You'll have plenty of time to be alone and decide what to do."

"And if I decide I'm not up to raising another man's child?"

"Then Dax and I will accept it. What we won't accept is you leaving Redemption's Edge. You're family, Bull, and family deals with their troubles together."

Chapter Fourteen

San Francisco, California

Lydia woke to a knock on her door. After retreating to her room, she'd wept until finally falling asleep. She'd meant to take a short nap, but the lack of sunlight streaming through her bedroom window indicated it had to be close to suppertime.

"Lydia...are you awake?"

Pushing to a sitting position, Lydia ruffled her short locks. "Yes, Caro. Please, come in." Walking to a nearby table, she poured water into a bowl, dampening a hand towel to wash her face.

Caroline Iverson swept into the room, not surprised to see Lydia's puffy eyes and tear-stained cheeks. "Are you feeling any better?"

"Somewhat." She turned to face Caro, a beautiful widow who'd grown up in New York. Gabe Evans had been a childhood friend, inviting her to visit Splendor when he learned her wealthy husband had passed away. Although she loved the small town, meeting Beau Davis, a man she cared a great deal about, nothing had changed her mind about continuing her journey to San Francisco.

"It's going to take time to settle in and get used to a large city."

"And to put thoughts of Bull behind me."

"My dear, no one expects you to forget Bull. In fact, Isabella and I are hopeful the future will be kind to you, allowing you to return to Splendor and marry him." Caro walked to the wardrobe, pulling open the door to select a lovely evening dress.

Lydia had made no secret of the reason she'd made the difficult decision to leave Splendor. Almost a month had passed since she and Isabella had left on the stage to Ogden, Utah, taking the train the rest of the way to the large city on the Pacific Ocean. Not a second went by that she didn't think about Bull and wonder if she'd made a drastic mistake.

"It's time we went out for a special supper, and this is the perfect dress." Laying it on the bed, she turned to choose matching evening slippers. "I've asked my driver to have the carriage ready in an hour. Will that give you enough time or shall I tell him later?"

Lydia had no desire to dine in an opulent restaurant, such as Delmonico's, one of Caro's favorites. A quiet supper in her room fit Lydia's mood better.

"An hour is fine. Where are we going?"

"Isabella wants to go to one of the French rotisserie restaurants. It's not fancy, but I hear the food is excellent. And there's a small theatre company next door. They're performing a comedy that has gotten wonderful reviews." She sent a pointed, yet kind look at Lydia. "I thought a few laughs would do all of us some good."

"You must miss Beau terribly." Lydia slipped off her day dress, running a brush through her hair. Although still short by current fashion, it had grown to where it no longer stuck out beneath her bonnet.

Lydia watched as Caro fiddled with the fabric of her dress, a habit she resorted to when someone mentioned Beau's name. Letting out a deep sigh, Caro sat on the edge of the bed, watching as Lydia continued to style her hair.

"He is a wonderful man. I'd be lying if I said I didn't miss him."

Setting the brush down, Lydia turned to face her. "Then why did you leave?"

"Sometimes I wonder the same. The truth is, Beau and I couldn't be more different. He loves Splendor, the small town where everyone knows everybody else. He prefers a quiet supper in a family restaurant, an evening walk down the boardwalk, or a ride in the country. Big cities hold no appeal to him."

"And you prefer the bustle and action of a large town."

Caro let her gaze drift out the window to the magnificent view of the San Francisco Bay. "I grew up with servants, a carriage always waiting, dressmakers, and fancy restaurants. One reason I like Delmonico's so much is my father, and then my late husband, took me to the original one in New York for special occasions. Until arriving in Splendor, I don't believe I ever spent a birthday anywhere else since I turned thirteen. But..."

Lydia waited, giving Caro time to continue. She suspected her friend had come to doubt her decision to leave Splendor, but Caro had never come out and said as much.

"It may sound strange, coming from a woman with my background, but I've come to realize how much I miss the Montana wilderness."

"And a certain man."

Standing, Caro laughed, placing a hand on Lydia's shoulder. "Yes. And a certain man."

Hearing the door click shut, Lydia glanced at herself in the mirror. The young woman filled with expectations of a wonderful future had vanished. In her place, she saw a woman old beyond her years with a drawn face and eyes filled with deep sadness. Touching a shaky hand to her chin, she winced, knowing Bull saw the same when he looked at her. The shy, happy girl he'd fallen in love with had been replaced by a woman who doubted her own worth, who had lost the ability to smile.

Placing a hand on her stomach, she forced away the negative thoughts. Soon, her condition would be obvious to everyone she met. They'd expect her to be happy, looking forward to the baby's arrival. They'd ask about the father, and Lydia would repeat the story she, Caro, and Isabella had invented—her husband had work in Montana, planning to join her before the baby's birth. *If only it were true*, Lydia thought as she slipped on the evening dress, preparing to put on her best smile, transforming into an actress as good as the ones who'd be on the stage tonight.

Redemption's Edge

Bull rolled over in his bed, grasping his head in both hands as the effects of downing a full bottle of whiskey took control. Sitting up, he groaned at the folly of the night before.

After several nights of solitary misery in town, he'd returned to the ranch, picking up his work without a hitch, ending almost every night with a bottle of whiskey on the table. He'd rarely drank before Lydia left him. It had now become a ritual, a way to make it through each night without her image haunting him. Standing, he made his way to the stove, planning to start a pot of coffee, then winced when a loud knock sounded at the door.

"Bull, Dax and Luke want to see you."

Blowing out a breath, he turned to a chair where he'd recklessly thrown his clothes the night before. "Thanks, Travis. Let them know I'll be right there."

"Sure thing, boss."

Bull snorted. He didn't deserve to be called boss with the way he'd been acting. Even though he'd made the decision to return to the ranch and his job, the men went through their day with little direction from him. It was probably why Dax and Luke wanted to see him—to tell him they gave his job to Travis and it was best if he moved on.

Slipping on his pants and shrugging into a clean shirt, he grabbed his boots. His movements were slow, deliberate. He could control how he went about his day, but couldn't do the same with his confused thoughts about Lydia.

Bull knew he'd surprised Luke and Dax when he hadn't been able to say he'd accept the baby regardless of the father. It had nothing to do with his love for Lydia. The way his heart ached all day and every night, he doubted any man could love a woman more. His hesitancy had everything to do with his own shortcomings, his doubt as to whether he'd truly be able to accept a child created by the union of Lydia and White Buffalo.

Strapping on his gunbelt, he checked his revolver, holstered it, then started for the door, walking into the sunlight. Ginny's sister, Mary, came running up to him, throwing her arms around his leg and tugging.

"Come with me, Uncle Bull. Me and Margaret are playing cowboys and Indians. You can be the Indian." She placed a hand over her mouth, giggling, tugging his leg harder. At seven, Mary still had a vivid imagination, a love for life, and a never-ending supply of energy.

Bending, he scooped her up in his arms. "I'd like to play with you, but I need to meet with Dax and Luke. Maybe later, after I get my work done."

Her eyes locked with his before she sighed. "Oh, all right." Then her eyes lit up. "We might play nurse with Aunt Rachel later. You could be the patient."

Bull shook his head, thinking he'd need to stay out on the range longer than anticipated today. "Maybe, sweetheart." Setting her down, he brushed some dirt from her cheek. "You have fun today, and don't get in too much trouble."

Waving, she ran off, all thoughts of Bull already forgotten.

Luke let go of the curtain and turned to Dax. "There isn't a man on this ranch who loves children more than Bull."

"True." Dax didn't look up from the papers on his desk. They had to make some decisions on the old Frey spread sooner than anticipated. Although a great piece of property, it took over an hour to ride from one ranch to the other, assuming the weather was clear.

"He'd make a great father."

"That he would." Dax scratched some notes, then continued reading. He and Luke wanted to move their horse breeding operation to the new property, but that would mean sending Travis over there. They'd planned for Bull to move into the original Frey ranch house, but they couldn't have them both over there. Rubbing his brow, he leaned forward, trying to come up with another solution.

"Lydia told Ginny they hoped to have three, maybe four children. She said Bull wanted a lot more, but she put her foot down."

Dax sat back, frustrated at Luke's constant prattling. "What is it you're trying to tell me?"

Luke crossed his arms, irritated Bull's dilemma didn't seem to concern his brother. "It's been almost a month since Lydia left and he's still struggling with what to do. I thought he'd come to his senses and be on his way by now."

"Is that what you would do if it had been Ginny taken by the Crow? Ginny who'd been with White Buffalo?" Dax stood, leaning against the edge of his desk. "I know what you're saying, but he's in a helluva spot. I'm thinking the more time he takes, the more certain he'll be of his decision."

A knock on the door stopped further discussion, but not the warning look Dax shot Luke. "Come on in, Bull."

"Dax, Luke. Travis said you wanted to talk to me. If this is about how I'm handling Lydia's leaving me..."

Dax shook his head. "It's not. What you decide is up to you. There'll be no judgment one way or another. Although, I have to tell you, Rachel wants Lydia back here no matter who the baby's father is."

Bull knew he'd been given a warning. If Rachel wanted Lydia back here, she'd move mountains to make it happen. "I haven't figured it all out yet. Doesn't mean I won't go after her."

Luke studied his friend's face, seeing the fatigue and flashes of pain. They'd worked together most of the time since Bull returned to the ranch, talking little of Lydia's departure.

Today, he could see the dire toll it took on the man.

"Understood." Dax moved back behind the desk, glancing down at the papers on the Frey ranch. "We're thinking of moving the horse breeding to the Frey place. If we do, it means Travis will have to move over there."

"And I'd stay here," Bull added. "I'll do whatever is best for the ranch."

"If you have no real objection, Luke and I think it best to go ahead with moving Travis over there. He'd need three men, which we'd let him choose. Anyone you don't want to lose?"

"Billy's hankering to work with the horses, so he'd be a good choice to go with Travis. I'd like Tat and Johnny to stay here. They're good with the cattle."

Bull walked to the window, watching as Mary ran around the front of the barn, glancing behind her as Margaret came whooping up from behind. *Cowboys and Indians*, he thought, shaking his head. He felt as if his life had become a game he didn't know how to play.

"Sounds good. Luke, would you let Travis know. Other than Tat and Johnny, he can pick two men to go with him—assuming Billy *does* want to work with horses."

"Bull's right. Billy won't have any issue working with Travis. Other than Bull," Luke nodded toward him, "I don't believe there's another man he admires more."

A bitter snort left Bull before he could stop it. "Billy's got a lot to learn. Travis will make a good teacher."

"You know, he's struggling almost as much as you with Isabella leaving."

Bull rounded on Luke, his gaze narrowing. "What's that supposed to mean?"

Holding up his hands, palms out, Luke backed off. "Nothing, Bull. It just occurred to me that Beau, Travis, and you all have women in San Francisco, and none of you are happy about it."

"Isabella will be coming home before the first snow. I have no idea what Caro is planning. And Lydia..." His eyes took on a glazed look, indicating his struggle. "If Rachel has her way, Lydia will be coming back after the baby is born. None of it concerns you." Bull stormed to the door and pulled it open. "I've got work to do. I'll see you later tonight."

Luke winced as the door slammed shut. "Guess I should've kept my mouth shut."

Dax shook his head, his mouth twisting into a wry grin. "Guess so."

"You doing all right?" Dirk rode alongside Bull, feeling the agitation rolling off him. Everyone knew to keep their distance the last few weeks, and they all understood why.

"Doing fine. Just wish we could figure out who's taking the cattle and where they're keeping them. Two this week, three last, and three the week before. Feels as if they're bleeding us."

"Bleeding us is exactly what they're doing. You said Gabe mentioned no one else has complained of missing cattle, right?"

Bull nodded, taking off his hat to slide a sleeve across his forehead.

Dirk thought a moment, as if weighing his words. He didn't speak much, but when he did, all the men listened, including Dax and Luke.

"I'm thinking you, me, and about four more men set up a trap, see if we can catch whoever's rustling the cattle."

Bull reined Abe to a stop. "I'm listening."

"We move all except a dozen head to the west pasture. We keep the small group on the east border, closer to where we've been missing cattle. Let them graze, wander a little. All the while, we stay back a ways, but close enough to watch. Stay as long as needed until whoever's doing this shows up or we give up and herd them back with the others."

Bull thought over the idea. Dirk was the foreman for the east side of the ranch where Luke and Ginny's house was located. Bull handled the west side where Dax and Rachel lived. It had always been an odd situation, yet each man respected the other enough to work together for the good of the ranch.

"Anything is better than watching the herd shrink without any idea why. When do you want to start?"

"If Dax and Luke approve, we cut the small group from the herd tonight. It's been four days since we last noticed missing cattle. I reckon it's about time for them to try to take some more."

Bull grinned. "Except this time, they'll get a little more than they bargained for."

Dirk shifted in his saddle. "Do you want to ride back and talk to the bosses? I can stay here with the men."

"Naw. You go ahead." Bull had no desire to get back into it with Luke. He loved the man like a brother, but the younger Pelletier sometimes pushed too hard. Right now, Bull didn't want to be pushed, shoved, or nudged. He needed time to clear his head, which meant no more whiskey until he figured out what to do about Lydia. Staying out on the range a few nights sounded real good.

"I'll bring you back some whiskey." Dirk raised his brow and grinned, riding off.

Bull grimaced. He guessed everyone at the ranch knew how he'd been spending his nights, his mind numb from too much whiskey. "Guess I'll have to put a bullet through it if you do," he shouted back, hearing Dirk laugh as he disappeared down a slope in the valley.

Riding toward the rest of the men and the herd, he thought again of Lydia. Last night, his restless, alcohol-fogged brain had conjured up an image of her holding a baby, rocking it in a chair as another man stood behind her. The baby's hair was black, face a golden brown—White Buffalo's child. Yet the man standing behind her wasn't the Crow warrior. He was white with blond hair, his hand resting on Lydia's shoulder. Bull couldn't see the man's face as he leaned down to press a kiss to Lydia's cheek.

Bull had woken with a start, his body covered in sweat, his breathing ragged. On a normal night, he'd have two or three dreams, remembering none of them. Last night, he remembered each painful detail. Lydia had chosen another man over Bull, one who had the courage to raise the Crow child as his own. Or, as Bull thought later, she'd taken someone else because he had refused to step forward, share his love with both Lydia and the baby. Either way, the dream left him unsettled, lying awake the rest of night, imagining all kinds of scenarios as he stared at the ceiling. None gave him comfort.

Maybe tonight, on the open range under the summer stars, he'd find some peace, maybe come closer to a decision about his future. Feeling torn in a million pieces had grown old. He needed to make a decision, and it had to be made soon.

Chapter Fifteen

"What did Travis say this time, Isabella?" Caro rocked in a chair near the window, needlepoint in hand, the latest letter from Splendor capturing her interest. Travis had sent Isabella two, both brief.

"He says there's been some rustling. The sale of the Frey ranch is final and Travis is moving over there to oversee the horse breeding operation." Isabella glanced up, casting a wary look at Lydia. "Bull is doing well, spending most of his time out on the range with the men."

Lydia didn't respond. Any mention of Bull became more difficult to hear as the pregnancy continued. She'd received no word from him, having no one to blame except herself. Most surprising, neither Rachel nor Abby had written. Even though neither agreed with her decision to shut Bull out, Lydia thought they'd at least correspond, keep her in their thoughts. She glanced up at Isabella's laugh.

"Travis says Mary and Margaret have been playing cowboys and Indians almost every day." Isabella folded the letter, slipping it into a pocket. "Travis sure doesn't embellish. Sparse doesn't begin to cover what he shares."

Caro's hands stilled. "Be grateful. It's more than we get from Beau or Bull."

"I'm sorry, Caro. Would it be better if I kept word from Splendor to myself?"

"Certainly not, Isabella. We all want to know what's happening. At least one of us is getting the news. Right, Lydia?"

"It's true. I'm glad for the letters Travis sends you. Please don't stop sharing them with us." Lydia looked back down at the open book in her hands, wishing the story could capture her attention long enough to forget Bull and what she'd left behind. Instead, she read each page over and over until her eyes tired and the words blurred.

"We've been invited to supper by a gentleman I met at a reception not long ago." Caro set down her needlepoint, glancing out the window as the fog cleared over the bay, allowing the sun to brighten the day. "He's a successful businessman. Someone told me he's a widower with two children."

Isabella's brows furrowed. "Wouldn't you prefer to go alone? It would give you a chance to get to know him."

"Oh, I'm not interested in him in that way, although he is quite handsome and, well, suitable." Caro grinned at the word. She hadn't thought of someone being a *suitable* match in a long time. Not since she'd met her late husband. "There will be a number of guests. It will give us a chance to meet new people and learn more about the city."

Lydia sighed. All she wanted was a quiet supper and to retire early. "Sounds lovely."

"I know." Caro stood, walking to the door of the parlor to call her housekeeper. Speaking to the woman for a few seconds, she turned back to Isabella and Lydia. "I've been wanting to visit a new dress shop. We can meet the proprietress, be fitted for new dresses, then have dinner in one of the restaurants along the water. It's too beautiful a day to sit inside until the supper party."

"Oh, Caro. I don't know. You've done so much, and you know I have no funds for more dresses. I'd be happy to accompany you, though." Closing her book, Lydia set it aside, prepared to hear an argument.

"We've been over this several times. You and Isabella are my friends, and I am blessed to have the ability to choose how and when to spend my money. Please, let me do this."

Lydia didn't have the heart to argue. "If you're certain."

"Wonderful. The carriage will be ready and waiting." She shot a look at Isabella. "Would you like to send a return message to Travis?"

"I've a letter almost finished. It will be ready to post by the time we leave." She dashed from the room and up the stairs.

"I do believe Isabella has deeper feelings for Mr. Dixon than she lets on. Makes me wonder what will happen when she returns to Splendor."

"Do you think she and Travis will marry?" Lydia hadn't realized how much Isabella cared for him until they'd shared the trip to San Francisco. Insisting they were just friends, she hadn't come right out and professed her love for the man. The clues were in how Isabella spoke of the quiet, hardworking ranch hand, his kind ways and gentle manner. More revealing was her almost giddy eagerness when his letters arrived, her face taking on a wistful expression when reading them. Isabella's response to Travis couldn't have been in sharper contrast to the way Caro pretended indifference regarding Beau Davis.

"I truly don't know. I'd like to believe two people coming from such different backgrounds could make a life together. It's hard when you've grown up thinking otherwise."

"Like you and Beau?" Lydia bit her lip, wishing she'd kept silent.

Caro looked at her, her eyes showing the sadness she felt whenever someone mentioned Beau.

"I'm sorry, Caro. I shouldn't have said anything."

"No, it's fine. Few know of his background, but the Davis family had considerable wealth. They lost almost everything during the war, the same as Cash's family. Perhaps that is why the two became such close friends. Regardless, it's not his background where we differ." Caro didn't explain further before lifting her chin and flashing Lydia a stilted smile. "Enough of reminiscing. It's time to enjoy ourselves."

Redemption's Edge

"Three nights and nothing. Maybe I was wrong about setting a trap." Dirk whittled a piece of wood into the shape of a horse, intending to give it to Rachel for Patrick's growing collection. There'd been a full moon the night before, giving him the light he needed since they'd made the decision not to give away their location by starting a fire.

Bull lay on his bedroll, arms behind his head, watching a comet flash across the sky. "Give it time, Dirk. My instincts say whoever is doing this won't be able to pass up a few head so far from the main herd."

Tat, Johnny, and Billy had taken the same positions each night, spreading themselves in a circle around the dozen animals used as bait. All except Tat and Johnny rode back to the larger herd each morning, leaving the two to continue their watch.

"Maybe." Dirk lowered his knife and sat up straight, cocking his head at the sound of the cattle mooing. Relaxing, he went back to his work. "I don't mind staying out here a few more nights."

Bull chuckled. He'd slept better out in the open than in his own bed, and he hadn't had a drink since they'd made the decision to trap the rustlers. The time away from nightly suppers with Dax and Rachel had given him more time to think about Lydia and the baby.

It still tore at his insides knowing she hadn't trusted him enough to confide in him, choosing to leave instead of taking a chance he'd reject her. After weeks of struggling with his decision, Bull somewhat understood her reasons for staying quiet, yet he hadn't been able to forgive her.

"You hear that?" Dirk stood, facing the spot where the cattle grazed.

Bull shook his head, clearing his mind of memories of the past to focus on the present. The short, sharp sound of panicked cattle ripped through the otherwise silent night.

With a quick glance at Dirk, the two dashed for their horses, mounting silently. The sounds of the cattle drowned out any noises they made, making it easy to get close. Reining to a stop, the two stared.

"Well, I'll be." Dirk leaned forward, trying to make sense of what he saw.

Bull rubbed his eyes, then looked again, confirming the sight before them. "They're children."

"One looks a little older. I count four." Dirk looked beyond the cattle, seeing Tat, Johnny, and Billy hidden in the trees twenty yards away, waiting for a sign to ride out.

"Yep. There are four of them. Appears they're cutting out a few head. As soon as they start herding them out, we'll circle around...and no guns." Bull pulled a handkerchief from his pocket, waving it in the air twice, indicating to hold up until he gave a second signal. "What are four boys doing rustling cattle?"

"Don't know, but I'm darn sure going to find out." The firm set of Dirk's jaw indicated his level of frustration at finding children stealing their cattle.

"Looks like they've got the ones they want." Bull raised the handkerchief, waving it four times in the air, then stuffing it back into his pocket. Without another word, he and Dirk moved out, staying to the west while Tat and Billy stayed on the east, and Johnny rode behind the rustlers, who were oblivious to the fact they were being stalked.

A few minutes passed before Dirk whistled, giving the signal to close in.

At the shrill sound, the leader of the rustlers whipped around, seeing three men, missing the two coming up behind. "We've been seen. Ride!"

In the next instant, a rope slipped over slim shoulders and jerked, forcing the slender body to the ground.

"Got him." Dirk rode to the body writhing on the ground while the men captured the other three. Reining to a halt, he held the rope tight as he approached, setting a boot on the rustler's back. "Hold still. You aren't going anywhere."

Bending down, he pulled the boy to a sitting position, then grabbed his collar, yanking him to his feet, ignoring the hat toppling to the ground. His jaw dropped when he saw the mass of golden brown hair falling around an oval face, huge light blue eyes glaring back at him.

Dirk stepped back, swallowing his surprise. "Bull. Get over here."

The girl didn't try to get away or show any shame. Instead, she lifted her chin and squared her shoulders. Looking behind Dirk, her eyes softened when she saw her brother being pulled along by a man she recognized from the Pelletier ranch.

"I see you got..." Bull's words died in his throat when he saw who Dirk held captive. "Rosemary Thayer?"

"You know her?"

Bull nodded, sucking in a breath before pulling his own captive forward and removing his hat. "Ben? Tarnation, boy." His angry gaze focused on Rosemary. Holding Ben by the collar, Bull dragged him toward his sister. "I'm out of patience. Now, you *will* tell me what's going on here."

Jutting out her chin, Rosemary tried to stare him down. "I don't have to tell you anything." The caustic tone stunned Bull, who'd only known the nineteen-year-old to be shy and a hard worker, having the responsibility of her younger brother and two other orphans.

Dirk grabbed her shoulders, pulling her close, his eyes blazing. "You'll answer Bull, or by God, I'll tie you up, toss you over my saddle, and ride you through town so everyone can see. First, though, I'll give you a spanking you won't soon forget."

Ben struggled against Bull's hold, fighting to get close to Rosemary. "No, you won't. You aren't going to lay a hand on my sister or I'll…I'll…"

"Enough, Ben," Rosemary cautioned through gritted teeth. "Keep your mouth shut. There's nothing they can do to us."

"Oh no?" Dirk moved so fast, Rosemary didn't know what had happened until he tossed her over his shoulder and ambled to a fallen tree, laying her across his lap.

"You wouldn't!" The bravado so thick in her voice a moment before fell away, replaced with shocked disbelief.

"The heck I won't. You're nothing but a pack of thieves, stealing cattle from hardworking people without a care for who it hurts." Dirk brought a flat hand down hard on her backside.

"Stop it!" Ben's scream drew the attention of the other men, who dragged two other boys toward them, tossing them a foot away from Bull.

He looked them over, not recognizing either one. "What are your names?"

"Don't tell them, Jimmy." Ben realized what he'd said a moment too late.

Bull cocked a brow, sending Ben a menacing smile. "Jimmy, is it? Well, here is how it's going to be. Dirk is going to spank some sense into Rosemary until one of you fesses up and tells us what's going on here." He nodded at Dirk, who drew his hand up, bringing it down with a little more force than the time before.

"You can't do that. She's just a girl." The one called Jimmy pushed himself up, charging toward Dirk until Tat grabbed him by his ankle, forcing him to the ground.

"Now, Jimmy, I don't believe you understand who's in charge here. Dirk and I are the foremen of Redemption's Edge." Bull watched as Jimmy's eyes flickered, then darted between the men circling them. "Do you know what that means?"

Jimmy glanced at Rosemary, who offered a weak smile. Looking back at Bull, he shook his head.

Bull settled fisted hands on his hips, a wicked gleam in his eyes. "It means we caught you four stealing our cattle. Out here, we're the law. We don't need to take you back to town. It's our right to string you up for your crimes, bury you in a shallow grave, and get on about our business. It that what you want?"

Jimmy's body trembled, his face draining of color. Lowering his gaze to the ground, he shook his head. "No, sir. It's not what I want."

"Good." Bull reached out a hand, helping Jimmy to his feet. "Dirk, you and the men keep watch on these other three. Jimmy and me are going to have a talk. Man to man."

Tat shot Johnny an amused look. They respected Bull and Dirk, and all had been on the receiving end of Bull's anger at least once. Slow to burn, once he reached his limit, Bull didn't hold back, his words causing more damage than his fists ever could. And every one of the men standing around knew he'd never do what he told Jimmy. By the look on the boy's face, they knew he believed Bull was leading him to his death.

They kept walking until Bull found a gully fifty yards away, drawing Jimmy into it. Using his hands to force the boy to the ground, Bull crossed his arms, his jaw hard as he let the silence build. Minutes passed without either talking, Jimmy's face twisting in pure misery until he couldn't take the quiet any longer.

"We needed the cattle for food." His voice cracked.

"Don't lie to me. It would take the four of you a *year* to eat one of our steers. Try again."

Jimmy drew his knees up to his chin, lowering his forehead. "We sell them."

Bull almost missed the mumbled whisper. "Say that again. And look at me when you talk."

Lifting his head, Jimmy's eyes filled with fear. "We sell the cattle to a man in Big Pine."

Shaking his head, Bull leaned against a nearby boulder. "Start from the beginning. I want to hear it all."

An hour later, Bull followed Jimmy out of the gully, his hand on the boy's shoulder. He glanced at Tat, Johnny, and Billy. "Take these three boys down the trail a spell. I need to speak with Dirk and Rosemary."

Waiting until the others disappeared, Bull paced back and forth for a good five minutes, calming the anger at Jimmy's confession. Snatching a small rock from the ground, he drew his arm back, letting the rock fly through the air, having no idea where it landed. He continued to pace until he felt calm enough to speak.

Dirk had tied Rosemary's hands and ankles, propping her up against a large rock. Walking to within a foot of her, he crossed his arms and planted his feet shoulder width apart, his glare holding all kinds of threats.

"So, you're the leader of this group of children."

She blinked several times, showing the first signs of cracking.

Bull looked at Dirk. "Jimmy Odell is fifteen. His brother, Teddy, is fourteen. I know for a fact Rosemary Thayer is nineteen and works for Suzanne." Dirk's eyes widened at the news, but he held his silence. "Ben is her brother. The last I heard, he's nine. Do I have it right so far, Rosemary?"

Her face paled. Swallowing a lump of fear lodged in her throat, she nodded.

"Rosemary takes care of the three boys with what she makes at the boardinghouse."

"Jimmy and Teddy work when they can, but nobody wants to hire boys who aren't part of their family." Rosemary's clipped response surprised Bull. Jimmy hadn't told him about trying to find work.

"A few months back, a man from Big Pine cornered Rosemary at the boardinghouse, offering her a way to make money." He looked at the girl. "Do you want to finish this?"

She shook her head, doing her best to hide the tears threatening to stream down her cheeks.

Bull continued, still finding it hard to believe what the four had agreed to do. "He offered them good money for up to twenty head of cattle every four weeks. He and his men meet them east of Splendor, trade money for the cattle, then drive the herd to Big Pine."

"Twenty head? Hardly worth the risk of getting caught." Dirk scrubbed a hand down his face.

"Jimmy doesn't know the man's name or what he does with the cattle." Bull shot a nasty gaze at Rosemary. "He says *you* do."

Her lower lip trembled, showing true fear for the first time. "He said they'd come back and kill us if we talked to anyone."

Bull lowered himself to the ground beside her, his face softening. "Then I guess we have a problem. I believe if we can find the men, arrest them for accepting stolen cattle and threatening you, there's a good chance the Pelletiers might drop the charges." He waited a moment to let her consider his words. "What do you say, Rosemary? Are you going to help us?"

Chapter Sixteen

"It was a lovely party, Caro. I'm so glad you insisted we accept his invitation." Isabella unpinned the hat Caro had insisted she buy, setting it on a table in the parlor before collapsing in a nearby chair. "The entire day was fun...and exhausting."

"According to our host, it's not unusual to be invited to two or three soirees each week." Caro stifled a yawn as she took a chair next to Isabella. "In fact, we've been invited to one in two weeks." She glanced at Lydia, who'd said little on the trip home. "Did you enjoy yourself, Lydia?"

Picking up the book she'd been reading earlier, she sat on the edge of the sofa, her face and slow movements showing her fatigue. "I did, although I do believe I could use a night at home."

"We certainly do not have to accept all the invitations. I do think the party in two weeks will be quite fascinating. We've been invited to the mayor's home."

Isabella sat up, the announcement snapping her out of her lethargy. "The mayor? I'd love to see where he lives."

Caro lifted a brow, her mouth tilting up into a smile. "So would I. The word is he's quite interesting. An Irishman who married the daughter of the former mayor. Their chef is rumored to be one of the best in the city. Oh, I almost forgot, Lydia. The guest I sat next to during supper is a doctor. I think it's time you made some decisions about, well...when the time comes."

Lydia hadn't considered the baby's birth. Splendor had one doctor, Rachel's uncle, Doc Worthington. Her parents' farm had been miles from a small town with one doctor. Lydia had never considered the ability to have a choice.

"You mean I have a choice of who to use?"

Caro laughed. "This is a big city. There are many doctors, some more established than others. I have gathered a few names for you."

"What about your doctor?"

"Unfortunately, he's retiring and moving to a small town north of here. The doctor I met tonight is taking over for him."

"Caro is right, Lydia. You should make a decision soon, in case there are any complications." Although she'd desperately wanted children, Isabella had never been able to with her late husband.

"You're both right. Would it be convenient to meet with someone next week?"

"Of course." Caro reached into her purse. "Ah, here it is." She pulled out an engraved card.

"I think it embarrassed the doctor when I asked if he had a card. Some still regard them as tasteless. However, I find them quite useful. Let's see. Mr. Gavin McLean. Monday morning, I'll send an invitation for him to come by to meet with us." Caro raised her hand, stifling a yawn. "Well, if you two will excuse me, I believe it's time for me to get some rest."

"Goodnight, Caro." Lydia stood, walking up to her friend, touching her arm. "You've done so much for me. I don't know how I'll ever repay you."

"Lydia, my dear, I'd never allow you to repay me. You're my friend. Besides, I can't express to you how much I enjoy having you and Isabella visiting." Caro glanced at Isabella. "I know you're planning to return to Splendor before the first snow, but I do hope you both know you're welcome to stay with me as long as you'd like."

Isabella grinned. "Don't offer something you may regret later."

Caro threw back her head and laughed. "I think you know me better than that. Believe me, if I didn't want you here, I never would've mentioned it. Now, I really must go upstairs."

"I believe I'll do the same, Caro." Isabella laid a hand on Lydia's shoulder. "Have you thought again about sending Bull a letter, telling him why you left?"

Lydia's face fell, her throat constricting when she tried to respond. She shook her head as tears formed.

"It's all right. You have time to decide what's best. It's just, well…I can't help but believe if Bull knew, he wouldn't hesitate to come for you."

Swiping at the tears trailing down her cheeks, she nodded, knowing Isabella meant well. Lydia still couldn't get past the fear Bull would never be able to accept White Buffalo's child.

"Don't forget. There's a good chance the baby is Bull's."

Lydia's face heated. Her circumstances dictated her closest friends know she and Bull had been intimate before their marriage. There were no recriminations, no judgment. She'd received unconditional support and love. Plus, Rachel had made a good point before Lydia left for San Francisco, saying if she and Bull hadn't made love, there'd be no question as to the baby's father.

"I know you're right, Isabella. I could've already been pregnant when I rode to the Crow village." She drew in a shaky breath. "I pray every night the child is Bull's, and if it is, he'll take me back." Her voice cracked, prompting more tears. "I'm sorry. I don't know why I'm so weepy all the time."

Isabella grinned. "It's quite normal. Your emotions will control you until the baby comes. You might as well get used to it."

As tired as she felt, Lydia couldn't bring herself to follow Isabella up to bed. Lowering herself onto the sofa, she placed both hands on her stomach. The slight bulge grew a tiny bit each day, stretching her dresses until they felt uncomfortably snug. Caro had noticed and, always gracious, had taken Lydia to her dressmaker. Now there were a dozen dresses hanging in her wardrobe. She had yet to wear even one.

Leaning back, she looked at the ceiling, closing her eyes, wondering if the life inside her was a boy or girl. Lydia grinned, thinking of how the people at Redemption's Edge would react. If a girl, Mary would mother her to death. A boy would become a full-fledged cowboy by the time he turned five—Bull would make sure of it.

Rising, she walked to the stairs, her heavy heart laden with thoughts of Bull and what he must think of her. Doubt about her decision to leave plagued her. Perhaps Isabella was right. She'd been a coward to slip out of Splendor, taking a child with her who might belong to the man she loved.

Closing the bedroom door behind her, she walked to the window, gazing out on the town and bay below. Squeezing her eyes tight, she rubbed her temples to relieve the intense pain. The truth hit her as sharp as a lance to her heart. The decision she'd made had been emotional, selfish, and wrong. After all he'd done, the patience he'd shown, the love that never wavered, she'd abandoned him as if he meant nothing to her.

Turning from the window, she took a seat at the small desk, pulling paper from the drawer and picking up the pen. It was time Bull learned the truth.

Redemption's Edge

The sun crested the eastern horizon, ushering in another day. Bull had yet to find any sleep. Once Rosemary began to confess how she and the boys had become rustlers, she hadn't stopped, talking well past midnight.

Dirk listened with a stoic expression, asking a few questions, commenting more than once about the lunacy of what the children had done. From his perspective, Rosemary had acted as a willful, undisciplined child. Bull had a different opinion.

He saw four scared kids doing what they had to in order to survive. No matter how hard she worked, Rosemary couldn't make enough to feed all of them, not to mention clothes, shoes without holes, or doctor care if one fell ill. The fact few would hire fifteen-year-old Jimmy bothered Bull more than a little. Certainly Stan Petermann at the general store, the barber, or the telegraph office could have hired him to clean and sweep the boardwalk.

The only two people who'd stepped forward were Doc Worthington and Alison Coulter. Jimmy cleaned the clinic twice a month, and helped Alison in her dress shop once a month. It was as much as either could afford. He'd been surprised to learn Jimmy hadn't approached Nick or Gabe about a job at their new hotel. Bull promised himself to speak with Gabe as soon as he went to town, assuming he hadn't already locked the four up.

"Bull, you about ready to start back to the ranch?"

Dirk handed him a cup of coffee. So lost in his own thoughts, Bull hadn't noticed the fire Dirk started or the coffee he brewed. The four children lay huddled together on one side of the clearing, Johnny and Tat began to stir a few yards away, and Billy held his position watching the cattle.

"I'm more than ready to get to the ranch and figure out what to do next. I'll wake the others, give 'em some hardtack and coffee, then we'll move the cattle back to the main herd." His job as foreman still came first. Turning in the rustlers and talking to Gabe had to come second. Nudging Rosemary, he pulled back the blanket she shared with her brother, Ben. "Time to get up. We have to head back to the ranch."

Rosemary sat up, her gaze darting around, trying to figure out what happened. Then she noticed Bull and her jaw went slack. Her stomach clenched as the truth of the situation slapped her in the face.

"Here." Bull handed her the hardtack. "Coffee's ready. Hurry up. We need to get the cattle back to the herd." He walked a few feet away, then spun back around. "And don't get any ideas about trying to ride off. You wouldn't get far, and it would just make Dirk mad. And, trust me, you don't want to rile him any more than you already have."

She glanced at the boys as they stood, rolling up the bedrolls. Her heart broke at the scared looks on their faces, their sluggish movements.

"Rosemary, what are we going to do?" Jimmy's voice hitched. Running a hand through his long hair, he accepted the hardtack she handed him and took a bite, choking on the brittle biscuit.

"There's coffee ready." She nodded toward the fire, glancing at Dirk, then quickly turning away. Rosemary had never met a man who unnerved her the way he did. Judgmental and arrogant, he looked at her as if her brains were scrambled. She cringed, remembering what he'd said to her last night. *You, missy, don't have the brains of a grasshopper.* What could she say? As much as she hated to agree with him, Dirk was right. She'd made a poor decision. Now the boys might end up suffering for her stupidity.

"You done feeling sorry for yourself?"

She spun around, almost colliding with Dirk standing mere inches from her. Crossing his arms, he glared down at her.

"'Cause if you are, we need to get on the trail. You'll ride next to me."

"But..." She glanced away. Riding next to him, even for a couple hours, would be pure torture. The man hated her, and she felt the same about him.

His brow arched as his lips twisted into a wry smile. "You going to argue with me?"

Shaking her head, Rosemary turned away. Grabbing her bedroll, she tied it to the back of her saddle, scolding herself for being exactly what Dirk called her—stupid. She'd brought this on herself. At least she could do her best to make sure the boys didn't suffer for her blunder. She'd accept the blame, confess it was all her doing. As long as the boys went free, she didn't care what they did to her.

"Let's ride."

At Bull's command, she swung up into the saddle. The time had come to pay her penance.

Gabe leaned a hip against Dax's desk, his arms crossed as he looked at the three boys and young woman. By no definition would anyone consider her a child. She was a woman, plain and simple. A woman who should've known better than to rustle cattle.

"You all know the penalty for rustling, right?"

The four nodded, no one daring to look at him. Few rustlers escaped the hangman's noose in Montana, and the town of Splendor took cattle theft seriously.

"How many head did you turn over to Boyden Trask?"

Rosemary lifted her head. "Thirty."

"All stolen from the Pelletier ranch." It wasn't a question. Gabe already knew the answer.

She nodded, her body trembling under his scrutiny.

"I'm tempted to haul you into jail until the circuit judge comes through."

"Are you going to lock us up?" Teddy couldn't look Gabe in the eye. Shy and without a shred of self-confidence, he seemed much younger than fourteen.

"That's my job. And make no mistake. You are my prisoners whether or not you're in the jail."

"They going to hang us?" Jimmy crossed his arms in a hopeless attempt to stop the fear racing through him.

"It's not my decision." Gabe glanced up when the door opened. Dax and Luke walked in, each casting long, hard looks at each prisoner. "These are the people you stole from. Hardworking men who depend on the cattle they raise to feed their own families and the people who work for them. The money they get from selling their cattle is spent at the livery, lumber mill, restaurants, and general store. That money pays the employees at those places. They use it to feed their families and keep them clothed. Do you have any idea what I'm trying to explain to you?"

They all nodded. Only Rosemary lifted her face. "Yes, sir, we do. We didn't just steal from the Pelletiers. What we did took money from people in town, good people who depend on the money the same as everyone else." She blinked, doing all she could to stop the tears from breaking free and rolling down her cheeks. Gripping her stomach, she cast a despondent look at Dax and Luke. "I'm so sorry. I wish there was a way to get your cattle back, make up for all I've done, but I'm afraid it's too late." She turned her attention back to Gabe, her eyes pleading with him for understanding. "Please don't punish the boys. It was my idea, not theirs. Do what you want with me. Just, please, let them go."

Gabe glanced at Dax and Luke, who shook their heads. No matter the sincerity behind her plea, they weren't going to let any of them off so easily. Dax stepped forward, pinning each with a hard glare. He didn't say a word for several minutes, letting them stew in their own misery. By the time he spoke, they were trembling in fear.

"Rosemary, I can't even begin to tell you how disappointed I am. I can't imagine what Suzanne will say when she finds out the woman she trusted to clean rooms and help downstairs has been stealing cattle. What I want to know is have you also been stealing from her boarders?"

"No! I'd never do that." Her eyes flashed.

"That so? Yet you stole our cattle."

"We...I..." She sucked in a shaky breath. "You're right. It makes no sense what I did."

"You mean what you *all* did. The boys are as guilty as you, Rosemary. They're old enough to make their own decisions. Even Ben, who's what? Nine?"

Ben's voice shook. "Yes, sir."

"As far as Luke and I see it, you're as guilty as any other person who steals. That means each one of you must accept your punishment." Dax turned his back to them, walking around his desk and lowering himself into his chair as a sob broke from Ben's throat.

Luke stepped around the big chair where Ben sat and crouched in front of him. "Look at me, son."

Ben shook his head, unable to meet Luke's eyes.

"There's no shame in crying, as long as it's for the right reasons. If you're crying because you know you made a mistake and wish you could change things, then it's all right. If you're crying because you got caught and you're scared, well, those aren't the right kind of tears. Do you understand what I'm saying?"

Ben hiccupped. "I think so, sir."

"So, which is it?"

Ben glanced at his sister, then back at Luke. "I'm sorry for stealing your cattle. Real sorry."

Luke patted Ben on his knee, then stood. "What about the rest of you?"

"What we did was plumb wrong. Wish I could change it, but that fella already has the cattle." Jimmy cast a sorrowful look at Teddy, whose face had turned ashen.

"Rosemary, tell us again what Boyden Trask said."

She looked at Luke, swallowing hard, remembering the man's words. "He told us if we didn't steal the cattle and sell them to him, he and his men would find and kill us."

"Tell us once more about how it all started." Luke's voice held no trace of sympathy.

"We...I mean, I found a stray at the edge of your property when Suzanne asked me to take some of her baked goods out to Miss Rachel. The animal was all the way to town by the time I rode back." She looked up at Luke. "I swear, it didn't have a brand. I checked it real good and there was nothing."

Cocking his head, he crossed his arms, not sure whether to believe her or not. "Go on."

"I...um...herded it to the old shack where the boys and I live. We weren't sure what to do with it. I mean, it was too big for us to butcher and eat without most of it going to waste. The next day, I overheard Mr. Trask talking about needing better quality beef for his restaurant in Big Pine." She shot a look at Gabe, then Dax. "I don't know what made me do it, where I got the courage, but I told him about the steer we had. He came and looked at it, then offered us money to bring him more."

"She refused," Jimmy burst out, trying to make sure they all knew they hadn't planned to become rustlers.

"Mr. Trask said he'd tell the sheriff we stole the one at the cabin, and he'd kill us if we said otherwise. He gave us money and took the steer, then told us he'd be back in two weeks and wanted six more. That's when he told us again what would happen if we didn't have the cattle. He said just one more time, six head, and he'd never be back to see us." She sucked in a breath. "I should've gone to Sheriff Evans right off." She bit her lip hard, doing whatever she could to hold back the tears. "Of course, he lied."

"He kept coming back, demanding more cattle, threatening us if we didn't have them." Jimmy jumped to his feet, pacing back and forth. "I should've killed him. It would've been better if I had."

Gabe walked up to him, placing a hand on his shoulder. "No, son. Killing a man is never the right solution. Not unless he's going after you or someone else. What you should have done is come to me or one of my deputies."

Jimmy hung his head, staring at his ragged shoes. They were filled with so many holes, Gabe didn't know how he even kept them on.

Dax slapped his hand on the desk and stood. "We've heard enough." He walked around the desk, never taking his gaze off Rosemary. "All right. This is how it's going to be."

Chapter Seventeen

Suzanne stared into her cold cup of coffee. It seemed as though not a week went by where she didn't suffer another blow to her pride.

Nick began each day with a perfunctory greeting when she poured his coffee, then he'd disappear down the street to look in on one of the businesses he owned with Gabe and Lena. He no longer ate dinner or supper at the boardinghouse, preferring the food at his hotel. Not once had he mentioned their missed supper or the woman who'd captured his attention that night.

Trying not to be obvious, she'd asked around about the dark-haired beauty, learning she'd come in on the stage, stayed at the hotel two nights, then traveled toward Big Pine. Suzanne hadn't discovered the woman's name or anything else about her. A few days later, Nick rode out of town, not returning for several days.

Covering her face with both hands, she groaned, embarrassed she'd even embarked on a quest to find out more about the woman. No matter how much she cared about him or the pain his rejection caused her, who Nick saw or spent time with was none of her business. She'd bury her feelings for him deep inside, as she'd done since he'd first come to Splendor.

As if the fiasco with Nick hadn't hurt enough, Luke had ridden into town this afternoon. The news he'd brought shocked and saddened her. Never would Suzanne have suspected Rosemary of rustling. If she'd known how desperate Rosemary was, she'd have been more diligent about making certain whatever food could be spared went home with the young woman. Instead, Suzanne had gone about each day, oblivious to the plight of Rosemary and her charges.

"Are you all right, Suzanne?"

The deep voice with a slight southern lilt surprised her. For weeks, Nick hadn't said more than three or four words to her each day. Straightening in her chair, she glanced at him for a brief moment before turning away. "I'm fine, Nick." Standing, she smoothed her dress with her hands before starting for the kitchen.

"Suzanne, wait."

Not turning around, she stopped, hearing him walk up behind her.

"I owe you an apology and an explanation."

Her heart racing, she reminded herself too much time had passed without him coming forward to offer a reason for his actions. Did his words even matter to her now?

"You owe me nothing. Honestly, it's forgotten." She hoped he didn't detect her lie. As she started to move away, she felt his hands rest on her waist, holding her steady.

"No, it's not forgotten, and it's my fault." Pulling her back against his chest, he breathed in the scent uniquely Suzanne's. "Give me a chance to explain."

Turning to face him, she stepped out of his hold, feeling his hands fall away. She didn't want to hear how he'd met someone, a young woman who captured his interest. All she wanted was for the hurt to go away. "Perhaps another time. I need to help Fannie in the kitchen."

Reaching out, he grasped her hand. "Fannie can wait. I know you're upset with me and my silence has made it worse." Squeezing her hand, he stepped to within a few inches of her. "The reason for what happened had nothing to do with you and me, and it hasn't changed how I feel about you. All I'm asking for is a few minutes of your time."

Letting out a breath, she studied him, seeing nothing except lines of stress and a sincere desire to explain. "All right."

His face relaxed, a smile curving his mouth. "Thank you." He turned her toward the kitchen, tucking her arm through his.

Brows furrowed, she shot him a confused glance. "Where are we going?"

"I'm taking my lady for a walk along the river. Then, if I'm lucky, I'm hoping she'll allow me to take her to supper."

Her heart flipped. Although she did her best to ignore the tug of hope, she felt like a girl being courted for the first time.

Leading her through the kitchen, ignoring Fannie's stunned expression, Nick stepped outside, escorting her toward the river several yards away. Stopping at the edge, he turned her toward him, stunning her by placing a soft, lingering kiss on her lips.

"Thank you for giving me a chance to make things right."

"Are you certain you don't mind taking over? I'll be gone two, maybe three months." Doc Worthington sat at a table in Suzanne's restaurant, staring at Clay McCord—Doctor Clayton McCord, sitting across from him. Until a few months before, he'd been thought of as Stan Petermann's employee at the general store. When Noah and Bull had been attacked, Clay hadn't hesitated to help, revealing his background as a Union Army surgeon. Since then, he'd helped Doc Worthington often, spending less time at Petermann's and more time at the clinic.

"I'm honored you asked me, Charles. You need a break, and I need to spend more time helping others. It's what I trained for, what I'm good at." Clay sipped his coffee, his gaze shifting outside, spotting Rosemary Thayer climbing down from a wagon driven by Dirk Masters. Frowning, he pulled his attention back to the conversation with Charles. "I don't want you to worry about the clinic while you're gone. This is supposed to be a relaxing trip."

Charles grinned. "Visiting family isn't considered relaxing. At least not for me."

Clay chuckled. "Well, try to relax. It will make my job easier knowing you aren't concerned about not being here."

"Here you are, gentlemen. Let me know if you need anything."

"Thank you, Suzanne. This looks wonderful." Clay breathed in the enticing aroma of the rich stew.

"I'll let Fannie know. She's holding pie for each of you, so make sure you save room." Smiling, she turned away, leaving them to their food and conversation.

Clay couldn't stop his gaze from darting back outside. Dirk escorted Rosemary into the sheriff's office, which seemed odd for a couple reasons. Seeing Dirk in town, driving a wagon, was unusual. He usually sent one of the Pelletier ranch hands to pick up supplies and mail. That wasn't as curious as Rosemary not being in the restaurant to help Suzanne with the dinner customers.

"Have you seen Rosemary lately?"

Charles looked up. "No, I haven't. Not in several days. Why?"

"Dirk Masters drove a wagon into town with Rosemary sitting next to him. They went into the sheriff's office."

Charles scratched his chin as another thought crossed his mind. "You know, I haven't seen Jimmy Odell either. He missed his day cleaning the clinic. I hadn't thought much about it...until now."

"More coffee?" Suzanne hovered over them, a pot of coffee in her hand.

Clay held up his cup. "Is Rosemary not helping you anymore?" He saw the slight quiver of her jaw before she covered it with a nervous laugh.

"She hasn't been in for a few days. Luke told me she and Ben are staying at the Pelletier ranch for a while." She filled Doc's cup, then took a step back.

"You must miss having her here to help." Clay sipped his coffee, watching her eyes flicker, then widen. Following the direction of her gaze, he saw Rosemary and Dirk leave the sheriff's office, Gabe right behind them.

Tearing her gaze away from the scene outside, she looked at Clay. "Yes, I do miss her. She's a hard worker and the customers love her." *And I've grown to care about her*, Suzanne thought as she walked away and into the kitchen, then stopped when Fannie turned to face her.

"You going to tell me what happened with you and Nick last night, or are you going to make me guess? You know, my imagination can come up with some interesting thoughts."

Suzanne shook her head, fighting a smile at Fannie's humor. "You know I won't talk about what boarders tell me in private."

Fannie tossed down the towel she'd been holding. "I knew it. He's sweet on you, isn't he? I've seen it coming since the day I first started working in your kitchen. The man can't keep his eyes off you."

Suzanne bit her lip, recalling the night before. They'd walked along the river, holding hands as if they were years younger. He'd apologized again for the missed supper, promising to make it up to her. They'd followed the river for a ways, then turned around. As they approached the back of the Dixie, he'd let out a deep breath and turned her to him.

"I need to tell you about the woman you saw."

Her heart had pounded in her chest. "You don't have to, Nick."

"Yes, I do. It's important you know who she is."

As she nodded for him to continue, a series of shots rang out from inside the saloon, followed by shouts and more gunfire. He looked over her shoulder, muttering an oath.

"You have to go, Nick."

When another shot rang out, he brushed his lips against hers. "We aren't finished."

By the time he returned to the boardinghouse, she was asleep. When she woke up at dawn, she found a single red rose and a note on her dresser. She had no idea how Nick had been able to open her locked door.

"You have nothing to say?" Fannie waved a hand in front of her, bringing her back to the present.

"There's nothing *to* say. Nick and I took a walk, a fight broke out at the Dixie, and he had to leave. You know, I do believe we're going to need a couple more pies for supper."

Fannie snickered. "All right. I'll let you get out of telling me this time, but I am going to learn what's happening between you two." She shook her head, smacking her lips. "My, my. That is one handsome man you got there."

Suzanne was about to reply when the door swung open. Her face sobered when Rosemary walked in, her head cast down. "I'm sorry I haven't been here for a few days."

Taking her hand, Suzanne led her to the table, lowering herself into a chair, tugging on Rosemary's hand. "Sit down." She nodded at Fannie, who didn't hesitate to pour Rosemary a cup of coffee. "I want you to know Luke Pelletier came in a few days ago and told me what happened."

Rosemary's eyes flew open, her gaze darting between Suzanne and Fannie. "I'm sorry. So sorry for everything."

Suzanne patted her hand. "He said they knew who forced you and the boys to do it, and Gabe had already alerted the sheriff in Big Pine. That man is going to pay for what he did."

"I wish it were true."

Suzanne cocked her head. "What do you mean?"

Rosemary looked up, her face filled with misery. "Dirk Masters brought me into town to see Sheriff Evans. He received a telegram from Sheriff Sterling in Big Pine. Boyden Trask left town. Closed down his restaurant and disappeared."

"Perhaps it's good the man has taken off. I'm sure he isn't foolish enough to come here. Not with the sheriff looking for him."

Rosemary snorted. "Miss Suzanne, I don't believe Trask has any more brains than a prairie dog. There's no telling what he'll do once he learns I told the sheriff all about him."

"Don't you worry. I'm guessing he hightailed it as far away from this part of Montana as possible and will never return."

Fannie nodded. "I agree with Suzanne. He's got no reason to come looking for you with so many lawmen after him."

"Well, no one is going to hurt you or the boys." Suzanne stood, straightening her apron. "Luke told me the four of you are staying at the ranch. Is that right?"

"Yes, ma'am."

"Redemption's Edge is a safe place. You do exactly what the men say and no harm will come to you." Suzanne picked up a pie from the shelf, handing it to Rosemary. "You take this back with you. It'll ease Rachel's load not to have to worry about fixing dessert for all of you."

Rosemary accepted the pie, hesitating. "What I did wasn't right. The boys and I are going to do what we can to make up for it." She raised her gaze to Suzanne's. "Someday, I hope you'll trust me enough to let me come back to work."

Suzanne gripped her shoulder. "Listen to me, Rosemary. You admitted your mistake and are doing what you can to make it right. When you're ready to come back to town, this job will be waiting for you."

Rosemary's bottom lip trembled as tears pooled in her eyes. "Thank you. I won't let you down again." Turning, she hurried out.

Suzanne and Fannie followed, watching out the front window as she climbed into the wagon next to Dirk.

"That girl has the world on her shoulders. It's much more than any child should have to bear."

"You know, Fannie, I always thought Ginny carried the largest burden of any young women I knew, what with having to care for her sister, Mary. Now, I'm thinking Rosemary may have outdone her." Suzanne took one last look out the window as the wagon disappeared down the street.

"That's it, Teddy. Dig right into the nasty stuff and toss it in the back of the wagon." Tat leaned against one of the stalls. The ranch hand didn't know if he'd somehow drawn the short straw or done something wrong, but he'd been put in charge of watching over Teddy, Jimmy, and Ben as they cleaned stalls.

Jimmy stopped, resting the shovel on the ground and leaning on the handle. "Where does all this shi...uh...horse dung go?"

Tat pushed his hat off his forehead, his eyes crinkling at the corners. "Well, now, some of it goes behind the house near Miss Rachel's garden. The rest is dumped on the other side of the fence back there." He nodded toward the corral behind the barn.

Sighing, Jimmy wiped sweat from his brow, glancing at the other two boys. Teddy shrugged, then returned to scooping and tossing. Quiet and methodical, his younger brother kept plodding along, making a good amount of progress. Ben dawdled, finding the ropes and tack hanging on the barn wall of particular interest.

"Ben, you gotta do your share. Teddy and I can't do it all." Jimmy sent him a sharp look.

"But I can't do as much as you, Jimmy. I'm a lot smaller."

"You're not as small as you think, Ben." Tat walked to a room where additional tack, saddles, and a few more tools were stored. Looking around, he picked up a shorter shovel. "Here you are. Now you'll be able to do as much as they can."

Ben groaned, hearing Jimmy and Teddy snicker. Taking the shovel from Tat, he got back to work, then stopped at the sound of a wagon approaching. Looking up, he saw who he hoped. "Rosemary!" Dropping the shovel, he took off at a run.

"Hey, Ben. You get back here." Tat hurried after him, slowing to a stop when Rosemary jumped down, wrapping her brother in a hug.

Dirk took one look at the boy, then at Tat, and shook his head. "Ben, stop wasting time and get back in the barn. Tat doesn't have all day to stand around watching you dawdle."

Placing fisted hands on her hips, Rosemary glared up at Dirk. "He doesn't *dawdle*, and you don't order him around." She knew her mistake the instant Dirk jumped to the ground and stalked toward her.

"Do you want to say that again?" He leaned in, his face inches from hers. When she clamped her mouth shut, he stepped away, shooting a hard look at Ben. "Did you hear me, boy?"

Nodding, Ben turned and ran into the barn.

"You sure got a way with little boys, Dirk." Tat grinned, tipped his hat to Rosemary, then followed Ben, chuckling.

Rosemary's gaze followed the tall, lean cowboy as he disappeared into the cavernous barn. She hadn't realized how handsome and charming Tat was until that instant.

"He's not for you."

Her head whipped around to see Dirk's grim features fixed on her. Once again, she found the taciturn foreman overstepping his bounds, telling her what she could and couldn't do.

"I have no idea what you're talking about, Mr. Masters." Lifting her chin and picking up the edge of her skirt, she turned away, taking fast strides up the steps and to the front door.

Crossing his arms, he smirked as she walked away, appreciating the sway of her backside.

"I'd say Rosemary isn't for you, but it seems you may have already made up your mind."

Dirk cringed at Bull's voice, but didn't take his gaze off Rosemary until she disappeared inside. Dropping his arms, he glanced at Bull, his face a mask.

"She's young, willful, and without experience in much of anything—except rustling. If I were interested in a woman, which I'm not, it wouldn't be a girl with more sass than brains. I like my women easy and undemanding, not handing out a heap of trouble at every turn." He took one more look at the house, then started walking away.

Bull's mouth curled into a knowing smile. "I hear that's how it starts." Laughing at Dirk's less than friendly response, he walked toward the house where Dax and Luke waited inside for him. They'd sent a rider out to the north pasture to fetch him, saying the bosses had important business to discuss.

Bull couldn't imagine what else the two might be planning, but those men always had something they were working on, which usually resulted in more responsibility for him. These days, he welcomed the added duties. Anything that kept his mind off Lydia was welcome.

Knocking on the closed door of Dax's study, he strolled in when Luke pulled it open and stepped aside.

"We've been waiting for you." Without asking, Luke handed Bull a glass of whiskey. "Drink that."

Bull looked at the amber liquid, then at Luke. "It's a little early, don't you think?"

"Not when you hear our proposition. Or more accurately, Dax's proposition." Luke nodded at the glass. "Go ahead. I've already had one."

Bull raised a brow, then shrugged. "Why not? There isn't much that would surprise me." Swallowing his drink in one gulp, he set the empty glass on Dax's desk. "All right. What is it you want to say?"

Dax stood, walked around the desk, and clasped Bull on the shoulder. "You and I, my friend, are on our way to San Francisco."

Chapter Eighteen

Bull's stomach plummeted. "The hell I am. You said it would be my decision whether or not to go after Lydia." He had no intention of telling either man he'd already made up his mind to go after her. A man might not have much, but he had his pride. The decision to run after a woman who'd left him, no matter the reason, needed to be guarded.

"You think we're going because your woman's pregnant?" Dax dropped his hand, not letting the stricken look on Bull's face sway him. "Your personal situation has nothing to do with the trip. And you're right. Going for her *is* your decision. Neither Luke nor I will interfere." Dax crossed his arms, leaning a hip against the edge of the desk.

"Then why would we travel over a thousand miles in the middle of one of the busiest times of year to a place we have no reason to go?"

Dax glanced at Luke, who nodded at him. "Go ahead, big brother. This is your idea."

"All right. Bull, why don't you sit down?"

Instead, Bull picked up his glass, poured one more shot, then tossed it back. "I don't need to sit, Dax. Tell me what's so important we have to leave the ranch."

"Did we ever tell you about our shipping business in Savannah?"

"Luke mentioned it to me." Bull glanced at his friend. "He didn't go into detail."

"The quick version is the war devastated much of our businesses. Our shipping business was one of the largest on the Eastern Seaboard. Most of it burned to the ground when Sherman's troops marched through. Luckily, our family didn't lose everything. We were able to salvage a decent portion of the shipping business, but I had no desire to return to the sea. We still own sizable amounts of property. Before the war, George and Polly worked the land as slaves. When they were freed, Luke made a deal with them."

"*We* made a deal, Dax." Luke relaxed into the chair.

"All right. *We* made a deal where they'd earn ownership of the land for continuing to work. After we settled in Splendor, we made another agreement with a longtime friend of our father's, Arthur Yancey. We supplied the funds, and he helped rebuild our shipping business. Luke traveled back to Savannah a few times to help with major decisions. Other than that, Yancey's been the man in charge of rebuilding." Dax watched Bull as he explained the events.

"What does that have to do with now?"

"The shipping company is once again a major competitor. We've been talking to Yancey about expanding."

Bull's gaze narrowed as he began to see where this might be leading. "You want to expand into San Francisco."

"It's the logical place," Luke said. "Dax captained one of our ships and ran the shipping operation before the war. I was in charge of other aspects of the business, including the warehouse, working with suppliers, and setting up contracts."

"Yancey's getting older. He's asked Luke or me to come back and take over. We've made it clear that won't happen, but we can expand to San Francisco. I've already contacted Suzanne's brother-in-law, a well-known businessman there."

"Quentin Briar."

"You've met him?" Dax asked.

"Once." Bull sat down, still wondering how this involved him. "I didn't form an opinion, but Suzanne thinks highly of him."

"She does. Since he visited Splendor a couple years ago, his businesses in San Francisco have expanded a great deal. He's willing to help us in any way he can, perhaps even becoming a partner. Nick Barnett has done business with Quentin before and believes we can trust him."

"Still doesn't explain why I need to go out there with you. I don't have any experience in the shipping industry."

"What you *have* is experience building around the docks of Cincinnati. You know how to design the buildings, order materials, talk to the workers."

Bull held up his hands, palms out. "Whoa. That was a long time ago, before the war. And it was my father's business, not mine."

"Are you saying you can't draw the plans and hire men?"

Bull let out a deep breath, then scrubbed a hand down his stubbled jaw. His shoulders slumped, knowing he couldn't turn Dax or Luke down. "I'm not saying I can't. I'll do whatever you and Luke need."

Luke stood, holding out his hand. "Thanks, Bull. You won't regret it. When you return, you'll still have your house and job. Nothing will change."

Bull took Luke's hand, then glanced at Dax, who nodded. "When do you want to leave?"

"The stage leaves on Monday. We'll be on it."

We'll be on it. Bull thought over Dax's words as he walked outside. Heading toward his house, he detoured around it to a path leading into the tall trees.

Passing a berry bush, he remembered the times he and Lydia had taken buckets to gather the fruit for pies. She'd always teased him with them, holding a juicy, ripe berry to his mouth before popping it into her own, laughing as she dashed away.

It had become a game. Each played their part, knowing what would happen. The last time had been a week before Sam had been kidnapped. Bull had led her further from the ranch, behind thick boulders and lush bushes, making love to her until they couldn't move.

The memory felt like a knife twisting in his gut and shredding his heart. He lost track of time as he continued along the trail, hearing the gentle breeze ruffle the aspen leaves. Entering a clearing, he lifted his face to the sky, watching a hawk circle above before flying away. Shoving his hands into his pockets, he stared at the ground, unable to focus on much of anything until a strong gust of wind reminded him to move on. A moment later, a thick stand of aspen closed around him, giving Bull a strange sense of comfort.

Lydia loved running her hands over the smooth, pale aspen bark as she watched the feather-like leaves flutter in the wind. He loved the way she found joy in everything and insisted on sharing it with him. Lifting a hand to his chest, he pressed hard, trying to relieve the pain pulsing through him. For a few days on the open range with Dirk, he'd been able to push the loss aside, finding a small measure of peace. Returning to the ranch, the emptiness returned, reminding him each day and night of how alone he was.

You don't have to let her go. Lydia believes she's doing this for you. Only you can decide if she's right. Bull thought over Rachel's words, the ones said when she'd brought over a pot of stew when he didn't show up for supper. He suspected she'd been searching for a reason to speak with him alone, perhaps make amends for the hurt her silence caused. By the time she arrived, his mind was already clouded from too much whiskey and too little sleep. Still, he remembered her words.

"She's doing this for me." Bull whispered the words, repeating them. Pressing his fingers to his throbbing temples, he settled back against the trunk of a large pine. He closed his eyes, willing his mind to focus on an image of her the day of Cash and Alison's wedding. Her happiness overflowed, filling him as they held hands, talking of plans for their own marriage a few weeks away. It hadn't happened the way they'd hoped.

Whoever the father is, the baby will still be half Lydia, Luke had reminded him after Bull had returned from catching Rosemary and the boys rustling. Most on the ranch didn't say a word to him about Lydia leaving—except for Luke. He made it a point to prod Bull more than the others, making sure he looked at it from every perspective. Although irritating, Bull knew he hadn't allowed himself to think much beyond the fact she'd left without confiding in him about the baby. The betrayal kept his mind rooted in one place, stopping him from considering all the consequences of letting her go.

Groaning, he pushed away from the tree, walking back the way he'd come. In a few days, he'd be on a stage to Ogden, then a train to San Francisco, the same city as Lydia. Would he go see her? Should he track her down, confront her about the baby and her decision to leave? He didn't even know where Caro lived, although he felt certain Rachel did.

An odd feeling he couldn't define washed over him as he made his way to the front of his house. Although he knew it wasn't real, an image of Lydia standing in his kitchen, smiling while holding a baby, assailed him, causing him to stumble up the steps. Bracing his hand on the door, he sucked in an unsteady breath, then walked inside, his heart breaking at the sight before him. Emptiness, the same as every day since Lydia left.

"Oh my. You look beautiful." Fannie walked around Suzanne, nodding her head in approval. "Where did you get such a fine dress?"

Suzanne blushed at the fuss her friend made over a simple store-bought dress from Alison Coulter's shop. Except nothing ever left Allie's without her putting some distinctive style onto it. She'd added lace and fine pearls to the sleeves and collar of the blue and white silk dress. The colors and refinements enhanced Suzanne's deep blue eyes and strawberry blonde hair.

"Add a little rouge and Nick won't be able to take a breath."

"Rouge? Oh, I don't know, Fannie. I don't even own any."

Lifting a small bag she held in her right hand, Fannie stepped forward, eyes twinkling. "I have it right here. Now sit down and I'll fix you right up."

Fannie continued to chatter as she applied the rouge and made a few adjustments to Suzanne's hair. Suzanne stayed silent, hearing her friend, yet letting her thoughts stray elsewhere. For a brief moment, she remembered the sharp pang of disappointment when Nick forgot their supper a few weeks before. Her stomach twisted, wondering if that would be her fate again this evening.

"I'm telling you. When it comes to you, Nick Barnett is well and truly caught."

Suzanne forgot her fear of being hurt again as her attention snapped back to Fannie. "What did you say?"

"Nick Barnett. Anyone can tell by the way he looks at you that he wants to carry you away somewhere private...if you know what I mean."

Suzanne could feel her face heat. "He's younger than me."

"Nothing wrong with that. It doesn't seem to worry him, so it shouldn't worry you." Fannie picked up a small bottle of perfume Nick had given Suzanne the previous Christmas. "Now just a little of this."

"Do you think it's necessary?" Suzanne hadn't used a drop of the expensive liquid, guessing what it had cost him.

Fannie cocked her head to one side, raising an eyebrow. "Believe me. He wouldn't have given it to you unless he wanted to get a whiff every now and then." Stepping back, she took one more critical look at Suzanne, then smiled. "You are simply going to shock him into silence tonight."

Laughing, Suzanne stood, smoothing her dress with both hands. "That would surely make it an awkward evening." The words were said in a light tone, as if his reaction to her meant little. In truth, what Nick thought of her meant a great deal. More than she would ever admit to him or anyone else. "I guess it's time to go downstairs." Placing a hand on her stomach to quell the butterflies, she followed Fannie into the hall, stopping at the top of the stairs.

"I'll go on down and nod if he's waiting."

"Thank you, Fannie. I may need a couple minutes before coming down." She knew her hesitancy had to do with the fear he wouldn't be waiting for her. If he failed to honor his invitation a second time, there'd be no third chance, and the thought chilled her. The damage to her pride, and her heart, would be too great for him to continue living in the boardinghouse. She'd ask him to vacate his room, knowing he'd have no trouble moving into the hotel he owned with Gabe and Lena.

Suzanne took hold of the banister, waiting. When Fannie reached the first floor, she looked around. It seemed to take forever before she looked over her shoulder, a smile on her face.

Letting out a relieved breath, Suzanne tightened her grip on the banister and took the steps on shaky legs. Stopping midway, she scolded herself for acting like a schoolgirl. At her age, she shouldn't feel this anxious at having a man such as Nick show an interest in her. Several single women in town had made no secret of their interest in him. And why not? Handsome, single, and wealthy, he didn't have to work hard at finding female companions. Yet, in all the time he'd been in Splendor, Suzanne had never heard of him showing an interest in anyone—except her.

She was about to finish her descent when she glanced down to see Nick standing at the bottom of the stairs, looking up at her and holding out his hand, an appreciative smile on his face, causing her heart to beat faster. Keeping her gaze focused on him, she took the remaining steps, taking his hand.

"You look stunning, Suzanne." His gaze drifted over her, then settled on her mouth before lifting to her eyes. Seeing surprise on her face, he took her other hand in his. "You have no idea what a gorgeous woman you are, do you?"

Uncomfortable with the praise and the intimate stance any of the dining room guests could see if they turned to look their way, she tried to pull back. His fingers tightened around hers. Shaking his head, Nick chuckled, tucking her arm through his, turning them toward the door.

"I've waited too long for this evening, Suzanne, and I mean to let everyone know I'm courting you." Opening the door, he escorted her outside, taking a slow stroll down the boardwalk.

Her eyes widened. "You're courting me?"

He came to a stop, turning to face her. "Suzanne Briar, let me make my intentions clear. You are the most intriguing woman I've ever met. You're smart, generous, hardworking, courageous, and beautiful. Few men are worthy of you, and certainly not me. I can be brutal when needed. I've done things that might make you turn away, yet here I am, staking my claim in public, hoping you won't turn me down. Make no mistake. I *am* courting you, unless you tell me otherwise."

Her lips parted. She'd never heard anything so wonderful, so heartfelt. Her mind whirled with the implications of his declaration. She couldn't form words, so she nodded.

"Then we're agreed?" He lifted one of her hands to his lips, brushing a kiss across the palm.

The instant heat rushing through her body stunned her. Suzanne hadn't been interested in a man in years. Not one man since her husband died sparked any interest within her broken heart until Nick Barnett walked into her boardinghouse. Since then, she'd done everything possible to build a barrier to feeling anything other than friendship. The wall was crumbling fast.

"Suzanne? Are we agreed?"

"Yes, Nick. I believe we are."

Suzanne couldn't recall the last time she'd eaten so much or laughed so hard. They'd made a grand tour of the town, stopping several times to greet people they knew before he escorted her into the St. James Hotel, directing her to the dining room. Taking his time, he strolled past tables of strangers, greeting them, introducing Suzanne as he held her close to his side. Spotting Noah and Abby watching them from a table near the window, Nick walked straight toward them, holding out his hand, seeing Noah's right arm still confined in a sling.

"Tonight must be a special occasion, Noah."

Standing, Noah held out his left hand. "We're celebrating Abby's birthday. I couldn't think of a better place to bring her for such a special occasion. No offense, Suzanne."

"None taken, Noah. Are you enjoying your evening so far, Abby?"

Abby hadn't been able to break her gaze away from the sight of Nick's arm around Suzanne's waist. She'd known the older woman her entire life. After Abby's mother died, and until her father had sent her away to school back east, she'd spent a great deal of time in the boardinghouse kitchen. Suzanne had become a second mother to her.

"Um...yes. I'm having a wonderful time. Are you having supper here...together?"

Nick spoke before Suzanne could. "Mrs. Briar has agreed to allow me to court her. I hope we have your approval, Abby."

Suzanne blushed at his words, but didn't attempt to move away.

Setting her napkin aside, Abby stood, giving Suzanne a hug. "I think it's wonderful." Stepping back, she looked at Nick. "What took you so long?" Seeing the surprise on his face, she got on her tiptoes to place a kiss on his cheek.

Nick glanced at Suzanne, then shifted his gaze back to Abby. "Fear."

"Fear?" Abby and Noah asked at the same time.

"Of course. I was afraid this beautiful woman would turn me down."

Abby smiled. "I don't believe there was ever much chance of that."

"Abby..." Noah's deep voice warned her she may have gone too far.

"It's all right, Noah. She's right." Suzanne cast a shy look at Nick, whose mouth turned up at the corners when he heard her confession.

"We'll let you two finish your supper." Nick turned Suzanne toward a private alcove in the far corner, taking her wrap, then pulling out a chair. The table had been set with the finest silverware and china. A vase filled with native flowers sat in the middle of the table, candles on either side.

"Nick, this is lovely."

He didn't respond as he took a seat next to her, then nodded to a server standing a few feet away. Without a word, wine was poured, their meal appearing several minutes later.

Picking up his glass, Nick tilted it toward her. "Here's to the first of many evenings together, Suzanne."

She held up her glass, touching the rim to his. "Many evenings," she murmured, her voice unsteady.

Nick continued to hold his glass to hers, unwilling to break the moment. "And many days, and whatever else you're willing to give me."

Her mouth went dry as she understood the meaning of his words. If she'd been eighteen, or even in her twenties, she might have found his words insulting. Tonight, as a much older, perhaps wiser woman, she felt her body tingle with desire, spiraling to heights she hadn't experienced in years. Without a trace of shame, she leaned toward him, her voice dropping to a whisper.

"I'm willing to give you as much as you'll take."

Nick had been lucky to save his wine from spilling into his lap. The unexpected offer, the sultry tone of her voice, caught him so off guard, he felt his face color, an occurrence that never happened. People could do or say anything, and he'd take it without flinching.

Those soft words, spoken over a quiet supper, undid him.

Setting down her glass, Suzanne took a generous bite of the steak covered with a wine and mushroom sauce. "Oh my. This is the best steak I've ever had. And the sauce..." Her eyes closed as she savored a second delicious bite.

Watching her reaction, Nick's breathing grew shallow, his body reacting in a way he didn't want her to see. His stomach growled, yet all he could do was sip his wine and enjoy the pleasure on her face.

"Nick? Aren't you going to eat?" She rested her knife and fork on the edge of her plate. "It's delicious."

Leaning forward, he raised a hand, brushing a dot of gravy from the corner of her mouth. "I can see it is."

Sitting back, he took his first bite. It was, indeed, good, but not as satisfying as Suzanne's appreciation of it. They continued eating and talking until both plates were clean.

"Are you ever going to tell me about the woman?"

Nick's hand stilled on his wine glass. A young female face with clear, green eyes and molasses-colored hair flashed before him, bringing a warm feeling with it. His thoughts must have shown in his expression.

"From the look on your face, I assume she means a great deal to you."

He nodded. "I'm sorry, Suzanne. I should have told you before now. She *does* mean a great deal to me."

She tried to keep her features still as her stomach clenched. "Are you going to tell me who she is?"

"She's a young woman I care about very much. Someone I want to get to know better." He leaned forward, taking both her hands in his. "Her name is Olivia. She's my daughter."

Chapter Nineteen

Bull twisted the leather strap between his fingers as he watched the scenery rush past from his seat in the stagecoach. They'd been cooped up in this coffin on wheels for days. He'd been ready to get off after the first twelve hours.

He'd never felt comfortable without his horse nearby, giving him the ability to control where he went and when. Instinctively, his hand moved to the gun strapped to his waist, the feel of the handle giving him comfort. He glanced at his rifle resting on the seat next to him. It and his revolver were as much a part of him as his boots.

He and Dax had been alone in the jarring coach for most of the trip, allowing the long-legged men room to stretch out. Dax had filled his time reading, jotting numbers in a journal, or doing his best to nap. Although his body craved it, Bull found it hard to sleep...or take his mind off Lydia. Since the moment Dax told him they'd be leaving, Bull couldn't push images of her from his mind. At some point, he'd decided he didn't want to.

"Ogden ahead!"

Bull and Dax sat up at the guard's announcement, grabbing their rifles. Neither had been to Ogden, a growing town of over twenty-five hundred. The opening of the railroad had doubled the population, and more people were expected to settle in the area as the west continued to expand.

"Here you are, gents." The driver tossed them each a bag. "Where are you staying?"

"Hotel Ogden." Dax leaned down, clutching the bag as he looked around.

"It's a couple blocks that way." The driver pointed down the street. "Railroad is on past it."

Dax tossed the man a coin. "Appreciate it."

They didn't draw much attention as they took the boardwalk to their hotel. A town built on farming, ranching, and the Mormon faith, they didn't notice much difference between Ogden and Splendor, other than the size.

"We have time for a drink?" Bull stopped in front of the nearest saloon.

Dax answered by moving past him and pushing open the door, taking a place at the bar. Bull wedged his way between Dax and an older man, setting his bag on the ground between his legs.

"Two whiskeys." Dax held up two fingers to the bartender.

"I don't believe I've seen either of you in here before."

Dax and Bull turned at the husky feminine voice, seeing a woman almost as tall as them, with flaming red hair, her dress drawn up in front.

"My name's Ava Glenn. I own this place." She nodded at the bartender as he set glasses on the bar for Dax and Bull. "Where you boys from?"

"Montana," Dax answered, tossing back the whiskey.

Bull did the same, letting his gaze wander around the large room, then up the stairs. Larger than the Dixie or Wild Rose, it couldn't match the style Nick and Lena had brought with them from New Orleans.

Ava looked them up and down without a shred of shame. "You two see anything you want, let me know. I'm certain I can accommodate you."

I doubt that, Bull thought, holding his glass toward the bartender for another pour. Ava sashayed away, the sight making no impression on him.

"I could use a bath before supper."

"I'm with you, Bull." Dax picked up his bag, making his way outside. "We meet with the commandant of Fort Douglas tomorrow. He isn't happy with the quality of horses he's getting."

Bull stopped, turning to face him. "Are you thinking of driving horses this far south?"

Dax laughed. "Might be...if the price is right. Could be they need better beef. Either way, it's worth a meeting."

Bull blew out a frustrated breath. The delay would add one more day to their trip. Another day before he could locate Lydia and force her to admit what she'd been too ashamed to tell him earlier.

San Francisco

"When will the doctor arrive?" Lydia took a seat next to Caro, who didn't glance up from her needlepoint.

"About ten minutes less than the last time you asked."

Isabella bit back a smile. "She's nervous, Caro. The same as I would be. It's not as if any of us have had a baby."

Setting down the embroidery, Caro sighed. "True. It's a bit stressful for all of us. I do wish there were women doctors for this type of thing."

"There are some."

"Apparently not in San Francisco, Isabella. Or they aren't familiar to the women I've met. All have male doctors. Do you care, Lydia?"

She took a moment to answer. The only times she'd seen a doctor in the past was for an illness or injury. Doc Worthington had always been wonderful.

"I never thought about it. Fact is, I've never met a woman who was all that interested in medicine...except maybe Rachel. All I ask is for the doctor to be competent."

"I do believe a cup of tea would be perfect right now." Caro walked to the door, spoke to her housekeeper, then sat back down. "How do you feel, Lydia? You haven't mentioned being sick in the longest time."

"It's been weeks since I felt ill." She settled both hands on her expanding stomach. "I believe the baby is about four months along, maybe more." She prayed it was more. Counting back, it had been at least six months since the first time Bull had made love to her, weeks before she'd made the decision to ride into the Crow camp. If she were lucky...

"Mrs. Iverson, Dr. McLean is here."

"Please, show him in." Caro waited until the housekeeper left, then stood. "It appears we won't have time for our tea after all."

"From what I can tell, you appear to be close to six months along, Mrs. Mason."

Lydia cringed at the use of Bull's last name...the name Caro had given the doctor when he arrived. The news, however, caused her breath to catch and her eyes to grow wide.

"Do you really believe it's been almost six months?"

"I do. It's a miracle you are still so slim."

"Is that a problem?"

"Not at all, Mrs. Mason. Some women don't show much until the last few months. Appears you may be one of them." Standing, he picked up his bag before hearing a quiet sob. "Are you all right, Mrs. Mason?"

Lydia bent forward, placing one hand on her stomach and another over her mouth. A moment later, she saw the white handkerchief he held out, snatching it from him.

"Thank you. I don't know what's happening to me. It seems so foolish. I never used to cry, and now it seems it's all I do."

Gavin knelt down in front of her, taking one of her hands in both of his. "Would you like me to get Mrs. Iverson?"

"No, please. I just need a minute. Besides, Caro and Isabella will only worry if they see me crying again."

Clasping her hand firmly, he held her gaze. "It's quite normal for a woman who's expecting to be more emotional than normal. I can't truly explain it as I don't understand the reasons."

Smiling as she tried to swipe away her tears, Lydia glanced away, then back at him, her face still flushed with embarrassment.

"It's all right. I feel better knowing I'm not some silly woman."

"Oh, I doubt that's even possible, Mrs.—"

The door burst open as Caro dashed inside, her gaze darting to Lydia, then over her shoulder to whomever stood behind her. "Lydia..." Her voice trailed off as their visitor pushed past her and stepped into the room.

Bull stopped, his face hardening at the sight before him. A man kneeling in front of *his* woman, holding her hand.

"Bull!" Lydia stood, forgetting the doctor, focusing on the angry man before her. "You came for me."

Taking his gaze off the other man, Bull glared at her. "Did you think I wouldn't?"

Gavin stood, trying to understand what was going on in front of him. Straightening to his full height of close to six feet, he stepped forward, extending his hand.

"I'm Doctor McLean."

Bull glanced at the outstretched hand, deciding it best to accept it. "Bull Mason."

Gavin's eyes widened in understanding. "Ah, you're the husband."

Bull couldn't keep his gaze off Lydia. She'd grown even lovelier since he'd last seen her, and even though still slim, the fact she carried a child was obvious—at least to him. Watching her uneasy gaze shift between him and Dr. McLean became increasingly difficult as the time dragged on. He ached to hold her, tell her how much he'd missed her, and assure her any fears she had were unwarranted.

"I'm so glad you'll be able to be with your wife when the baby comes. She and Mrs. Iverson mentioned your work in Montana might keep you away for some time."

Bull didn't shift his gaze from Lydia, who seemed to squirm under his scrutiny. "Doctor, nothing is more important to me than my *wife* and our baby."

Gavin nodded. "As I was about to tell Mrs. Mason, it's important for her to rest and not overdo." He stood, picking up his bag. "Perhaps you and I should speak in private."

When Lydia began to protest, Bull held up his hand, silencing her.

"Whatever you have to say may be said in front of Lydia."

A slight blush crept over Gavin's face as he looked at her and the other two women. "Very well. It's unusual for a woman to have a baby without anyone around who has helped deliver a child before. It may be different where you come from, but in San Francisco, most women have other, more knowledgeable women who can stay with them as the date approaches."

"I'll be with her."

"Perhaps I wasn't clear. I'm talking about someone who's helped deliver a baby, in case I'm unable to get here right away or you don't make it to the hospital in time."

"You've been clear, Doctor McLean. I have experience." Bull couldn't miss the skeptical looks of the women or the doctor. "Besides delivering two of my cousins, I helped with a delivery near a battle during the war. The circumstances weren't good, but the baby and mother made it. The fact we're close to you and a hospital is a luxury. I won't let anything happen to my *wife*." He glanced at Lydia on the last word. They needed to talk. To do that, he needed to get the good doctor to leave. Bull cast a pleading look at Caro, hoping she understood.

"Doctor McLean, we appreciate you being here. I do believe it is time for Lydia to eat and take her nap. As you said, she needs rest."

"How true, Mrs. Iverson." He extended his hand to Bull. "Please, don't hesitate to send someone for me if anything happens."

Bull engulfed the man's hand with his larger one. "Trust me, Doc. I won't."

"Wonderful. Mrs. Mason, it was a pleasure meeting you."

Bull didn't miss the sweep of Gavin's appreciative gaze over Lydia. "I'll walk you to the door." Moving his body between Lydia and the doctor, his movements gave Gavin little choice but to leave. "Thanks again, Doc."

Closing the entry door, Bull rested fisted hands on his hips and took a deep breath. Sensing everything he wanted was within his grasp, he returned to the parlor, taking Caro's elbow and escorting her into the hall, ignoring Lydia's surprised look.

"How soon can you get a minister here?" he whispered.

Caro's eyes narrowed. "Have you spoken with Lydia about this?"

"Do I need to?" His thick sarcasm had her taking a step back. "She calls herself Mrs. Mason and acknowledges me as her husband. Do you truly think she will refuse an actual marriage?"

Caro glanced over her shoulder to the closed door of the parlor. She didn't want to betray Lydia, yet Bull was right. It would only be a matter of days before word spread about Lydia's husband joining her in San Francisco. Keeping up appearances had always been important to Caro and, by extension, those living under her roof.

"All right, Bull. I'll send my driver out with a message to the reverend at the church I attend. I hope he will agree to come here post-haste. Do you have a ring?"

Slipping his large hand into the pocket of his trousers, he pulled out a simple gold band.

The lines on Caro's face softened in relief. "You *did* come here to marry her."

Bull shook his head. "I came here to take her home so we could marry. Seems not much I plan lately is working out."

Caro rested her hand on his arm. "Love has an odd way of smoothing out the most difficult times, Bull. Lydia loves you, and it's obvious you love her. This is all going to work out—I can feel it."

Bull snorted. "I sure do wish I felt the same. For now, I'll be happy with a minister and a marriage."

She leaned up and kissed his cheek. "You go back to Lydia. Isabella and I will take care of your wedding. Is there anything else?"

Bull thought a moment, then smiled. "Get word to Dax. He's at the Clayton Hotel. Make sure he gets here by the time the minister arrives."

"Don't worry. I'll make sure he's here. You have my word."

Lydia stood by the window, her hands clasped in front of her as she stared out at the bay. The churning water mimicked the way she felt—agitated and unsettled. She didn't know what Bull would say once he returned from talking to Caro, and could only imagine the shock he felt at being introduced as her husband. He'd taken it well, fallen into the role without a flinch, which gave her some hope.

Isabella had gone to prepare tea, providing words of encouragement before she left, giving Lydia a few moments alone.

Hearing the door open and close, she assumed Isabella had returned. "I don't know what to do, Isabella." When Lydia didn't get a response, she turned, a hand coming to rest on her stomach when she saw Bull leaning against the closed door.

As much as he wanted to go to her, Bull didn't say a word. His intense gaze studied her, noticing the way her hands shook and her eyes clouded over. He didn't see tears, only intense emotion as the minutes ticked by. Pushing away from the door, he couldn't miss the way she flinched, her body stiffening at his approach.

He cocked his head, stopping a few feet away. "I'd never hurt you, Lydia."

"I know, Bull. You've always made me feel safe." She lifted a hand to her chest, feeling the intense pain in the area of her heart. It had grown into a dull ache over the weeks they'd been apart. Now it had returned in full force, making it hard to breathe. Lydia stared at the ground, unable to meet his gaze.

"This isn't easy for me." He swept a hand around the room filled with expensive furnishings and irreplaceable art. "It's hard, coming here after you left without a word of explanation. Is it that you truly prefer living in a place like this instead of my small house on the ranch? Was this a way to get far away from the little I could provide?"

She lifted her head, seeing raw hurt in his eyes. "No! I love your house and the ranch." She took a step forward. "And I love you."

He didn't go to her, unsure if he could trust what he'd say.

"I know now it was wrong to leave without telling you about the baby."

"You didn't trust me." He took a tentative step forward, arms held out, palms up. "Did you think I'd abandon you?"

She shook her head. "No. It wasn't that." Her voice had lowered to the point he had to strain to hear her.

He continued forward, stopping a foot away to see her lower lip quiver before she lowered her head. "Then tell me. What made you run?"

The sob rose suddenly, followed by another, her hands coming up to cover her face. "I'm sorry. So very sorry."

Going to her, Bull wrapped Lydia in his arms, stroking her hair as her body shuddered. "It's going to be all right, sweetheart. I'm here now, and I'm not leaving." Moving her to the sofa, he sat down, pulling her onto his lap. "Cry it out, then we'll talk."

It took several minutes for her to calm enough to talk without her voice breaking. Lydia sat up, wrapping her arms around his neck, resting her head on his shoulder.

"Say it, Lydia. Just say it."

She hesitated a moment before the words came out. "The baby may not be yours."

"I know."

Straightening, she stared into his eyes. "You know? How could you?"

He would've smiled if their situation weren't so serious and if she didn't hurt so much.

"Did you think I believed White Buffalo wouldn't make you his or that nothing would happen within the privacy of his tipi?" He sucked in a shaky breath, desperately trying to rid his mind of the image of Lydia with the Crow warrior. "I knew what would happen. It's why I didn't want you anywhere near his village."

She nodded. Of course Bull would've known. She'd been foolish to think otherwise. "Did you know about the baby before you came for me?"

"Yes."

"How?"

"I'm not going to tell you, Lydia. I confess it took me a while to come to terms with the fact you didn't trust me. It hurt to know you thought I'd abandon you, not want you as my wife."

She winced at the intense pain on his face. "I never meant to hurt you. I only wanted to protect you."

"From what?" Bull reached up and ran his fingers through her hair, noticing how much it had grown since he last saw her.

"What if the baby isn't yours?"

"Then we'll raise him as ours and give him plenty of brothers and sisters who'll also love him."

Her eyes widened before a timid smile turned up the corners of her mouth. "What if it's a girl?"

"Then *she'll* have brothers and sisters to love, and I'll have to scare away all the boys who'll be after her."

Her body began to relax against his. Then a thought popped into her mind. "So you still want to marry me?"

Before Bull could answer, a hard knock sounded and the door swung open. Lydia's breath caught when Dax walked inside and smiled.

"Caro sent a message you needed me here. Since I walked up the steps with a preacher, I hope it's for your wedding."

Chapter Twenty

"I pronounce you man and wife. You may kiss the bride." The minister took a step back, still somewhat mystified at the urgency of the wedding and the obvious lack of preparation. The bride appeared in a brown cloak, secured up the front and tied with a bow at the neck. The groom wore clothes more appropriate for work on a ranch than life in the city. He'd decided to silence his questions out of respect for Caro.

Cupping Lydia's face in his hands, Bull brushed a kiss across her lips, seeing the moisture in her eyes.

"Are you unhappy, Mrs. Mason?" Bull whispered.

Her smile washed away his doubts. "Quite the opposite. I'm very happy, Mr. Mason."

Giving her another quick kiss, he turned them to their friends. Caro and Isabella rushed forward to hug them before Dax stepped toward him, offering his hand.

"You've made a good decision, my friend." Dax clasped Bull's shoulder, speaking in a low voice so no one else would hear.

Bull glanced at Lydia, her face alight with joy. "Letting her go was never an option."

"You're a good man."

Bull laughed. "I'm like any other man who has found a woman he loves and who loves him the same. Nothing more."

He turned at Caro's approach. "You and Lydia are welcome to stay here. I have more than enough room."

"Thank you for the offer, Caro, but I'll be moving Lydia in with me at the Clayton."

Her brows drew together before she masked her disapproval with a tight smile. "If you feel it would be best for Lydia."

"I'm sure you understand my need to have Lydia to myself. We'll be staying in San Francisco for several weeks, so I'm certain she'll be visiting you often."

"Weeks?" Lydia asked.

Bull wrapped an arm around Lydia's waist, pulling her to him. "Dax has business to finish before we go back home."

Dax glanced at Bull, deciding it would be best to speak with him alone about the need for Bull to stay longer. Today was a day to celebrate, not burden the bride and groom with unwelcome news.

"If everyone will follow me, there are refreshments in the dining room." Caro thread her arm through Dax's, leading the way. She glanced up at him, unsure whether to ask the questions burning to get free.

"Go ahead, Caro. Ask me what you want about Beau."

Her hand tightened on his arm. "Am I that obvious?"

He chuckled, placing a hand on hers. "Not obvious. I'd be disappointed if you weren't thinking of him."

"I miss him." She hadn't confessed her feelings to anyone, including Lydia and Isabella. Somehow, she felt safe admitting it to Dax.

As the others filed past them, Dax took a detour into the library, leaving the door open, waiting to see if she'd continue.

"Beau is so much more."

"More?"

She looked up at him, her thoughts jumbled. "It's hard to explain as I don't quite understand it myself." Taking a few steps away, she stared at a tapestry of mountains covered in snow, a small town at the base. "Most of the men in Splendor are so different from those in the cities. Even Gabe, who I've known since we were children, isn't what I would have expected. Don't misunderstand. You're all honorable, hardworking men, and you'd do anything for those you care about. There's just a hardness...a toughness not seen in the men where I grew up."

Dax chuckled, trying to figure out what she meant.

"Oh, I'm not explaining this too well."

"Take your time, Caro. So far, it sounds interesting."

Glaring at him, she crossed her arms. "I'm used to men who are more refined, not given to violence as easily as those in Splendor. I don't know if I could ever get used to it."

Dax walked up beside her. "War can do that to a man. Beau fought for the South, as did Cash, Luke, and I. We lost a great deal. Family, friends, property. Those losses changed us. Gabe, Noah, Bull, and others fought for the North. They also lost much."

"Perhaps not as much as those who fought for separation."

Dax nodded. "Perhaps. We all saw and did things we'll never be able to erase from our memories. War does something to a man, changes his priorities. Your experiences in New York may have separated you from atrocities many men in Splendor witnessed."

"You're telling me there are good reasons."

"I don't know if they're good. They just...are. You're the only one who can decide if you're up to taking on the challenges associated with men who'll never be the same as they were before the war."

Hearing the laughter from the dining room, she walked toward the hall, then turned back. "He asked me to marry him."

Dax didn't respond, although her comment surprised him.

"I told him no." She sucked in a shaky breath.

"I'm sure you had your reasons."

"I thought I did. Now, well…I'm not so sure."

Dax took her arm, slipping it through his. "Then it appears you have more thinking to do."

"Yes. It appears I do."

Splendor

"Oh my," Rachel whispered, glancing up at Bernie Griggs. "Bull and Lydia got married. I have to go let everyone know." She dashed outside, hurrying across the street, dodging riders on horseback and wagons filled with supplies on her way to the sheriff's office. Pushing the door open, she stopped at the sight of Gabe, Cash, and Beau huddled around the desk. They all stood as she stepped toward them.

"Rachel. What brings you in here?" Gabe walked around her, closing the door.

She held up the telegram from Dax. "It's Bull and Lydia. They're married."

Rachel saw Beau's features go slack, then harden. He forced a smile. "That's great news." Grabbing his hat, he walked to the door. "I'd better make the rounds."

No one spoke until Beau closed the door behind him.

"What did I say?"

"It's not you, Rachel. Beau can't get his mind off Caro. The news of Bull and Lydia brought it back up. He's got to find a way to move past her leaving." Cash held out his hand. "Now, let me see what you have." Cash read the brief telegram, handed it to Gabe, then picked up his hat. "I'm going to let Allie know."

"We need to plan a celebration when they return." Rachel's eyes lit up. "Something special."

"Sounds like you need to speak with Lena, Suzanne, and the other ladies. I'll let Noah and Abby know." Gabe opened the door, letting Rachel precede him outside, then stopped. "I want you to keep Rosemary and the boys close to the ranch."

Rachel's face sobered. "Why?"

"I received a telegram from Sheriff Sterling in Big Pine. A couple people spotted Boyden Trask."

"I thought he left the territory."

"May have. It's best to be safe in case he circles back and comes after them." Gabe let his gaze wander up the street, then down. Cash and

287

Beau already knew of the possible danger. He had to let others know, as well. "Can you get Luke and Ginny to come to your place to stay until Dax returns?"

"They ride over almost every day. I'm sure they'll stay if I ask."

"Do it, and let all your hands know about Trask. We have to keep Rosemary and the boys safe."

Beau stopped at the house he used to share with Cash before his friend married Allie. He'd hoped to share it with Caro someday. Few people knew how much time they spent together—quiet suppers, walks when the weather allowed, and on clear days, rides on the trails around Splendor. As winter turned to spring, they'd taken the stage to Big Pine, telling people Caro had business to attend to and felt better with him accompanying her.

They'd kept it quiet, hiding how close they'd become, even from Cash, which hadn't been easy. No matter how many times he reminded himself she'd be leaving, moving to San Francisco when the snow melted, Beau had fallen hard for the beautiful widow from New York. He believed she felt the same.

After all he'd witnessed during the war, he thought little could affect him. Beau had been wrong. Watching her discomfort as she turned down his marriage proposal had nearly destroyed him. She'd been kind, telling him how much he meant to her, even saying she loved him. For Caro, love wasn't enough to give up her dreams.

Reaching into a cupboard, he pulled out a fresh bottle of whiskey. Not bothering with a glass, he downed a good portion, then carried the whiskey to a chair and slumped into it. Beau rolled the bottle between his palms, thinking of Bull and Lydia and all they'd been through. They deserved to be happy, to live their lives together, to raise a family. He envied them.

Leaning his head against the back of the chair, he looked at the ceiling, closing his eyes. When he watched Caro leave on the stage, Beau had told himself it was for the best. She had a dream, a vision of her future. One where he held no place.

As much strength as she'd shown traveling across the country alone, the vivacious blonde with violet eyes had a delicate side, one that drew her to a wealthier circle of people who enjoyed the city and all its trappings. The theatre, opera, balls, restaurants offering exquisite meals—all of these meant a great deal to her, more than any feelings she had for him.

In contrast, Beau lived a simple life. Time spent with friends, a glass of whiskey, an occasional game of cards, and his job as deputy kept his life in order, giving him a purpose for getting up each day. He could have been happy in Splendor, living a modest life with Caro by his side.

She'd chosen another path and he had to accept it.

Lifting the bottle, he took another long swallow, wiping his mouth with his sleeve. Disgusted with himself, Beau stood, placing the bottle back in the cupboard and shutting the door...hard. He'd thought of getting drunk, slipping into a stupor and sleeping off the day. Instead, the whiskey had little impact, other than producing a slow burn of melancholy he didn't want.

Beau had been a captain in the Confederate Army, led men into battle, held his head high, even during the terrible defeat of Atlanta. He was a better man than what he'd shown his friends over the past several months.

It was past time for him to bury his feelings and get on with his life. The same life Caro rejected with a few well-chosen words.

Picking up his hat and tightening the gunbelt around his waist, Beau stepped outside. The warm afternoon air felt good. He took a deep breath, clearing his mind, ready to shrug off the pain Caro had left in her hurry to leave.

Walking past the livery, he made his way up the main street of Splendor, taking time to speak with those he'd all but ignored since Caro left. Today, he'd start over with a new purpose, maybe even talk to Dax and Luke about the piece of land he'd been ready to buy if Caro agreed to marry him.

The land would be a start. He'd build a house, raise a few head of cattle, and maybe even buy a cow. For the first time since before leaving to fight for the South, he'd be a landowner in a town he liked, around people who were his friends. In time, he might even find a special woman to fill the empty place Caro created.

The thought came out of nowhere, but it stuck. Nothing serious, and not one of the women who worked at the Dixie or Wild Rose. An independent woman with no interest in marriage, who planned to make Splendor her home. Someone to share his free moments with, who wouldn't expect his love in return.

A thoughtful expression crossed his face as he considered the challenge he'd given himself. Beau would think it over a few days, maybe more, then start to put his own dreams into action. He'd talk to Horace Clausen at the bank, then with Dax and Luke about a piece of land. The rest would fall into place.

"You're certain you saw some of White Buffalo's men?"

"Believe me, Luke, after being their hostage, I know who I saw." Mal hadn't said a word to any of the other men. "We were bringing in some strays from the far northeast pasture when I spotted them."

After not seeing any sign of the Crow riders for months, Luke had pulled the sentries stationed at locations around the ranch's perimeter. They now worked as ranch hands.

"Looks like I'm going to be needing more men to keep watch. I'll talk with Dirk, see who we can spare. If I have to hire more men, I will. We aren't letting White Buffalo get near our women or the children ever again." Luke stalked out of the barn.

He and Ginny had moved back in with Rachel and Patrick after the news about Trask. The sighting of the Crow scouting party increased the urgency to consolidate the herd in the western pastures.

"For the first time, I'm glad Lydia decided to visit Caro. We sure don't need to have her around with White Buffalo keeping watch on the ranch. Sure wish Bull were here, though." Mal slid from his horse, then looked over his shoulder. "Let me know what you want me and the men to do after you've talked to Dirk."

"I'll have an answer for you after supper tonight. Make sure all the men know what you saw."

Luke had sent a congratulatory telegram to Bull and Lydia the day after Rachel had announced the news of their marriage. Now, another telegram needed to be sent advising them of what Mal had seen.

The news from Dax made it clear he'd be returning home as soon as he hired a manager, leaving Bull to finalize designs and hire a foreman to handle construction. The delay in his return could benefit everyone. Perhaps if White Buffalo realized Lydia had moved away from the ranch, he'd give up and return to his village.

Luke stopped halfway up the steps to the porch, taking his time to look around. The hairs on the back of his neck danced, as they always did when he thought someone watched him. Seeing nothing, he continued into the house, wishing he knew a way to get a message to the Crow warrior that the prize he sought was well out of his reach. Unless his intentions were even more sinister, such as revenge on anyone who took part in rescuing his captives.

"What's wrong?" Ginny set down her sewing. She'd always been much too perceptive.

He walked up to her, trying to conceal his concern as he kissed her. Breaking away, he smiled. "Hmmm...You taste good."

"It's the lemonade, and don't change the subject. Tell me what's happened. Is it Trask? Did someone see him?"

Luke didn't want to alarm her, but she needed to know. "Mal spotted a group of White Buffalo's warriors on the northern edge of the ranch."

"Did I hear you right?" Rachel walked in from the hall, holding a squirming Patrick. Setting him down, she watched as he took hesitant steps to Luke, then wrapped his arms around his uncle's legs.

Luke stroked his nephew's hair. "You did. I'm going to have Dirk post guards, the same as before Dax left. We need to keep all the children close to the house, and that includes Sam."

"He won't be happy. With Dax and Bull gone, Travis and Billy at the old Frey place, and Mal acting as the second foreman, he's been taking on more work as a ranch hand." Rachel dashed over to Patrick before he toppled a small table. "Sam will fight you on this."

"I suspect he will. The truth is, I need him here to keep watch on you two and the children. Pulling men to keep watch around the property is going to leave us short until I can hire more."

"Jimmy is fifteen, Luke, the same age as Sam. Rosemary says he's good with a gun and even speaks some Crow." Ginny said it as if everyone knew.

"The boy speaks Crow? How did he learn it?" Luke crossed his arms, his brows knitting together.

"According to Rosemary, his father traded with several tribes, including the Crow. Haven't you noticed his dark coloring?"

"His coloring is the same as Teddy's, Ginny. Come to think of it, they're almost twins with their reddish-brown hair, green eyes, and golden brown skin." He pinched the bridge of his nose. "Tell me what you know."

"Rosemary thinks their mother was Crow. She hasn't asked Jimmy or Teddy outright, and they keep quiet about what happened to their parents. There have been times one of them has said something to make her think their father was white and their mother wasn't."

Luke thought a minute, feeling a sense of guilt about how little he knew about the four orphans who'd been rustling their cattle. He'd heard the stories about Rosemary and Ben's father taking off with a woman he met in one of the saloons, leaving his family to fend for themselves. Their mother had been too ill to take care of them, eventually dying without the medical care she needed. When Suzanne heard of their plight, she'd stepped forward, offering Rosemary a job. He didn't know anything about Jimmy and Teddy.

"Where is Jimmy now?" Luke grabbed his hat from the peg, then walked to the door.

Rachel bent down, pulling Patrick away from falling into another table. "Find Tat and you'll find both the boys."

Stepping out into the late afternoon sunshine, Luke checked the barn first. Finding no one inside, he walked out the back doors, seeing Tat, Jimmy, Teddy, and Ben near the fence where Sam had been taken. Putting two fingers in his mouth, he let out a high-pitched whistle, drawing their attention, waving for them to return to the barn. Taking off at a run, Ben led the others to Luke's side.

"Tat, take Teddy and Ben to the porch and ask Ginny for some lemonade. I want to talk to Jimmy."

Tat glanced at Teddy and Ben. "You heard the boss. Let's go."

Luke took one more look around. His stomach churned, all his senses on alert. He knew, without any doubt, someone watched them, yet he saw nothing.

What he didn't see were the three sets of eyes hidden in the bushes, crouched low, keeping watch.

Chapter Twenty-One

San Francisco

"Come here, sweetheart." Bull wrapped his arms around Lydia, pulling her back against his chest as they lingered in bed on a rare morning when he didn't have to meet with Dax.

Hiring a manager, purchasing and provisioning ships, and locating suitable captains had taken a long time due to Dax's desire to go with the best. What they thought would take a few weeks had stretched into months. During this time, Bull completed the plans for the warehouse, hired a well-experienced manager to oversee construction, and ordered materials.

Suzanne's brother-in-law, Quentin Briar, had been brought in as a partner, having the authority to work on behalf of Dax and Luke in their absence. His work complete, Dax had taken the train east the day before. He'd meet again with the commandant of Fort Douglas to finalize the contract supplying horses to the troops. Dax had already sent a telegram to Luke stating the need for Travis to plan for fifty horses to be delivered to the Utah outpost. The order would take almost all the stock available, but the opportunity was too great to be ignored.

For Bull and Lydia, the time since their wedding had passed in a blur as they became reacquainted, settling into life as a married couple. They, along with Isabella, planned to leave for Splendor in a few days. Lydia wanted to be there for the birth of their baby, wanting Rachel by her side during the delivery.

"What shall we do today?" Lydia felt Bull's hands splay across her expanding stomach. It seemed her body began to grow the moment they married, making up for all the months her pregnancy didn't show. With Bull sitting next to her, an arm around her shoulders, Doctor McLean had visited several times, assuring her she and the baby were progressing fine. Once he learned of Lydia's desire to be in Splendor for the delivery, McLean had been the one to encourage the trip home as soon as possible. Taking Bull aside, he'd cautioned him the baby may come earlier than anticipated...a conversation Bull hadn't shared with Lydia.

"I've ordered a buggy, and the hotel kitchen is preparing a picnic for us. There's a park I'd like to visit before we leave. We'll lay out a blanket and spend the day." His soft breath washed across her neck, producing shivers as he pressed a kiss to the sensitive skin below her ear. Letting his lips draw a path to her shoulder, he felt her body melt against his, trembling at his touch.

"Bull..."

"Hmmm..."

Lydia moaned as his hands stroked across her belly, her body heating as he continued.

"We could always stay here," Bull whispered as a hand moved lower, causing Lydia to push back against him, then stiffen. He could hear her breath catch, her moans turning into a cry of pain. "Lydia..." He moved his arms, turning her so he could see her face. "Lydia, what is it?"

She sucked in a breath, her face contorting, her legs drawing up as a sharp pain ripped through her. "Bull. Get Doctor McLean."

Conflicting emotions flashed through him as he jumped out of bed, grabbed his trousers, then slipped into a shirt. He whipped around at Lydia's groan of discomfort.

"Hurry, Bull."

Not bothering with his boots or hat, he ran into the hall and down the stairs, interrupting the clerk as he helped another couple. "My wife, Mrs. Mason...she needs Doctor McLean."

The clerk didn't look at Bull, holding up his hand. "A moment please."

"Now!" Bull's roar turned heads in his direction.

The clerk's pen shook, his mouth dropping open. "Yes, sir, Mr. Mason." He signaled a uniformed young man. "Go for Doctor McLean right away. Tell him it's Mrs. Mason and it's an emergency. Do not come back without him."

"I need urgent messages sent to Mrs. Caroline Iverson and Mrs. Isabella Boucher."

"Yes, yes, of course. I have what I need from your last message."

Satisfied the doctor would be coming and unable to stand around any longer, Bull dashed back up the stairs, taking them two at a time. Shoving through the door of their room, Bull hurried to the bed, dropping to his knees.

"Doctor McLean will be here soon, sweetheart." He stroked her hair, feeling the dampness and the beads of sweat on her forehead. Standing, he poured water into the basin, then grabbed a towel. Soaking it and wringing it out, he gently wiped her face and neck. "Try to relax, Lydia, and breathe."

She moaned, her panicked gaze locking on his. Reaching out a hand, she gripped his arm. "I think the baby might be coming early."

Bull swallowed the fear her words produced.

"What will we do if the doctor doesn't get here in time?" She groaned again as another sharp pain ripped through her.

"Shhh, sweetheart. He'll be here."

Bull continued to stroke her face, neck, and shoulders with the damp cloth, whispering words of encouragement as the minutes passed. Each time her body curled in pain, Bull's chest tightened to the point he couldn't draw a breath. After an hour with no sign of Doctor McLean, Bull's calm vanished. He waited until another agonizing episode passed, then leaned to her ear.

"Lydia, I'm going to talk to the clerk to see if there's word from the doctor. Will you be all right for a few minutes?"

A knock on the door had him on his feet and crossing the room in seconds. Pulling it open, he saw two anxious females.

"Where is she? Is the doctor here?" Caro moved past him, tossing her hat and gloves aside as she made her way to the bed.

"How is she doing, Bull?" Isabella placed a hand on his arm.

"She's in pain. I don't know how much more she can handle." His shoulders slumped. The truth was, Bull didn't know how much more of her suffering he could stand.

Isabella saw the distressed look on his face, something few people had witnessed in the strong man who never gave up. Steeling herself, she stepped back.

"Bull Mason, you need to get in there and do whatever you must to help deliver your child."

His eyes widened at Isabella's strong tone.

"I believe you told the doctor you've delivered three babies. That gives you more experience than either Caro or I. If the doctor doesn't get here, it's all up to you."

They both turned as an agonized scream pierced the air. Taking a quick look at Isabella, Bull sucked in a deep breath and nodded. "Will you help me?"

"Caro and I will do whatever you need."

Hours passed with Isabella and Caro taking turns sitting by Lydia's side, holding her hand as she squeezed tight, her body contracting in pain over and over. Bull didn't move from her side, knowing it could be hours before the baby came. After another tortured cry, Lydia stared at him, her face covered with a damp sheen.

"Bull, I can't do this."

Pushing away damp strands of hair from her face, he kissed her forehead. "You're doing fine, sweetheart. It takes time." He covered her hand with his, keeping his voice low and calm. "Keep breathing and try not to worry. The baby will come when he's ready."

"You keep saying *he*." She tried to smile, her face twisting as another spasm ripped through her. "Bull, I think the baby is coming." Her deep groan had him reaching for the sheet as the door of the hotel room burst open.

"How is she doing?" Gavin McLean hurried to the bed, set down his bag, and pulled back the sheet. After a short examination, he looked up at Bull. "It appears the baby is ready to join the world. Mr. Mason, you've done an admirable job, but you may want to step outside."

"I'm not going anywhere, Doc. As I told you before, I've been through this three times. Tell me what you need." Bull felt some of the tension ease at the presence of McLean. Somehow, delivering three babies didn't amount to much when Lydia was the one suffering.

Gavin studied him for a moment, then nodded and looked around. "We'll need more warm water. The towels you have here should be fine."

"I'll get the water," Isabella said, dashing into the hall. Caro continued to mop Lydia's face and neck, whispering to her in a soothing tone.

"Mr. Mason, please move behind your wife's head and brace your hands under her shoulders. She'll need your strength when she pushes. It shouldn't be much longer."

Bull closed his eyes and prayed. It seemed he hadn't stopped talking to God since Lydia's pains started. His silent plea never changed. *I don't care who the father is. Please don't let Lydia or the baby die.* He repeated the words over and over until they became a chant inside his head.

And Bull believed every word. No matter the actual father, the baby was his. There had never been a doubt, only a period of acceptance. He knew, with absolute certainty, if anything happened to either Lydia or the baby, his life would never be the same. They were his family.

"Not much longer, Mrs. Mason. You're doing quite well." Gavin wiped his brow, blinking several times to clear his vision.

Instead of finding comfort in the doctor's words, Lydia glared at him, preparing to scream her thoughts when another contraction stole her breath.

"That's it. Push hard now."

Lydia gave one more hard push before the baby burst free and into the doctor's hands.

Another whispered prayer crossed Bull's lips as he lowered his head to stare into Lydia's eyes, seeing her exhaustion, then relief when the baby let out a fractured cry. Bull's gaze jerked up to see the doctor holding a screaming infant in his arms.

"Mr. and Mrs. Mason, you have a son." Gavin walked closer, handing the baby to Lydia.

Bull heard the words, but his gaze was fixed on the thick patch of strawberry blond hair and hazel eyes—the exact image of Lydia. His eyes filled with tears, which he quickly swiped away.

"He's so beautiful, Bull."

His watery gaze slid to Lydia, a smile curving his mouth. "That he is, sweetheart." Bull leaned down, kissing his son on the forehead. "He is a miracle. Our miracle."

Splendor

"You're certain they've disappeared?" Dax had been home less than thirty-six hours before the conversation turned to White Buffalo. Luke and he stood on the lower rungs of the corral, watching as one man after another attempted to break a string of horses.

"Men were posted as soon as Mal saw them on the north border a few weeks ago. Since that day, nothing. Not once have any of the men seen a trace of the Crow scouts." Luke pulled off his hat in salute when Johnny calmed the second horse, riding in circles until the animal stopped fighting him.

"It makes no sense. Why come looking for Lydia, then disappear?"

"I wish I knew. I had formed a plan to get word to White Buffalo about Lydia moving far away. I'm glad the scouts disappeared without me having to use it."

Dax quirked a brow. "How would you have gotten word to him?"

"Jimmy."

Dax's gaze narrowed. "Jimmy?"

Spotting Rachel and Ginny walking toward them, Luke jumped to the ground. "We'll talk later."

Dax slipped an arm around Rachel, pulling her to him. "It's good to be home." His soft whisper sent shivers down her spine.

"It's good to have you back. I know the trip was important, I just didn't expect you to be gone so long." She tightened her arm around his waist. "Ginny and I need to go into town."

"I can ride along if you want company."

"I'd love to have you with us, Dax, but I know you're needed here. We won't be gone long. I want to see how Clay is doing at the clinic with Uncle Charles gone, and I'm hoping there's another telegram about the baby."

Caro had sent a telegram the morning after the baby arrived, although it was woefully lacking in details. *Lydia had the baby. A boy. Both are doing well. No name yet.* Rachel and Ginny had been disappointed in the lack of details.

"You're right. I shouldn't leave so soon, but I can send someone else along. Tat! Johnny!" He waved at the young cowhands standing at the fence and motioned them over. "Rachel and Ginny are going into town. I want you two to ride along."

Tat nodded. "We'll get our horses."

"You don't need to send them with us, Dax."

"Between the threats of Trask and White Buffalo, I'd feel better with them riding with you." He brushed a strand of hair off her face. "Humor me, darlin'."

"Rachel." Rosemary came running toward them from the barn. "Tat said you're going to town. May I come with you?"

"Well, I'm—"

"All my chores are done and I won't be any trouble. Please, Rachel." Rosemary shot looks at both Dax and Ginny, who tried to hide their amusement at her enthusiasm.

"We leave in five minutes. If you can be ready by then, you can come."

Rosemary dashed to the house, reappearing a few minutes later in a wool dress and bonnet. "I'm ready."

Rachel chuckled at the excitement on the young woman's face. "All right. Climb up on the wagon and we'll get going."

"Hold on." Luke walked up, handing a rifle to each woman.

"I already have a shotgun, Luke." Ginny pointed to the weapon she'd already placed below the seat.

"Keep it, but take these also." Luke shifted his gaze to Tat and Johnny. "You boys keep watch. With all that's gone on, we can't be too careful."

"Yes, sir. We won't let anything happen to them." Johnny reined his horse around, taking a position behind the wagon, letting Tat ride in front.

"Hold up, Tat. I want you to check with Sheriff Evans. Find out if he's heard any more about Boyden Trask."

"Yes, sir."

Dax and Luke stood shoulder to shoulder, watching the wagon disappear down the trail.

"My instincts tell me we shouldn't let the women go into town."

"I know the feeling, Luke. As you said, nothing has happened in weeks and we can't keep them imprisoned around the ranch forever. Tat and Johnny will be careful. Remember, they were part of the search party to find Sam."

"I hear what you're saying, Dax. Still, I don't like feeling vulnerable where the women are concerned. I'll be glad when Trask is found."

"And the threat of White Buffalo returning is over."

"I wish I had more information for you, Tat, but I haven't heard any more about Trask. Sheriff Sterling sent another telegram a few days ago saying Trask hadn't been seen in Big Pine since a couple people thought they saw him weeks ago. Sterling thinks he and his men have left the territory." Gabe kept pace with Tat as they walked past the Wild Rose to the telegraph office.

"What do *you* think?"

Gabe stopped. "I don't have the faith Sterling does. Trask has a grudge, and those kind of men are dangerous. I'm afraid we haven't heard the last of him." Continuing down the boardwalk, he nodded at Johnny, who'd taken a position outside. "The women still inside?"

"Yes, sir, except for Rosemary, who's in the clinic. She wanted to talk with Dr. McCord."

Gabe put his hands on his hips, shaking his head. "I still can't get used to Clay being a doctor. I'm sure glad he's here, though. Doc Worthington definitely needs the help." Leaving Tat and Johnny outside, Gabe pushed the door open. "Ladies."

Rachel and Ginny turned to see Gabe a few feet away.

"It's from Bull." Rachel handed him the piece of paper.

"And this one is from Caro." Ginny held up the telegram, but didn't offer it to Gabe.

He scanned Bull's message, then chuckled. "Joshua Joseph Mason. It's a good, strong name. Says they'll be coming back to Splendor as soon as possible. What does Caro say?"

Ginny shot a quick look at Rachel, not wanting to reveal Caro's private questions about Beau. "Lydia and Joshua are doing well. The baby's hair and eyes are just like Lydia's."

Gabe blew out a breath, choosing not to comment. "It would be good if they could get home before the heavy snows start."

Ginny nodded, folding Caro's telegram and sliding it into her reticule.

"I'm going over to the Dixie to let Lena know the news."

"Can you tell Cash and Noah, Gabe? I want to be sure Alison and Abby know."

"I'll be happy to tell them, Rachel. How much longer will you ladies be in town?"

"I want to speak with Clay, see how he's doing, then stop by and let Suzanne know the news. Why?"

Gabe looked through the window. Tat and Johnny stood outside, their gazes scanning the busy street. The scene bothered Gabe more than a little. Waiting for danger was never an easy feeling.

"Have Tat or Johnny let me know when you're ready to head back to the ranch. Beau told me he wants to ride out to speak with Dax and Luke. He might as well ride along with you." Gabe touched the brim of his hat before stepping outside, facing Johnny. "Either of you seen Beau?"

"Last I saw, he was headed into the bank."

"Thanks. Don't leave town before letting me know. He may be riding back with you." Gabe left the two, making his way to the bank, stopping when Beau stepped outside.

"Rachel, Ginny, and Rosemary are in town. Tat and Johnny are with them, but it might be a good idea if you rode back to the ranch when they return. We still don't know where Trask went, and I'm not convinced he left Montana."

"I'm not convinced either. Sure, Gabe, I can ride back with them. It will give me a chance to speak with Dax and Luke."

Both fell silent as they walked back to the jail, Gabe seeing Tat and Johnny now standing outside the clinic across the street.

"Are you still planning to buy some land from them?"

"Clausen says I'm good for a loan, and I've already selected a few acres not too far from town. If they're still interested in selling, I'm going to buy it and build a place."

"Good decision."

"I believe it is. I'll be a landowner again, which will keep my mind off things better left in the past."

Gabe clasped Beau's shoulder. "Let me know if you need anything."

"Thanks, Gabe. Right now, luck and time are all I need."

Chapter Twenty-Two

"We'll be coming up on Splendor in less than an hour." Bull kept his arm securely around Lydia as she held Joshua. He'd somehow slept most of the trip. With the sun approaching noon, Bull knew he'd wake up soon, expecting another meal.

"Have you traveled this trail before?"

"Not on the stage, but I've ridden out this way many times. We got farther east than this when we searched for Abby's father, King Tolbert." He glanced out the window, remembering the way Tolbert had met his death and the men responsible. Shaking off the gruesome memory, he looked down at his son. Lydia had been right. Joshua was a beautiful baby.

Isabella sat across from them, reading a book as the stage bounced along.

"Do you mind that Rachel and Ginny want to throw a party for us at the ranch?"

"I guess we can't expect them not to want to do something. They missed the wedding and Joshua's birth. And I'd like to show him off." Bull glanced out the window, seeing a cloud of dust approaching from the north. He moved to grip his rifle without Lydia noticing.

"Their telegram said they'd wait until we arrived to set a date."

Without taking his gaze from the distant cloud growing closer, he nodded. "That's good."

"Bull, is everything all right?"

Without looking at her, he touched the back of her head. "I want you to crouch on the floor with Joshua. Stay down until I tell you otherwise. You, too, Isabella."

"You're scaring me." Lydia's wide eyes searched his as she cradled Joshua tighter.

"Please, Lydia. Just do it." He pushed her gently, waiting until all three were out of sight, then turned back to the window.

"Riders coming." The guard's shout came a little late for Bull, who already had his rifle trained toward the men on horseback.

As they drew closer and slowed down, the dust began to clear. Bull blinked a few times to make certain he wasn't seeing things.

Luke, Noah, Cash, and Travis reined to a stop in front of the stage.

"It's all right, Lydia." Reaching down, he helped both women to their seats. "It's Luke and a few friends." He looked at Isabella. "Travis is one of them." Bull jumped out of the stage. "We didn't expect a welcoming party." He held his hand to Luke, then the others.

"We decided an escort might be the safest way to get you back home. That, and Travis didn't want a crowd around when he greeted Isabella." He jerked his thumb to where Travis held Isabella's hands through the window of the stage. "I doubt it'll be long before those two get hitched."

"I need you to get back on the stage." The driver shot a look at Bull. "I've got to keep on schedule."

"See you in Splendor." Bull jogged back to the stage and jumped inside while Travis swung back up on his horse. "We're almost home, ladies." Sitting against the seat, he let out a breath, relaxing for the first time since they boarded the stage in Ogden.

The men surrounded the stage on the short trip, keeping watch, their guns ready. Even though White Buffalo hadn't been seen in recent weeks, it didn't mean the Crow warrior and his braves weren't watching, preparing an attack.

"There they are." Suzanne pointed toward the stage, Nick's arm around her as they stood near the livery. A good number of friends joined them, ready to welcome Bull, Lydia, Joshua, and Isabella home. Toward the back of the crowd,

Rosemary and Dirk stood near Dax, Rachel, and Ginny. All clapped or cheered as the stage stopped and Bull got out, extending his hand to Lydia, then Isabella, who walked straight to Travis.

Wrapping an arm around Lydia, they faced their friends. "I'd like to introduce my bride, Lydia Mason, and our son, Joshua." Bull didn't get another word out before they were surrounded by friends.

"We expect to see you and your family in church, Bull." Reverend Paige held out his hand while his wife fussed over Joshua.

"He looks just like you, Lydia. Such a sweet baby." Ruth Paige touched the soft hair on his head. Reaching into a small satchel, she pulled out a wrapped package. "This is for you."

Lydia adjusted Joshua in her arms, glancing at the gift. "Mrs. Paige, what a wonderful surprise. May I open it?"

"Please don't. I'll be embarrassed. It isn't new, but a blanket I made for our boy when he was a baby." Her eyes misted over as she spoke. Lydia was one of the few people in Splendor who knew their only child died of cholera when he was ten.

Lydia clutched the package to her. "This means so much to me. I'll take good care of it."

Reaching out her hand, Ruth touched Lydia's arm. "I know you will, dear. The Reverend and I are so happy for you and Bull."

"We should leave, sweetheart." Reverend Paige settled a hand on the small of Ruth's back. "Remember what I said, Bull. I expect to see you in church."

"Yes, sir. We'll be there."

Nick and Suzanne walked up, their hands clasped tight. A young woman moved to Nick's side, her gaze darting between Bull and Lydia, resting on a sleeping Joshua.

"How any baby can sleep through all this commotion is beyond me." Suzanne reached out her arms, careful not to wake Joshua as she cradled him. "Is he always this good?"

"So far, but he's barely a month old." Lydia watched the young woman next to Nick, noticing the strong resemblance.

"Lydia, Bull, I'd like to introduce you to my daughter, Olivia. Olivia, this is Bull and Lydia Mason."

"Daughter?" Bull and Lydia said in unison.

Nick chuckled, noticing Olivia squirming next to him. "It was a surprise to me, too. But a wonderful surprise." He bent to kiss her cheek. "I persuaded her to move to Splendor."

Bull tipped his hat as Lydia stepped forward. "It's a pleasure, Olivia. I hope we become friends."

The young woman's eyes flickered. "That would be lovely, Mrs. Mason."

"Please, call me Lydia."

"Bull, do you have a few minutes to talk with Gabe and me before you leave for the ranch?"

"Sure, Nick."

"We'll be at the hotel when you're ready."

Watching Lydia, Olivia, and Suzanne, who still held Joshua, Bull smiled. "Why not now?"

"You've already spoken with Dax and Luke about this?" Bull stared at the two men, then let his gaze wander again to the rough drawings before him.

"We wouldn't be talking if they hadn't agreed." Gabe moved around the table to stand next to Bull. "Along with Noah and Abby, they'll be helping us fund the new clinic. It will be next to Sarah Murton's house behind the bank."

"It's pretty ambitious. Four patient rooms, a large waiting area, and two separate rooms for surgeries." Straightening, Bull looked between them. "You know I'm not an architect."

"Dax and Luke say you are, which is good enough for us. Even without formal training, we'd want you to prepare the plans and help us build the clinic." Nick pulled open a drawer, handing Bull a one page document. "It's a contract for your work. We hope it's suitable."

He frowned. "I've never worked under a contract."

"It says what we'll pay you for the plans and supervising construction." Nick pointed to the main parts, then held it out to Bull once more.

Taking it, Bull read through it, his eyes widening. "That's a good amount of money."

"It's worth it to us." Gabe looked up when the door opened and Dax walked in, followed by Luke and Noah. "Glad you could join us."

Bull held up the paper to Dax and Luke. "Are you sure about this? What about my job at the ranch?"

"As with the work in San Francisco, your job will be waiting." Dax glanced at Luke, who nodded. "Until this is done, Dirk is going to pick up most of your work with Mal helping out."

Bull pursed his lips. He didn't quite know what to make of the changes over the last several months. "I'm just a ranch hand," he breathed out.

Luke laughed. "You're much more than a ranch hand, Bull. When the clinic is done, you can return to herding cattle and breaking horses."

"Doc's clinic is in need of improvement, and the town is expanding." Bull studied the document once more. "With Clay joining Doc Worthington, they'll need more space."

"Rosemary's been talking with Clay and Rachel," Dax said. "She wants to be a nurse, and Rachel still wants to help out when needed. As far as we know, Doc Worthington isn't planning to retire any time soon."

"What about Lydia and Joshua when I need to be in town? We still don't know what White Buffalo plans."

Luke stepped next to him. "They'll be protected, Bull. There won't be a repeat of what happened with Sam."

Bull nodded, letting out a slow breath. "If you're all sure."

"We are." Nick held out a pen.

"Hope you know what you're getting into." Bull took the pen, scribbling his name at the bottom of the page. "Now, may I take my bride home?"

Joshua and Lydia still slept as Bull quietly dressed. They'd been back a few days and all seemed quiet, yet he couldn't shake the continued feeling of dread. No matter how many times he told himself the additional ranch hands Dax and Luke hired were enough, his instincts told him otherwise.

Stepping outside, he covered the distance between his house and Dax's in a few long strides. Before he could knock, the door opened.

"Dax and Luke are in the study." Rachel held a cup of coffee toward him. "There's more if you need it." She didn't wait for a response, returning to the kitchen and preparations for the party planned for Lydia and Bull.

"Rachel and Ginny haven't stopped since you agreed to the celebration." Dax held the door to his study open. "This won't take long. We know you're busy working on the clinic."

"Gabe received a message from Sheriff Sterling. Still nothing about Boyden Trask. Sterling still thinks he's left the territory, but..." Luke's voice trailed off.

"You don't feel the same." Bull sipped his coffee, his instincts the same as Luke's.

"Neither of us believes he's gone. He's lying low, waiting for the right time to come after Rosemary and the boys. Look at this." Luke handed him a list of dates and numbers of missing cattle.

Bull scanned the list, shaking his head. "Too many missing for it to be anything except rustlers."

"Dax and I agree."

"What do you want from me?" Bull handed the paper back to Luke.

"Gabe, Cash, and Beau are on alert, but they have their regular duties. With the town growing, Gabe is considering hiring more deputies. He's sent a telegram to a friend of his, hoping he's interested in moving west." Dax crossed his arms, leaning a hip against the edge of his desk. "We're asking you to be vigilant when you're in town working on the clinic. Nick and Clay are doing the same."

Bull cocked his head to the side, taking a seat. "You know I'm always on guard, Dax. What are you not telling me?"

"Told you he'd figure it out." Luke lowered himself into a chair, stretching out his legs.

"I haven't figured anything out—yet. I *do* know there's more."

"Do you remember the Penderville gang?" Dax asked.

Bull sat up straighter. "Of course I do. They're the ones who shot Noah and me."

"The Penderville brothers didn't do the shooting. They were up on the mountain when you were shot. Men who rode with them ambushed you. They were never arrested."

Bull stood, pacing to the window, looking out toward his house a few yards away. "What else?"

"At least two couldn't keep their mouths shut about what they did. More than one person went to Sheriff Sterling, saying the two admitted shooting you and Noah. When he and his deputies went to arrest them, they'd disappeared." Dax grabbed something from his desk and handed it to Bull.

"A wanted poster?"

"Gabe received this before I returned from San Francisco. Clem and Louis Dawson are the two who talked about shooting you and Noah. Louis tells everyone his name is Jones, but those who know him say he and Clem are brothers. They've formed a new gang."

Bull smirked. "The Dawson gang."

Dax nodded. "They've been hitting ranches in the Dakotas, Wyoming, and Montana."

"You and Luke think they're the ones responsible for the missing cattle?"

"Rosemary is sure Trask doesn't rustle. He reaps the benefits of forcing others to do it for him. If he hasn't left the territory and is dumb enough to come this way, it will be for Rosemary and the boys—not for cattle. The Pendervilles, and the Dawson brothers, did whatever they needed to make money. Robbed banks and stages, stole cattle—anything that paid." Dax paused a moment. "I think the Dawsons are here."

Bull cursed, his jaw set. "If they are, I won't be left out. They almost killed Noah and me. I'm not letting them get away this time."

Epilogue

"It's so good to have you home." Ginny cradled Joshua to her chest, her voice shaky as she held the infant. Her eyes glistened when she glanced up. "You are so fortunate."

Lydia watched as Ginny turned her attention back to Joshua, compassion rolling through her knowing Ginny still hadn't recovered from her own loss. "I know. Some days, I can't believe I'm here with Joshua and married to Bull. A few months ago, I'd lost all hope."

Ginny looked up with a genuine smile. "There's always hope, Lydia."

"How's my son?" Bull walked up, resting his arm around Lydia's shoulders.

"He's wonderful." Ginny handed him back to Lydia as Rachel walked up.

"I can't believe how many made it today." Rachel looked around at the crowded house. "The children are still outside. Sam, Jimmy, and Teddy are taking care of the new foal, and Margaret is somewhere with Selina." She saw the concern on Bull's face. "Tat, Johnny, and some of the other ranch hands are guarding them, Bull. They'll be fine. Today is about celebrating your marriage and Joshua's birth." She stopped, hearing another knock. "More guests." Striding across the room, she pulled the door open. "Come in." Cash and Allie walked inside with Beau following, Sarah Murton, the town schoolteacher, at his side. Rachel masked her surprise, greeting Cash and Allie before they joined Luke and Ginny in the living room.

"Miss Murton, I'm so glad you could join us to celebrate with Bull and Lydia."

"I hadn't planned to come, what with the snow on the trail, but Allie offered to let me ride with them." Sarah slipped out of her coat, handing it to Rachel. "It was also nice to sit with Deputy Davis." She glanced at Beau and smiled, then turned her gaze to the people standing in the living room.

"I'm certain it was. Please, go on inside. Refreshments are on the table." Rachel waited until Sarah stepped out of earshot, then held out her hand for Beau's coat. "Seems you had a chance to get to know Miss Murton."

Beau shrugged. "She's a nice lady who didn't have anyone to escort her." He watched Rachel's brow arch. "What?"

She chuckled. "Nothing. You've been so busy planning your house, I didn't think you had time to court."

Beau shook his head. "I am *not* courting Miss Murton, Rachel. Working for Gabe and getting ready to build in the spring takes all my time." He didn't say how much time he still spent thinking of Caro, hoping she'd found happiness in her decision to leave. Over the months she'd been gone, he accepted love wasn't for him—especially with a woman who saw social status as an important part of her life. Stifling a bitter laugh, he shifted from one foot to the other. "Believe me, I've learned my limitations."

"I'm glad to hear it." She hung up his coat, then gestured toward Bull and Lydia. "Why don't you go on in and greet the guests of honor." Lowering her voice, she leaned toward him. "I'm sure Dax can find you some whiskey."

He picked up her hand, made a slight bow, then kissed it. "Thank you, Rachel."

Laughing, Rachel nudged him away. "Go on with you."

Walking into the front room, he spotted Bull and Lydia in a corner talking with Sarah, and headed toward them.

"He's such a beautiful baby, Lydia. May I hold him?" Sarah reached out her arms, taking Joshua and cradling him to her chest. "What do you think, Mr. Davis? Isn't he just the sweetest little boy?"

Beau glanced at Bull, who smirked. "Uh...yes, Miss Murton. He is a good looking lad."

Bull laughed. "You'd better say that. After all, he looks a lot like Lydia."

"True." Beau nodded as Sarah cooed in Joshua's ear, producing a grin from the infant. As the women talked, he turned toward Bull. "How are you doing? We haven't talked much since you got back into town."

"Real good. We're both glad to be home." They turned their backs to the women as they spoke. "Dax and Luke still have the men watching for White Buffalo. I wish there was a way to know for certain he no longer wanted her."

A commotion at the door had everyone in the house shifting their attention to the newest guests. Several of the women gasped and backed away. The men straightened, waiting to see what happened next.

"Will you look at that?" Bull moved forward, a broad smile on his face.

"Running Bear. You are welcome in our home." Dax motioned the two Blackfoot inside.

"We are pleased to be here." Running Bear turned toward the young man accompanying him. "This is Swift Bear. He is my grandson."

"You are both welcome."

Running Bear stood still as Bull approached.

"I am honored you have come to celebrate with us. Will you let me introduce you to my son, Joshua?"

Running Bear nodded, his back straight as he followed Bull toward Lydia, stopping when Luke approached.

"We're honored you came, Running Bear." Luke turned to the other guests. "Everyone, this is Running Bear, the Blackfoot chief. Without his help, we might not have rescued those who White Buffalo took from us."

The tension in the room disappeared as Bull introduced him to individuals until they reached Lydia. "I believe you know my wife, Lydia."

Stepping forward, Lydia stood on her toes, surprising everyone by placing a kiss on Running Bear's cheek. The chief's eyes widened briefly before his features stilled.

"I can't thank you enough for rescuing me. I wouldn't be here with my husband and son if you hadn't offered your help."

He nodded, then turned to Bull. "We must speak."

Bull glanced around, seeing Dax nod toward his study. "Follow me." Cutting a path through the people, he opened the door, letting Running Bear and Swift Bear precede him. "Please, sit down."

"We will stand."

"Then, tell me, what is it you need from me?"

"I have news for you, Bull Mason. White Buffalo will no longer bother your woman."

Bull's mouth opened, then closed before he took a breath, his heart pounding, hoping what Running Bear said was true. "I don't understand."

"Know the man who took your woman will no longer come onto your land." Running Bear turned to his grandson, motioning it was time to leave.

"Wait." Bull stepped forward, holding out his hand. "I don't know how to thank you."

Running Bear clasped Bull's hand, then looked at Swift Bear. "It is this one you should thank. He is a man of great heart. One day, he will lead our people."

"Thank you, Swift Bear." Bull held out his hand.

The young brave's expression didn't change at his grandfather's words or when he grasped Bull's hand. "We will go now, Grandfather?"

A slight smile crossed Running Bear's face. "Take care of your woman, Bull Mason."

Without another word, the two left the house, mounting their horses and riding north, the other braves who came with them trailing behind.

Bull stood on the porch, hands on his hips as he watched them ride away.

"Why did they leave?" Dax asked when he and Luke joined him.

"I don't really know. He told me we no longer need to worry about White Buffalo. Said his grandson, Swift Bear, was the one to thank."

"I'll be," Luke said, slapping Bull on the back. "That is the best news you could have gotten."

The sound of an approaching wagon got their attention, all three waving when they saw who had arrived. Two women sat in the seat of the wagon, Gabe riding alongside on Blackheart.

"I need to speak with Lydia." Bull disappeared inside. Luke continued to watch as the Blackfoot warriors rounded the bend in the trail.

"It's about time you got here, Gabe." Dax walked to Lena's side of the wagon to help her down, then glanced at the woman sitting next to her. "Caro. We didn't expect you. What a wonderful surprise."

Caro scooted over, letting Dax grasp her around the waist to settle her on the ground, then threaded her arm through his.

"I hope so."

Dax looked down at her, knowing she must be concerned about Beau's reaction to her arriving. "He's inside. Are you ready to see him?"

"As ready as I can be. I've made some major decisions. I only hope it isn't too late."

Stepping inside, Dax motioned for Rachel.

"Look who arrived with Gabe and Lena." Before Dax could say more, Gabe grasped his arm.

"We need to talk." Walking down the hall, Gabe turned to Dax. "Boyden Trask and his men were spotted."

"What direction were they headed?"

"Toward Splendor."

Dax nodded. One danger had been eliminated. Now they faced another. "Did you come for Cash and Beau?"

Gabe nodded. "I can give them a few minutes, then we have to leave."

Watching the men step down the hall, Rachel pushed her worry aside, looking at her friend. "Caro, you look wonderful." Turning, she called out to the others. "Hey, everyone. Caro just arrived from San Francisco."

Beau's head snapped toward Rachel, his gaze locking on Caro. Beside him, Sarah linked her arm through his. Instead of pulling away, he settled a hand over hers.

Beau's chest seized the instant Caro saw him. She offered him a hesitant smile, walking forward until her gaze moved to the woman beside him, then down to their joined hands.

Stopping abruptly, her smile faded before she turned away.

Thank you for taking the time to read Promise Trail. If you enjoyed it, please consider telling your friends or posting a short review. Word of mouth is an author's best friend and much appreciated.

Please join my reader's group to be notified of my New Releases at:
http://www.shirleendavies.com/contact-me.html

I care about quality, so if you find something in error, please contact me via email at
shirleen@shirleendavies.com

About the Author

Shirleen Davies writes romance—historical, contemporary, and romantic suspense. She grew up in Southern California, attended Oregon State University, and has degrees from San Diego State University and the University of Maryland. During the day she provides consulting services to small and mid-sized businesses. But her real passion is writing emotionally charged stories of flawed people who find redemption through love and acceptance. She now lives with her husband in a beautiful town in northern Arizona.

I love to hear from my readers.

Send me an Email
Visit my Website
Sign up to be notified of New Releases
Check out all my Books
Comment on my Blog
Follow me on Amazon

Other ways to connect with me:

My Facebook Fan Page
Twitter
Pinterest
Google+
Tsu

Books by Shirleen Davies
Historical Western Romance Series
MacLarens of Fire Mountain

Tougher than the Rest, Book One
Faster than the Rest, Book Two
Harder than the Rest, Book Three
Stronger than the Rest, Book Four
Deadlier than the Rest, Book Five
Wilder than the Rest, Book Six

Redemption Mountain

Redemption's Edge, Book One
Wildfire Creek, Book Two
Sunrise Ridge, Book Three
Dixie Moon, Book Four
Survivor Pass, Book Five
Promise Trail, Book Six

MacLarens of Boundary Mountain

Colin's Quest, Book One,
Brodie's Gamble, Book Two

<u>*Contemporary Romance Series*</u>

MacLarens of Fire Mountain

Second Summer, Book One
Hard Landing, Book Two
One More Day, Book Three
All Your Nights, Book Four
Always Love You, Book Five
Hearts Don't Lie, Book Six
No Getting Over You, Book Seven
'Til the Sun Comes Up, Book Eight, Releasing
2016

Peregrine Bay

Reclaiming Love, Book One
Our Kind of Love, Book Two

Tougher than the Rest – Book One
MacLarens of Fire Mountain Historical Western Romance Series

"A passionate, fast-paced story set in the untamed western frontier by an exciting new voice in historical romance."

Niall MacLaren is the oldest of four brothers, and the undisputed leader of the family. A widower, and single father, his focus is on building the MacLaren ranch into the largest and most successful in northern Arizona. He is serious about two things—his responsibility to the family and his future marriage to the wealthy, well-connected widow who will secure his place in the territory's destiny.

Katherine is determined to live the life she's dreamed about. With a job waiting for her in the growing town of Los Angeles, California, the young teacher from Philadelphia begins a journey across the United States with only a couple of trunks and her spinster companion. Life is perfect for this adventurous, beautiful young woman, until an accident throws her into the arms of the one man who can destroy it all.

Fighting his growing attraction and strong desire for the beautiful stranger, Niall is more determined than ever to push emotions aside to focus on his goals of wealth and political gain. But looking into the clear, blue eyes of the woman who could ruin everything, Niall discovers he will have to harden his heart and be tougher than he's ever been in his life...Tougher than the Rest.

Faster than the Rest – Book Two
MacLarens of Fire Mountain Historical Western Romance Series

"Headstrong, brash, confident, and complex, the MacLarens of Fire Mountain will captivate you with strong characters set in the wild and rugged western frontier."

Handsome, ruthless, young U.S. Marshal Jamie MacLaren had lost everything—his parents, his family connections, and his childhood sweetheart—but now he's back in Fire Mountain and ready for another chance. Just as he successfully reconnects with his family and starts to rebuild his life, he gets the unexpected and unwanted assignment of rescuing the woman who broke his heart.

Beautiful, wealthy Victoria Wicklin chose money and power over love, but is now fighting for her life—or is she? Who has she become in the seven years since she left Fire Mountain to take up her life in San Francisco? Is she really as innocent as she says?

Marshal MacLaren struggles to learn the truth and do his job, but the past and present lead him in different directions as his heart and brain wage battle. Is Victoria a victim or a villain? Is life offering him another chance, or just another heartbreak?

As Jamie and Victoria struggle to uncover past secrets and come to grips with their shared passion, another danger arises. A life-altering danger that is out of their control and threatens to destroy any chance for a shared future.

Harder than the Rest – Book Three
MacLarens of Fire Mountain Historical Western Romance Series

"They are men you want on your side. Hard, confident, and loyal, the MacLarens of Fire Mountain will seize your attention from the first page."

Will MacLaren is a hardened, plain-speaking bounty hunter. His life centers on finding men guilty of horrendous crimes and making sure justice is done. There is no place in his world for the carefree attitude he carried years before when a tragic event destroyed his dreams.

Amanda is the daughter of a successful Colorado rancher. Determined and proud, she works hard to prove she is as capable as any man and worthy to be her father's heir. When a stranger arrives, her independent nature collides with the strong pull toward the handsome ranch hand. But is he what he seems and could his secrets endanger her as well as her family?

The last thing Will needs is to feel passion for another woman. But Amanda elicits feelings he thought were long buried. Can Will's desire for her change him? Or will the vengeance he seeks against the one man he wants to destroy—a dangerous opponent without a conscious—continue to control his life?

Stronger than the Rest – Book Four
MacLarens of Fire Mountain Historical Western Romance Series

"Smart, tough, and capable, the MacLarens protect their own no matter the odds. Set against America's rugged frontier, the stories of the men from Fire Mountain are complex, fast-paced, and a

must read for anyone who enjoys non-stop action and romance."

Drew MacLaren is focused and strong. He has achieved all of his goals except one—to return to the MacLaren ranch and build the best horse breeding program in the west. His successful career as an attorney is about to give way to his ranching roots when a bullet changes everything.

Tess Taylor is the quiet, serious daughter of a Colorado ranch family with dreams of her own. Her shy nature keeps her from developing friendships outside of her close-knit family until Drew enters her life. Their relationship grows. Then a bullet, meant for another, leaves him paralyzed and determined to distance himself from the one woman he's come to love.

Convinced he is no longer the man Tess needs, Drew focuses on regaining the use of his legs and recapturing a life he thought lost. But danger of another kind threatens those he cares about—including Tess—forcing him to rethink his future.

Can Drew overcome the barriers that stand between him, the safety of his friends and family, and a life with the woman he loves? To do it all, he has to be strong. Stronger than the Rest.

Deadlier than the Rest – Book Five

**MacLarens of Fire Mountain Historical
Western Romance Series**

*"A passionate, heartwarming story of the
iconic MacLarens of Fire Mountain. This
captivating historical western romance
grabs your attention from the start with
an engrossing story encompassing two
romances set against the rugged
backdrop of the burgeoning western
frontier."*

Connor MacLaren's search has already stolen
eight years of his life. Now he is close to finding
what he seeks—Meggie, his missing sister. His
quest leads him to the growing city of Salt Lake
and an encounter with the most captivating
woman he has ever met.

Grace is the third wife of a Mormon farmer,
forced into a life far different from what she'd
have chosen. Her independent spirit longs for
choices governed only by her own heart and
mind. To achieve her dreams, she must hide
behind secrets and half-truths, even as her heart
pulls her towards the ruggedly handsome
Connor.

Known as cool and uncompromising, Connor
MacLaren lives by a few, firm rules that have

served him well and kept him alive. However, danger stalks Connor, even to the front range of the beautiful Wasatch Mountains, threatening those he cares about and impacting his ability to find his sister.

Can Connor protect himself from those who seek his death? Will his eight-year search lead him to his sister while unlocking the secrets he knows are held tight within Grace, the woman who has captured his heart?

Read this heartening story of duty, honor, passion, and love in book five of the MacLarens of Fire Mountain series.

Wilder than the Rest – Book Six
MacLarens of Fire Mountain Historical Western Romance Series

"A captivating historical western romance set in the burgeoning and treacherous city of San Francisco. Go along for the ride in this gripping story that seizes your attention from the very first page."

"If you're a reader who wants to discover an entire family of characters you can

fall in love with, this is the series for you." – Authors to Watch

Pierce is a rough man, but happy in his new life as a Special Agent. Tasked with defending the rights of the federal government, Pierce is a cunning gunslinger always ready to tackle the next job. That is, until he finds out that his new job involves Mollie Jamison.

Mollie can be a lot to handle. Headstrong and independent, Mollie has chosen a life of danger and intrigue guaranteed to prove her liquor-loving father wrong. She will make something of herself, and no one, not even arrogant Pierce MacLaren, will stand in her way.

A secret mission brings them together, but will their attraction to each other prove deadly in their hunt for justice? The payoff for success is high, much higher than any assignment either has taken before. But will the damage to their hearts and souls be too much to bear? Can Pierce and Mollie find a way to overcome their misgivings and work together as one?

Second Summer – Book One
**MacLarens of Fire Mountain
Contemporary Romance Series**

"In this passionate Contemporary Romance, author Shirleen Davies introduces her readers to the modern day MacLarens starting with Heath MacLaren, the head of the family."

The Chairman of both the MacLaren Cattle Co. and MacLaren Land Development, Heath MacLaren is a success professionally—his personal life is another matter.

Following a divorce after a long, loveless marriage, Heath spends his time with women who are beautiful and passionate, yet unable to provide what he longs for . . .

Heath has never experienced love even though he witnesses it every day between his younger brother, Jace, and wife, Caroline. He wants what they have, yet spends his time with women too young to understand what drives him and too focused on themselves to be true companions.

It's been two years since Annie's husband died, leaving her to build a new life. He was her soul mate and confidante. She has no desire to find a replacement, yet longs for male friendship.

Annie's closest friend in Fire Mountain, Caroline MacLaren, is determined to see Annie come out of her shell after almost two years of mourning. A chance meeting with Heath turns into an offer to be a part of the MacLaren Foundation Board and an opportunity for a life outside her home sanctuary which has also become her prison. The platonic friendship that builds between Annie and Heath points to a future where each may rely on the other without the bonds a romance would entail.

However, without consciously seeking it, each yearns for more . . .

The MacLaren Development Company is booming with Heath at the helm. His meetings at a partner company with the young, beautiful marketing director, who makes no secret of her desire for him, are a temptation. But is she the type of woman he truly wants?

Annie's acceptance of the deep, yet passionless, friendship with Heath sustains her, lulling her to believe it is all she needs. At least until Heath drops a bombshell, forcing Annie to realize that what she took for friendship is actually a deep, lasting love. One she doesn't want to lose.

Each must decide to settle—or fight for it all.

Hard Landing – Book Two

**MacLarens of Fire Mountain
Contemporary Romance Series**

Trey MacLaren is a confident, poised Navy pilot. He's focused, loyal, ethical, and a natural leader. He is also on his way to what he hopes will be a lasting relationship and marriage with fellow pilot, Jesse Evans.

Jesse has always been driven. Her graduation from the Naval Academy and acceptance into the pilot training program are all she thought she wanted—until she discovered love with Trey MacLaren

Trey and Jesse's lives are filled with fast flying, friends, and the demands of their military careers. Lives each has settled into with a passion. At least until the day Trey receives a letter that could change his and Jesse's lives forever.

It's been over two years since Trey has seen the woman in Pensacola. Her unexpected letter stuns him and pushes Jesse into a tailspin from which she might not pull back.

Each must make a choice. Will the choice Trey makes cause him to lose Jesse forever? Will she follow her heart or her head as she fights for a chance to save the love she's found? Will their independent decisions collide, forcing them to give up on a life together?

One More Day – Book Three
MacLarens of Fire Mountain Contemporary Romance Series

Cameron "Cam" Sinclair is smart, driven, and dedicated, with an easygoing temperament that belies his strong will and the personal ambitions he holds close. Besides his family, his job as head of IT at the MacLaren Cattle Company and his position as a Search and Rescue volunteer are all he needs to make him happy. At least that's what he thinks until he meets, and is instantly drawn to, fellow SAR volunteer, Lainey Devlin.

Lainey is compassionate, independent, and ready to break away from her manipulative and controlling fiancé. Just as her decision is made, she's called into a major search and rescue effort, where once again, her path crosses with the intriguing, and much too handsome, Cam Sinclair. But Lainey's plans are set. An opportunity to buy a flourishing preschool in northern Arizona is her chance to make a fresh start, and nothing, not even her fierce attraction to Cam Sinclair, will impede her plans.

As Lainey begins to settle into her new life, an unexpected danger arises —threats from an unknown assailant—someone who doesn't believe she belongs in Fire Mountain. The more Lainey begins to love her new home, the greater the danger becomes. Can she accept the help and protection Cam offers while ignoring her consuming desire for him?

Even if Lainey accepts her attraction to Cam, will he ever be able to come to terms with his own driving ambition and allow himself to consider a different life than the one he's always pictured? A life with the one woman who offers more than he'd ever hoped to find?

All Your Nights – Book Four
MacLarens of Fire Mountain Contemporary Romance Series

"Romance, adventure, cowboys, suspense—everything you want in a contemporary western romance novel."

Kade Taylor likes living on the edge. As an undercover agent for the DEA and a former Special Ops team member, his current assignment seems tame—keep tabs on a bookish Ph.D. candidate the agency believes is connected to a ruthless drug cartel.

Brooke Sinclair is weeks away from obtaining her goal of a doctoral degree. She spends time finalizing her presentation and relaxing with another student who seems to want nothing more than her friendship. That's fine with Brooke. Her last serious relationship ended in a broken engagement.

Her future is set, safe and peaceful, just as she's always planned—until Agent Taylor informs her she's under suspicion for illegal drug activities.

Kade and his DEA team obtain evidence which exonerates Brooke while placing her in danger from those who sought to use her. As Kade races to take down the drug cartel while protecting Brooke, he must also find common ground with the former suspect—a woman he desires with increasing intensity.

At odds with her better judgment, Brooke finds the more time she spends with Kade, the more she's attracted to the complex, multi-faceted agent. But Kade holds secrets he knows Brooke will never understand or accept.

Can Kade keep Brooke safe while coming to terms with his past, or will he stay silent, ruining any future with the woman his heart can't let go?

Always Love You— Book Five

**MacLarens of Fire Mountain
Contemporary Romance Series**

*"Romance, adventure, motorcycles,
cowboys, suspense—everything you want
in a contemporary western romance
novel."*

Eric Sinclair loves his bachelor status. His work
at MacLaren Enterprises leaves him with plenty
of time to ride his horse as well as his
Harley...and date beautiful women without a
thought to commitment.

Amber Anderson is the new person at MacLaren
Enterprises. Her passion for marketing landed
her what she believes to be the perfect job—until
she steps into her first meeting to find the man
she left, but still loves, sitting at the management
table—his disdain for her clear.

Eric won't allow the past to taint his professional
behavior, nor will he repeat his mistakes with
Amber, even though love for her pulses through
him as strong as ever.

As they strive to mold a working relationship,
unexpected danger confronts those close to them,
pitting the MacLarens and Sinclairs against an
evil who stalks one member but threatens them
all.

Eric can't get the memories of their passionate past out of his mind, while Amber wrestles with feelings she thought long buried. Will they be able to put the past behind them to reclaim the love lost years before?

Hearts Don't Lie– Book Six
MacLarens of Fire Mountain
Contemporary Romance Series

Mitch MacLaren has reasons for avoiding relationships, and in his opinion, they're pretty darn good. As the new president of RTC Bucking Bulls, difficult challenges occur daily. He certainly doesn't need another one in the form of a fiery, blue-eyed, redhead.

Dana Ballard's new job forces her to work with the one MacLaren who can't seem to get over himself and lighten up. Their verbal sparring is second nature and entertaining until the night of Mitch's departure when he surprises her with a dare she doesn't refuse.

With his assignment in Fire Mountain over, Mitch is free to return to Montana and run the business his father helped start. The glitch in his enthusiasm has to do with one irreversible mistake—the dare Dana didn't ignore. Now, for reasons that confound him, he just can't let it go.

Working together is a circumstance neither wants, but both must accept. As their attraction grows, so do the accidents and strange illnesses of the animals RTC depends on to stay in business. Mitch's total focus should be on finding the reasons and people behind the incidents. Instead, he finds himself torn between his unwanted desire for Dana and the business which is his life.

In his mind, a simple proposition can solve one problem. Will Dana make the smart move and walk away? Or take the gamble and expose her heart?

No Getting Over You— Book Seven
MacLarens of Fire Mountain
Contemporary Romance Series

Cassie MacLaren has come a long way since being dumped by her long-time boyfriend, a man she believed to be her future. Successful in her job at MacLaren Enterprises, dreaming of one day leading one of the divisions, she's moved on to start a new relationship, having little time to dwell on past mistakes.

Matt Garner loves his job as rodeo representative for Double Ace Bucking Stock. Busy days and constant travel leave no time for anything more

than the occasional short-term relationship—
which is just the way he likes it. He's come to
accept the regret of leaving the woman he loved
for the pro rodeo circuit.

The future is set for both, until a chance meeting
ignites long buried emotions neither is willing to
face.

Forced to work together, their attraction grows,
even as multiple arson fires threaten Cassie's new
home of Cold Creek, Colorado. Although Cassie
believes the danger from the fires is remote, she
knows the danger Matt poses to her heart is real.

While fighting his renewed feelings for Cassie,
Matt focuses on a new and unexpected
opportunity offered by MacLaren Enterprises—
an opportunity that will put him on a direct
collision course with Cassie.

Will pride and self-preservation control their
future? Or will one be strong enough to make the
first move, risking everything, including their
heart?

Redemption's Edge – Book One
**Redemption Mountain – Historical
Western Romance Series**

"A heartwarming, passionate story of loss, forgiveness, and redemption set in the untamed frontier during the tumultuous years following the Civil War. Ms. Davies' engaging and complex characters draw you in from the start, creating an exciting introduction to this new historical western romance series."

"Redemption's Edge is a strong and engaging introduction to her new historical western romance series."

Dax Pelletier is ready for a new life, far away from the one he left behind in Savannah following the South's devastating defeat in the Civil War. The ex-Confederate general wants nothing more to do with commanding men and confronting the tough truths of leadership.

Rachel Davenport possesses skills unlike those of her Boston socialite peers—skills honed as a nurse in field hospitals during the Civil War. Eschewing her northeastern suitors and changed by the carnage she's seen, Rachel decides to accept her uncle's invitation to assist him at his clinic in the dangerous and wild frontier of Montana.

Now a Texas Ranger, a promise to a friend takes Dax and his brother, Luke, to the untamed territory of Montana. He'll fulfill his oath and return to Austin, at least that's what he believes.

The small town of Splendor is what Rachel needs after life in a large city. In a few short months, she's grown to love the people as well as the majestic beauty of the untamed frontier. She's settled into a life unlike any she has ever thought possible.

Thinking his battle days are over, he now faces dangers of a different kind—one by those from his past who seek vengeance, and another from Rachel, the woman who's captured his heart.

Wildfire Creek – Book Two
Redemption Mountain – Historical Western Romance Series

"A passionate story of rebuilding lives, working to find a place in the wild frontier, and building new lives in the years following the American Civil War. A rugged, heartwarming story of choices and love in the continuing saga of Redemption Mountain."

Luke Pelletier is settling into his new life as a rancher and occasional Pinkerton Agent, leaving his past as an ex-Confederate major and Texas Ranger far behind. He wants nothing more than to work the ranch, charm the ladies, and live a life of carefree bachelorhood.

Ginny Sorensen has accepted her responsibility as the sole provider for herself and her younger sister. The desire to continue their journey to Oregon is crushed when the need for food and shelter keeps them in the growing frontier town of Splendor, Montana, forcing Ginny to accept work as a server in the local saloon.

Luke has never met a woman as lovely and unspoiled as Ginny. He longs to know her, yet fears his wild ways and unsettled nature aren't what she deserves. She's a girl you marry, but that is nowhere in Luke's plans.

Complicating their tenuous friendship, a twist in circumstances forces Ginny closer to the man she most wants to avoid—the man who can destroy her dreams, and who's captured her heart.

Believing his bachelor status firm, Luke moves from danger to adventure, never dreaming each step he takes brings him closer to his true destiny and a life much different from what he imagines.

Sunrise Ridge – Book Three
Redemption Mountain – Historical Western Romance Series

Noah Brandt is a successful blacksmith and businessman in Splendor, Montana, with few ties to his past as an ex-Union Army major and sharpshooter. Quiet and hardworking, his biggest challenge is controlling his strong desire for a woman he believes is beyond his reach.

Abigail Tolbert is tired of being under her father's thumb while at the same time, being pushed away by the one man she desires. Determined to build a new life outside the control of her wealthy father, she finds work and sets out to shape a life on her own terms.

Noah has made too many mistakes with Abby to have any hope of getting her back. Even with the changes in her life, including the distance she's built with her father, he can't keep himself from believing he'll never be good enough to claim her.

Unexpected dangers, including a twist of fate for Abby, change both their lives, making the tentative steps they've taken to build a relationship a distant hope. As Noah battles his past as well as the threats to Abby, she fights for a future with the only man she will ever love.

Dixie Moon – Book Four
Redemption Mountain – Historical Western Romance Series

Gabe Evans is a man of his word with strong convictions and steadfast loyalty. As the sheriff of Splendor, Montana, the ex-Union Colonel and oldest of four boys from an affluent family, Gabe understands the meaning of responsibility. The last thing he wants is another commitment—especially of the female variety.

Until he meets Lena Campanel...

Lena's past is one she intends to keep buried. Overcoming a childhood of setbacks and obstacles, she and her friend, Nick, have succeeded in creating a life of financial success and devout loyalty to one another.

When an unexpected death leaves Gabe the sole heir of a considerable estate, partnering with Nick and Lena is a lucrative decision...forcing Gabe and Lena to work together. As their desire grows, Lena refuses to let down her guard, vowing to keep her past hidden—even from a perfect man like Gabe.

But secrets never stay buried...

When revealed, Gabe realizes Lena's secrets are deeper than he ever imagined. For a man of his character, deception and lies of omission aren't negotiable. Will he be able to forgive the deceit? Or is the damage too great to ever repair?

Survivor Pass – Book Five
Redemption Mountain – Historical Western Romance Series

He thought he'd found a quiet life...

Cash Coulter settled into a life far removed from his days of fighting for the South and crossing the country as a bounty hunter. Now a deputy sheriff, Cash wants nothing more than to buy some land, raise cattle, and build a simple life in the frontier town of Splendor, Montana. But his whole world shifts when his gaze lands on the most captivating woman he's ever seen. And the feeling appears to be mutual.

But nothing is as it seems...

Alison McGrath moved from her home in Kentucky to the rugged mountains of Montana for one reason—to find the man responsible for murdering her brother. Despite using a false identity to avoid any tie to her brother's name, the citizens of Splendor have no intention of sharing their knowledge about the bank robbery which killed her only sibling. Alison knows her circle of lies can't end well, and her growing for Cash threatens to weaken the revenge which drives her.

And the troubles are mounting…

There is danger surrounding them both—men who seek vengeance as a way to silence the past…by any means necessary.

Promise Trail – Book Six
Redemption Mountain – Historical Western Romance Series

Bull Mason has built a life far away from his service in the Union Army and the ravages of the Civil War. He's achieved his dreams—loyal friends, work he enjoys, a home of his own, and a promise from the woman he loves to become his wife.

Lydia Rinehart can't believe how much her life has changed. Escaping captivity from a Crow village, she finds refuge and a home at the sprawling Redemption's Edge ranch…and love in the arms of Bull Mason, the ranch foreman. For the first time since her parents' death, she feels cherished and safe.

In an instant their dreams are crushed...

Bull is resolute in his determination to track down and rescue Lydia's brother, kidnapped during the celebration of their friend's wedding. He's made a promise—one he intends to keep. Picking the best men, they are ready to ride, until he's given an ultimatum.

Choices can seldom be undone...

As their journey continues, the trackers become the prey, finding their freedom and lives threatened.

And promises broken can rarely be reclaimed...

Can Bull and Lydia trust each other again and find their way to back to the dreams they once shared?

Reclaiming Love – Book One, A Novella
Peregrine Bay – Contemporary Romance Series

Adam Monroe has seen his share of setbacks. Now he's back in Peregrine Bay, looking for a new life and second chance.

Julia Kerrigan's life rebounded after the sudden betrayal of the one man she ever loved. As president of a success real estate company, she's built a new life and future, pushing the painful past behind her.

Adam's reason for accepting the job as the town's new Police Chief can be explained in one word—Julia. He wants her back and will do whatever is necessary to achieve his goal, even knowing his biggest hurdle is the woman he still loves.

As they begin to reconnect, a terrible scandal breaks loose with Julia and Adam at the center.

Will the threat to their lives and reputations destroy their fledgling romance? Can Adam identify and eliminate the danger to Julia before he's had a chance to reclaim her love?

Our Kind of Love – Book Two
Peregrine Bay – Contemporary Romance Series

Selena Kerrigan is content with a life filled with work and family, never feeling the need to take a chance on a relationship—until she steps into a social world inhabited by a man with dark hair and penetrating blue eyes. Eyes that are fixed on her.

Lincoln Caldwell is a man satisfied with his life. Transitioning from an enviable career as a Navy SEAL to becoming a successful entrepreneur, his days focus on growing his security firm, spending his nights with whomever he chooses. Committing to one woman isn't on the horizon—until a captivating woman with caramel eyes sends his personal life into a tailspin.

Believing her identity remains a secret, Selena returns to work, ready to forget about running away from the bed she never should have gone near. She's prepared to put the colossal error, as well as the man she'll never see again, behind her.

Too bad the object of her lapse in judgment doesn't feel the same.

Linc is good at tracking his targets, and Selena is now at the top of his list. It's amazing how a pair of sandals and only a first name can say so much.

As he pursues the woman he can't rid from his mind, a series of cyber-attacks hit his business, threatening its hard-won success. Worse, and unbeknownst to most, Linc harbors a secret—one with the potential to alter his life, along with those he's close to, in ways he could never imagine.

Our Kind of Love, Book Two in the Peregrine Bay Contemporary Romance series, is a full-length novel with an HEA and no cliffhanger.

Colin's Quest – Book One
MacLarens of Boundary Mountain – Historical Western Romance Series

For An Undying Love...

When Colin MacLaren headed west on a wagon train, he hoped to find adventure and perhaps a little danger in untamed California. He never expected to meet the girl he would love forever. He also never expected her to be the daughter of his family's age-old enemy, but Sarah was a MacGregor and the anger he anticipated soon became a reality. Her father would not be swayed, vehemently refusing to allow marriage to a MacLaren.

Time Has No Effect...

Forced apart for five years, Sarah never forgot Colin—nor did she give up on his promise to come for her. Carrying the brooch he gave her as proof of their secret betrothal, she scans the trail from California, waiting for Colin to claim her. Unfortunately, her father has other plans.

And Enemies Hold No Power.

Nothing can stop Colin from locating Sarah. Not outlaws, runaways, or miles of difficult trails. However, reuniting is only the beginning. Together they must find the courage to fight the men who would keep them apart—and conquer the challenge of uniting two independent hearts.

Brodie's Gamble – Book Two
MacLarens of Boundary Mountain – Historical Western Romance Series

Brodie MacLaren has a dream. He yearns to wear the star—bring the guilty to justice and protect those who are innocent. In his mind, guilty means guilty, even when it includes a beautiful woman who sets his body on edge.

Maggie King lives a nightmare, wanting nothing more than to survive each day and recapture the life stolen from her. Each day she wakes and prays for escape. Taking the one chance she may ever have, Maggie lashes out, unprepared for the rising panic as the man people believe to be her husband lies motionless at her feet.

Deciding innocence and guilt isn't his job.

Brodie's orderly, black and white world spins as her story of kidnapping and abuse unfold. The fact nothing adds up as well as his growing attraction to Maggie cause doubts the stoic lawman can't afford to embrace.

Can a lifetime of believing in absolute right and wrong change in a heartbeat?

Maggie has traded one form of captivity for another. Thoughts of escape consume her, even as feelings for the handsome, unyielding lawman grow.

As events unfold, Brodie must fight more than his attraction. Someone is after Maggie—a real threat who is out to silence her.

He's challenged on all fronts—until he takes a gamble that could change his life or destroy his heart.

Find all of my books at:
http://www.shirleendavies.com/books.html

Avalanche Ranch Press, LLC
PO Box 12618
Prescott, AZ 86304